This Crowded Night

And Other Stories

This Crowded Night

And Other Stories

✦ ✦ ✦ ✦ ✦

Elrena Evans

DreamSeeker Books
TELFORD, PENNSYLVANIA

an imprint of
Cascadia Publishing House

Cascadia Publishing House orders, information, reprint permissions:
contact@CascadiaPublishingHouse.com
1-215-723-9125
126 Klingerman Road, Telford PA 18969
www.CascadiaPublishingHouse.com

This Crowded Night
Copyright © 2011 by Cascadia Publishing House.
Telford, PA 18969
DreamSeeker Books is an imprint of Cascadia Publishing House LLC
Library of Congress Catalog Number: 2011006145
ISBN 13: 978-1-931038-77-5; **ISBN 10:** 1-931038-77-5
Book design by Cascadia Publishing House
Cover design by Gwen M. Stamm with Elrena Evans

The paper used in this publication is recycled and meets the
minimum requirements of American National Standard for Information Sciences—
Permanence of Paper for Printed Library Materials, ANSI Z39.48-1984.1984

"This Crowded Night" first appeared as an audio podcast on *Sniplits*, November
2008. "Constant Companions" first appeared as "The Journey Home" in *Literary
Mama*, August 2007. "When the Light was Still New" was originally published
by *The Wild Rose Press*, February 2008. "Bartimaeus the Blind" first appeared in
Conte: A Journal of Narrative Writing, December 2007.

Library of Congress Cataloguing-in-Publication Data
Evans, Elrena, 1978-
This crowded night, and other stories / Elrena Evans.
    p. cm.
Summary: "This Crowded Night uses fiction writing resources to bring the
women of the New Testament Gospels to life, offering the voices of mothers,
daughters, sisters, and wives struggling to find their way--and perhaps their
faith--in a society in which women's voices are less often heard" --Provided by
publisher.
    ISBN-13: 978-1-931038-77-5 (trade pbk. : alk. paper)
    ISBN-10: 1-931038-77-5 (trade pbk. : alk. paper)
    1. Women in the Bible--Fiction. 2. Christian fiction, American. I. Title.
PS3605.V3649T47 2011
813'.6--dc22
                                    2011006145

17 16 15 14 13 12 11   10 9 8 7 6 5 4 3 2 1

To my husband,
who gives all my stories happy endings

Contents

This Crowded Night

And Other Stories

1

This Crowded Night

The spring night was clear and unusually cold as my husband shut the door to the inn and leaned against it wearily.

"That's the last of them," he said, wiping a drop of sweat from his brow. "I can't possibly squeeze in another living soul." He closed his eyes and slumped down even further, his weight supported by the heavy wooden door.

I turned away and surveyed the room. The last of the travelers were making their way through groups of people huddled on the floor, looking for a place to lay our one remaining guest blanket and try to find some sleep. It was a group of three, a tall, determined-looking husband, a tired-looking wife, and a small boy whose tear stains marked the only dirt-free tracks on his face. His toenails were torn and his small feet covered in dried, caked blood. They'd traveled from Galilee, they'd told my husband, on foot since they had no money for a beast. Having set aside Caesar's tax, paid for food and drink for the journey and now for their lodging in our inn, they were close to destitute.

Any other time, their plight might have reduced me to tears, but having heard the same story countless times that day, my heart was calloused. Their story was no different from anyone else's, and many of the families now huddled around the fire pit in the center of the floor had traveled even farther, with more children, to pay a tax they also couldn't afford.

It's this Roman government. Yahweh, Yahweh. When will you come and free your people, who have waited and hoped for so long?

I turned back to my husband, still slumped against the door of the inn, and managed a smile.

"Not room for another single soul?" I questioned, running my fingers through the damp locks on his forehead. "Shall I tell the footsore husbands to lay off their wives?" I smiled at him, and when he raised his head, he was smiling, too.

"You'd better," he answered, reaching his arms out to me. "Another soul, no matter how freshly conceived, would fill this place beyond bursting."

He stood there with his hands heavy on my shoulders and looked at me, and for a moment the noise of bickering families, crying children, and restless travelers was stilled. Then he stood to his full height and stretched.

"Come, *isha*," he said quietly, taking my small hand in his. "To bed. I've done everything I can for these travelers, and before the cock crows tomorrow they'll be up wanting food and drink. Let's try and catch come rest."

I followed my husband through the crowds of people, stepping around frightened children, nursing babies, and gently snoring couples. It seemed as if the entire house of David lay nestled in our inn, from the weak, crying little ones to the weak, trembling elderly. *Curse Caesar. These people shouldn't be here, shouldn't have to pay this tax.*

Outside, a knock on the door thumped through the noise of the inn. "No room," my husband called back hoarsely as we lay on our bed, hidden behind a curtain in the back corner of the inn.

"But we are weary from traveling," a young man's voice called back. "Please. . . . "

"No room, *ish tov!*" an old man called from the floor. "We're full! Seek shelter elsewhere, or get here sooner!"

I hiccupped into my muffling hand, half laughing, half crying, no longer knowing what to feel. Then I abandoned the entire scene and slipped instead into slumber.

I slept fitfully, waking to hear the knocks on the door and the cries of the lodgers calling back, "No room!" Even the children took up the cry, worn out but unable to sleep in these new, strange surroundings, their treble voices carrying through the inn and echoing out into the darkness.

"No room! No room!" they called in a singsong chant. I buried my face into my sleeping husband's side and hugged the nighttime to my body, trying to find a place of rest.

In my dream I was out in the darkness, traveling from inn to inn, knocking on the doors of strangers' homes looking for shelter. Then I was out in the hills with my youngest son, watching him birth a lamb in the pre-dawn chill. "My *ben*," I called to him.

"No room!" I heard again, shattering my dreams and calling me back to the crowded surroundings of my home. It was quieter now, the earlier noise of the people replaced by the gentler sound of sleep.

"But please, have mercy!" a man's voice called through the door. "We have traveled from Nazaret and my wife is about to deliver! Please, she is going to have the child. Have mercy."

Despite the calls of the bedded travelers, the man outside would not give up. My husband rolled over and looked at me, sighing.

"What do I do?" he asked me. "I don't even have a spot on the floor they can use, especially for a birthing. Shall I send all the men and boys outside in the cold so his wife can give birth? It can't be done. I can't help him. Not now." He paused—"I'm sorry."

My heart twisted as I watched my husband's face. I didn't know if he was apologizing to me, to himself, to the man, or to the night, but he looked as if his sorrow held us all.

"The inn at the other end of town filled before ours," I said, thinking aloud. "And every family I know has a house packed with travelers."

I looked at my husband, entreating.

"We can't just leave a birthing woman out on the street."

He sighed and rolled away from me, pulling our one thin cover around himself and exposing my skin to the air. I didn't complain.

"The problem, *isha*, is not that there's no room for them in the inn." His voice fell dully in the darkness. "The problem is that there's no room for them in Beit Lechem."

A small child coughed in the darkness and began to whimper. I could hear a mother shushing it with an ancient lullaby.

"We could give them our stable," I suggested, running my fingertips lightly down my husband's turned back. "We could bed them in the hay, and it would at least be warm."

My husband rolled back to look at me. "We can't put a birthing woman in a cave, *isha*!" he said. "That just—it isn't right. This whole night, this whole thing, it isn't right."

"No, it's not," I said. "But the stable is better than the street. And who knows if the woman is actually going to birth tonight? It could be early pains instead."

A smile crossed my husband's furrowed brow. He placed his hand lightly on my abdomen in the darkness.

"You weren't even with Avigail eight moons before you swore you'd birth her that very night." His hand caressed my belly in memory.

"Oh *ba'al*," I said, smiling at him. "You know how it is with a woman's first. She thinks every small pain means the *yeled* is coming."

I smiled and let out my breath with a sigh, thinking of Avigail, coming not one moon before her time but almost a full moon after. I placed my hand on top of my husband's as he traced circles on my long-empty womb. I'd borne seven children in my time, four of whom lived to be adults. Now, with three married in their own dwellings and one out on the hills tending sheep, the inn seemed quiet at times, without their laughter. But not tonight.

I sighed at the memory of little toes and curled fists, and then thought again of the couple outside. I couldn't leave them there. I wouldn't. I nudged away my husband's hand and stood.

"I'm going to go see what I can do, *ba'al*. At least then I'll know if the woman looks like she will birth soon. No, stay," I said as my husband struggled to rise. "This always was and ever will be woman's work." I slipped my feet into sandals, tied the thongs tightly around my ankles, and grabbed a cloak from the foot of our pallet.

Outside, the night had grown colder. I tugged the heavy inn door behind me and looked at the couple. They seemed barely old enough to be married, the man still in his first beard and the woman even younger. He was brawny, his dust-covered traveling clothes doing little to hide his muscular form. *A fisherman, perhaps*, I thought to myself, *or a carpenter*. The light that spilled out from the oil lamps in the windows along our street showed his nails were broken and the tips of his fingers were scarred from small splinters of wood embedded in their calluses.

A gasp from the woman made me turn to look at her. She was seated astride a mangy, worn-out donkey with heavy-lidded eyes, clutching her swollen abdomen with both hands. As she moaned into the night she shut her eyes against the pain. Her sweaty brow reminded me of my husband's, her dark locks escaping her covering and clinging to her damp skin. She was breathing heavily, her eyes wide with fright and her lips trembling. She opened her mouth to speak—to me or to her husband, I couldn't tell, and then succumbed to a wail of anguish. She was plainly terrified. I rushed to her and lifted my arms to help her off the beast before she fell, but when her husband saw my intent he pushed ahead of me and lifted her gently down. He supported her as she stood on the ground in her flimsy sandals, clothes trailing in the dirt.

"I'm Yosef," he said, "of Nazaret. And this is my wife, Miriam. We have come to Beit Lechem to pay the tax because we are of the house of David—although I'm sure you've heard that countless times today." A wry smile twisted his otherwise creased face, and he relaxed his arms slightly. The woman named Miriam screamed in pain and clenched her fists even tighter against her belly before she sat down on the ground.

"This couldn't have come at a worse time," he continued, sinking to the ground to wipe Miriam's face as she keened in the dust. "Please," he said, looking up at me, "can you help us?"

I knelt to the ground myself and placed my hands on the small of the girl's back and began to apply a gentle, steady pressure. My knees creaked in protest.

"Our inn is full," I told Yosef, looking at him. "The best I can offer you is our stable. At the very least, she will be warm and off the street for the birthing."

"You are kind," Yosef said, and bent over his wife in concern. "Will the baby be born tonight?"

"There's no way to tell, but she looks as though the *chevlei leydah* are upon her. If it isn't tonight, it will at least be soon."

I looked at the young couple. "This is your first," I said. It was more of a statement than a question.

"Yes," Yosef replied, as Miriam shuddered and leaned more closely into his chest. "Our first."

"Then come," I said, standing up with the effort of age. "I will take you to the stable."

The cave was dark and smelled of animals. The rustlings of beasts greeted us; the cow lowed in welcome, and the goats rearranged themselves before returning to sleep. Our equally tired donkey lifted his shaggy head as if to inquire whether I'd brought a rider or a snack, and then, seeing the other donkey, blew out his breath and turned away to face the jagged rock wall. Although the scent of manure hung richly in the air, it was warm and the breath of the beasts seemed a welcome respite from the cold night.

"I'm sorry this is the best I can offer," I said, indicating the straw on the hard stone floor. "Perhaps she should lie in the manger—the hay will be cleaner, and it won't be so cold."

The squat wooden box, longer than the length of a man and filled with feed for our beasts, stood in the center of the stable. I put my arms around Miriam and guided her the few steps toward the manger, while Yosef, his head nearly touching the roof of the cave, absent-mindedly scratched the old donkey. I helped Miriam over the low wooden edge of the manger and laid her on her side, before lying down beside her myself.

"Put one arm here," I instructed her husband, wrapping my arm around her shoulders from behind, my body pressed against hers. "Place your other hand on the small of her back. Rub it gently, and push against her back when she has pains. If you breathe with her you will keep her breathing slower and the *chevlei leydah* will not be so intense. I must run and find the midwife, and look for cloths for the birthing and the swaddling."

I climbed out of the manger and indicated the vacated spot to Yosef. He positioned himself against his wife, tentatively, and placed his right arm almost reverently around her shoulders but didn't touch her. His face reminded me of my married son's when the wedding veil was lifted off his bride.

"You have to *hold* her," I said to him. "Hold her tight. You can't expect me to believe that, with her in this condition, you are still afraid to touch your own wife."

He didn't answer, but slowly let out his breath and wrapped his wife into his arms. I left them there, her cries piercing the cold night air, and went to look for the midwife.

Stepping out of the stable, the cold hit me like water. I bent to pick a piece of hay out of my sandal and, wrapping my cloak more tightly about me, went to find Shifra. The path was hardened by countless feet tramping over it during the day, and after the hectic bustle of a Beit Lechem inn I welcomed the quiet darkness.

Shifra wasn't the midwife's real name, but everyone called her that in remembrance of the legendary Shifra, the great midwife who disobeyed Pharaoh's orders to kill all the Yehudim babies long ago, and thus preserved our people. Our Shifra was also a great midwife and a good friend, and although nearing her time to leave this earth, she still approached her work with practicality and a sure hand.

I hurried along in the darkness, and thought back to the night of my first son's birth. The elderly midwife who birthed Avigail so skillfully, after being called to the inn several times for my false alarms, had passed on shortly after her birth. Thus for the difficult labor of my son, I had to rely on the arms of a stranger. My labor pains had been unbearable, and the woman who came to help me was young, scarcely older than I was. I screamed at her that I wanted someone skilled, not a baby just out of swaddling herself, but she ignored my cries and insults. Hours later, when she looked at me and spoke her first words of that long night, "*Eishes chayil*, behold your son," I wept and dubbed her my Shifra. Now that son was married with children of his own.

I brushed my hand against the rough door of Shifra's house and softly called to her. I could smell the goatskins drying inside; her husband was a tentmaker.

"She's not here," a familiar man's voice called back. "She's gone to midwife at the house of Itai ben Yitzhak." Shifra's husband was accustomed to disrupted sleep.

Yael? I thought. *She isn't due to birth for at least a moon.* I paused to murmur a prayer for her, but I had other concerns.

Itai ben Yitzhak paced nervously in front of his small house. He scuffed his sandals in the dirt and kicked at small rocks along the path. When he heard my footsteps, his face lifted and I saw his troubled eyes.

"Have you come to help?" he called, eagerly, desperation sharpening his voice.

"No, Itai, I've come looking for Shifra. She's here, is she not?"

"The baby's coming wrong," he said, and as his dark brows knit themselves together I heard him choke down a sob. "My Yael! I'm afraid the baby will kill her . . . I don't want to lose my *isha*!"

Itai grabbed me and started to cry like a young girl. I was overwhelmed by the grief shaking his strong, sculpted shoulders. The smell of salt air and stale fish clung to him as he clung to me, and I inhaled his scent in the darkness. I placed my hand on his young head. It seemed a night for difficult births. I forced myself to breathe deeply in an attempt to force the slow breaths into him.

"Shhhh," I told him. "I am sure that Yahweh holds both Yael and her baby in His infinite hands. My *ba'al* swore every time the baby would kill me, and here you see I am healthy and strong, and have lived to see to my children's children."

"No, you don't understand," Itai persisted. "The baby's coming wrong. It's not leading with the head. It's too early. Oh, my Yael!"

"Let me talk to Shifra," I said, gently but persistently disentangling myself from Itai. I walked the few short steps to the door and lifted the latch, ducking inside.

The smell of blood and birth hung in the air like a weight, and it tasted bitter. Yael lay on a pile of cloths in the center of the house, breathing heavily. Tears tracked in runnels down her sweat-stained cheeks. Shifra bent over the laboring woman, her hair slipping from its covering, and massaged Yael's belly in an attempt to turn the baby. The house was dark, and Yael's younger sister, Tziporah, stood by her head, wiping her forehead with a cloth. Tziporah's eyes reflected the fear in the room, yet she said nothing, merely dipping her cloth in the earthen jar at her feet and wiping Yael's face.

"Shifra," I said quietly.

She turned and saw me, her weary, lined face attempting a fleeting smile.

"Is what Itai said true? The *yeled* is coming the wrong way?"

Shifra nodded her head, not speaking.

"I have a young woman who is also about to birth, in our stable. "Her first. There was no room for her in our inn—she is younger even than Yael, and terrified. But you cannot come. . . ." It wasn't a question.

Shifra shook her head and gestured toward the laboring woman. "I can't," she said. "I am first needed here, and this birth will be long." She paused, and lifting her hands from Yael's belly, pressed them into her own back and arched against them. I felt her weariness.

"Shifra, what do I. . . ."

"You birth the baby," she answered simply. Her clear eyes

gazed at me unafraid. "I know you, *achot*," she continued. "If anyone can bring the *yeled* into the world without me, it's you."

"I've never midwifed," I started to protest, but Shifra held up her hand to silence me.

"Yael's older sister Rivka just went for more cloths—when she returns, I will send her with you and keep Tziporah here to help me. If anything should go wrong, send Rivka back here and I will come as soon as I can."

She paused.

"And may Yahweh grant strength to all who travail this night," she murmured softly.

"Amen," I answered, and heard Itai wail outside. "And to those who share in their suffering."

When Rivka returned, we hurried back to the stable. She carried a bundle of cloths, originally intended for Yael, but Shifra had instructed her instead to bring them along with me. They'd make do, Shifra said, a concession for which I was grateful, knowing full well we didn't have one spare piece of cloth in the inn, and neither would anyone else on this crowded night.

"Here, let me help carry those," I said, reaching for some of Rivka's bundle.

The cloths I grabbed felt soft to my fingertips, and in the dim light from the stars I could see they were new swaddling cloths, beautifully made. Any baby would be blessed to be wrapped in such softness, and I wondered where Rivka, barren, had found them.

"Rivka, these are beautiful. Where did you find such soft cloths on such an overfull night?"

She pushed her dark covering away from her face with her free hand as she balanced the rest of her bundle on her hip and looked at me for a moment. We walked on in silence, the soft tread of our feet against the ground her only answer for several paces. Finally she sighed and said, "I wasn't always barren. I bore a child, a daughter who died almost as she was being born. She was my only one, and she didn't even live to be named." The quiet of the night surrounded us.

"I made these," she continued, reaching out to touch the swaddling cloths in the darkness, "for her. She only got to rest in them a few moments, and then she was no more."

I was stunned—I didn't even remember Rivka ever being with child.

"She came before her time," Rivka continued, "and so she went to be rocked by Yahweh instead of by me. I packed these away that night and never brought them out again—but Yael was unprepared, her little one also coming early, and I decided my daughter would be honored to give up her cloths for my sister."

Rivka dropped the soft fibers back into my arms and started walking faster.

"And now, Rivka, you are giving them to a *yeled* you don't even know." I reached for her hand. "Yahweh will bless you for your gift."

Back in the stable, Yosef was holding Miriam in the manger and breathing with her. He looked up when he saw me.

"She's quiet now," he said, "but only for a moment. The pains are coming faster."

I nodded at him. "It's time. I have brought a woman to help me with the birth."

"The midwife?" Yosef asked, and his worried face seemed so young in the limited light of the stable I wanted to lie to him and say yes.

"No," I said truthfully. "Our Shifra is attending a difficult birth for another woman—this woman's sister. Rivka has agreed to come help me in her stead."

Yosef looked uncertain. "Will she be all right? Miriam, I mean?" Then he stopped and looked at Rivka, as if realizing how that must have sounded. "I'm so sorry," he sputtered, twisting his hands in the rough cloth of his traveling cloak. "I want them both to be all right. Thank you for coming."

Rivka nodded at him and smiled, and then turned to Miriam and back to me.

"It's time," she echoed, "Yosef, go and pray to Yahweh for

your wife and your child—we will call you when the little one is here."

Yosef turned and headed toward the opening in the cave. "What is your sister's name," he asked, hesitantly. "I want to pray for her also."

Rivka smiled, her strong teeth visible in the darkness. "Her name is Yael—and thank you."

As Yosef left the stable, fear gripped my abdomen until it hurt to breathe, reminding me of my own labor pains. I wouldn't admit it to Rivka, to Yosef, or especially to Miriam, but I was petrified. I'd given birth, of course, but birthing and midwifery are vastly different. I'd lost three of my own children—Rivka lost the only child she'd ever borne. Yael herself probably wouldn't make it through her birth tonight. I sank down to my knees beside the laboring woman.

Oh Yahweh, I keened silently. *Bless this woman who now shares the curse of Chavah. Make her travail light and bring us a healthy baby. Make me—make Rivka and me—strong. Keep us all safe this night. And pour your comfort on Yael.*

Miriam opened her eyes and looked at me.

"Where's Yosef," she asked, and then gasped as pains shook her body.

"Shhhh," I said, as her body heaved with pain. "Breathe, Miriam. Breathe with your *yeled.*"

When the pain subsided, I directed Rivka to run and get an earthen jar filled with water, to wash Miriam's face. In the few minutes of calm before the next pain I talked to the young mother.

"Miriam, Yahweh has sent you here this night for a reason. He will be with you while you birth, and so will I, and Yosef will be waiting right outside the stable praying for you and for your child. You must be strong for the little one. You must trust in Yahweh to fill you with His strength."

Miriam looked up at me and I saw a fierce determination in her eyes I hadn't noticed before. She pushed her covering away from her face and looked me clear in the eye. "I am not afraid," she told me, as strong as if she had no labor pains. "I am the Lord's handmaiden, and Yahweh's will be done."

She was interrupted by a pain, just as Rivka came back with the jar of water.

"Hold her hand," I instructed Rivka, "and when the pain is gone, wipe her face."

The night wore on. Miriam screamed and writhed in the manger. Bits of hay stuck to her sweaty form and the odor of her birthing body mingled with the smell of manure in the stable. She screamed again and arched her back, then collapsed, shuddering. Tears were pouring down her face and sweat drenched her clothes.

"Miriam," I said, when she was again quiet, "pray with me."

"The Lord is my strength and my song," I intoned—the song of Moses as he led his people into salvation from Egypt.

"He has become my salvation," Miriam and Rivka joined me.

"He is my God, and I will praise him, my father's God, and I will exalt him."

I took a deep breath.

"The Lord is my strength and my song," we began again, and I heard a man's voice joining in from outside the stable. We sang until Miriam had another pain, this one causing her to wrench herself into a seated position, pressing so hard on her abdomen I had to restrain her arms while she cried.

Finally, sucking air greedily into her lungs, she turned to me.

"Please," she said, her young chest heaving, "I don't know—what shall I call you?"

I paused for a moment. Then I looked at her. "You can call me Shifra," I replied, and turned to smile at Rivka. Tonight, I would be Shifra. Tonight I would save our people. I smiled again, glad that neither Miriam nor Rivka could hear my thoughts.

"Shifra," Miriam said, and then collapsed into another pain.

Although her pains grew stronger, they didn't seem to come

any closer together. Rivka bathed her face and I massaged her back and legs, yet the pains stayed the same distance apart for what seemed like hours. Miriam's strength was waning, and with each passing pain she cried harder. Her determination was still fierce, but the birthing was taking its toll on the young girl. I remembered the pain of my own first daughter, and the sharper pain of my son, and put my arms tighter around the sweaty, tear-stained body.

Eventually I turned to Rivka. "This isn't working," I said. "We're going to have to try something else. It's as if her body doesn't want to open and let the *yeled* pass through."

I sighed and shifted my position, trying to ease the strain on my own aching back. "I know the first one is often the most difficult," I said to no one in particular, "but if her body won't give soon. . . ." I looked at Rivka. She understood. Miriam's strength was failing. The child needed to come.

Another pain wracked Miriam's already contorted body and she cried out.

"I want my *em*!" she sobbed, drenched face buried in my shoulder.

"It's always our mothers we call for in these times, isn't it?" Rivka said to me. "All other times we call for our husbands, but not now. When I was in labor I understood my mother more deeply than at any other time. I wanted her to share in the pain." She looked down at Miriam.

"Our husbands," she continued as if to herself, "we may love them, but at this time we resent them because they did this to us. So we call for our mothers instead."

She broke off her musings to catch Miriam's hand and restrain it from pushing too hard again against her swollen belly.

I stroked the damp hair off of her face. "Miriam, can you stand?" She tried to sit up and nodded. Quickly, before another pain could ravage her, I helped her from the manger and stood her with her back to me, my arms under her armpits.

"Rivka," I called, "put fresh cloths in the manger and then come here."

She obeyed, and I continued my directions.

"Stand in front of Miriam. Miriam, when you have your next pain, put your arms around Rivka's neck and hold on tight. We will support you."

I looked at Rivka's strong body and smiled at her. "We can do this, right?"

She nodded.

"The pressure of the *yeled* will increase in this position," I explained. "It might help open her body so the little one can come sooner."

Miriam screamed and slumped down into my arms. I held her and murmured into her ear.

"God is our refuge and strength," I began the ancient psalm. "An ever-present help in trouble. Therefore we will not fear. . . ."

Rivka's voice entwined with mine beneath Miriam's next scream.

". . . Though the earth give way and the mountains fall into the heart of the sea, though its waters roar and foam and the mountains quake with their surging."

"*El-Shaddai!*" I called out. "Almighty God, help us!"

A flow of blood ran down Miriam's legs, soaking her already drenched garments. She struggled for air as if she was under water, and straightened up. I placed my hand on her abdomen. "Miriam," I exclaimed, "Miriam, the *yeled* has moved. It's coming, the little one is coming!"

"Would you like to lie down?" Rivka inquired.

Miriam shook her head. "No," she gasped, "no, this is better."

I looked at Rivka. "You'll hold her?" I asked.

Rivka nodded, and I transferred Miriam's weight to Rivka's arms. The two women leaned against each other, Rivka supporting, Miriam drawing strength from her arms. *What a pity Rivka's little one left this earth so soon,* I mused, kneeling before Miriam. *She would have made a wonderful mother.* I looked at Rivka's earnest face and realized that was exactly what she was doing now—she had become a surrogate mother to a lonely girl in a stable on a cold spring night in Beit Lechem.

Miriam's gasps came ceaselessly now, and as I massaged her legs I spoke to her.

"Breathe, Miriam. Breathe for the *yeled*. And when your body tells you it's time, you push."

Miriam nodded. All of a sudden, her eyes flew open wide, and I knew she was feeling the urge to deliver. I nodded. She pushed.

With a final, star-shattering scream, the labor was over and a small, healthy baby boy slithered into my arms, dripping with blood and fluid. Miriam burst into tears afresh and fell against Rivka so hard that the two of them landed in the manger together.

The child was a solid-looking tiny little man, with a shock of dark wet curls on his robust head. He wriggled in my hands and, as I lifted him up, still attached to his mother by the cord, he began to cry lustily. It wasn't a cry of protest, it seemed, merely one of announcement. *I'm here*, he seemed to say. *You've waited for me, and now I'm here.*

"Miriam, Miriam you have a *ben!*" I cried. "Surely *Yahweh-yir'eh* has heard our prayers this night."

I looked at Rivka and she was crying, her tears mingling with Miriam's sweat on both of their faces.

"Miriam, your *yeled* is here," I said. "Your firstborn, and a *ben.*"

Shaking, Miriam reached up her arms for the child. "I knew he was a boy," she said, and I stifled a wild desire to laugh. Every mother of a firstborn son claims she knew he was a boy, and apparently Miriam was no different.

"Come here," she said softly to her child. "Come to your *em.*"

Gently, I laid the boy on her chest, and together we began to massage the creamy white birth covering into his skin. Rivka reached out a tentative hand, stroked his dark, moist head, and then lifted one of his little arms and joined us in the massage. It was quiet in the stable with the smell of manure and birth surrounding us as we ministered to the new little one. For a while, none of us spoke. We were joined in the mystery of birth, life arising out of nothing. The miracle hung in the air as heavy as the smell, and we didn't speak, just slowly ran our hands over the baby's damp skin, fused together through the miracle of the night.

After what felt like an age, the sound of running footsteps pounded into our stillness. Tziporah's dark head appeared at the mouth of the cave. "Rivka!" she called. "Rivka!"

Rivka's body tensed until I could feel it, and she shut her eyes before turning to look at her little sister.

"What is it, Tziporah?" she started to ask, but the girl interrupted.

"Yael! She's all right! The baby is here—Shifra birthed the baby! Yael has a daughter and she's fine and Yael is fine!" Tziporah was babbling so fast she seemed on the verge of hysterics.

"Itai wants to name her Elisheva, what do you think of that?" she gurgled on. "Yael says on her name day Itai can name the *yeled* anything; she is just so happy to have her and to be alive."

Rivka looked at me.

"Yahweh is kind to all women tonight," I told her. "Perhaps someday Elishiva will be *airusin* to this little one, born on the same cold night in Beit Lechem."

I laughed and looked at Rivka.

"Go to your sister. And Rivka. . . ."

She paused at the edge of the stable and looked at me.

"*Todah*," I whispered. "Thank you."

They raced into the night, holding hands and laughing for the sheer joy of a loved one escaping death.

After Miriam passed the afterbirth and I swaddled the child in Rivka's baby's cloths, I wiped blood off my hands and went outside the stable to find Yosef. He was sitting on a large rock not too far from the door to the inn, his head in his hands.

"Did you hear him cry?" I asked him as he looked up. "Your firstborn is a *ben!*"

Yosef's broad shoulders shook and he stood up and clasped my hands. "I know," he said. "I know. *Todah.* . . . " His voice broke. "Thank you for what you did for Miriam."

I squeezed his rough palms between my own. "Go, now," I said. "Go and see them."

I felt strangely connected to this small, new family on this night, connected by virtue of housing them not only in my stable, but in my heart. To midwife was to witness a miracle, I realized, and now I knew why Shifra would continue on until Avraham stole her to his bosom.

Yosef faltered. He seemed shy, and scared.

"It's all right. They're both fine, and they want to see you."

Again I was struck by his resemblance to my son on his wedding day. His gaze darted around the night and he looked eager, yet filled with trepidation.

"Yosef," I said more firmly, my hand on his shoulder. "Go and see your wife. At the very least, you should be happy that when her time of impurity has passed, you may touch her again."

I grinned and gave him a gentle shove. That would have been more than enough encouragement for my husband, but Yosef, to my surprise, sank back down on the rock, his head again in his hands.

"But I haven't touched her," he jabbered, seemingly more to himself than to me. "I waited, like the angel said, and I. . . ."

"Yosef," I cut in, "the night has been long, and you're tired from traveling. You're not making sense. Go and sleep and the morning will bring you clarity and peace."

"She came to my bed!" Yosef remonstrated me. "We had the ceremony and she came to my bed and I slept by her side every night and didn't touch her!" His wild eyes looked up at me. "I don't know what I'm supposed to do! How can I be a father to *him*? He grabbed my hands again, his eyes pleading with me.

Through all his gibberish this final statement made sense, and I knelt down beside the rock and took him into my arms like he was my son.

"Yosef. No man is ever ready to be a father when the *banim* come. You just have to trust Yahweh and let Him guide you."

He was still in my arms.

"Have you thought of names for his name day yet?" I asked him, trying to calm him down.

"We were told what to name him," Yosef answered, pulling away from me and searching my face again, but for what I couldn't tell. "We are to name him Yeshua, the Moshiach, for he will save the people from their sins."

A cold wave of nausea suffused my body, and I released him. *No! Oh Yahweh, no. Not this baby, not the one I birthed!* The night seemed to swirl around me and I sank down even lower to the ground. I didn't speak.

I fought down the bile that stung the back of my throat. Had it all been for nothing? What we'd gone through tonight, was it really for nothing? Rivka, Miriam, and I had suffered together the intense miracle of childbirth; my fingernails were still seeped in blood and birthing fluids. I could feel the baby's soft skin in my hands. I had taken part in a miracle, for what? For the child to be quietly killed in the night while Miriam's body was battered to death in the streets? Everyone knew the penalty for claiming to be the Moshiach was death.

I looked at Yosef, his strong form swimming through the tears in my eyes.

"Go to your *isha*," I told him. "And Yahweh's blessings on your *ben*."

I turned and ran into the inn.

Stepping through the crowds of people, I made my way back to my pallet and collapsed next to my sleeping husband. I didn't even bother to untie my sandals.

The quiet form next to me stirred, and my husband rolled over and wrapped his arms around me.

"*Isha*," he said, nuzzling his face against my neck.

"Oh *ba'al*," I replied, and started to cry.

"My *isha*, what's wrong?" My husband was fully awake now, and sitting up, he pulled me close to him. "Did the woman birth? Did Shifra come?"

Salt tears were dripping into my mouth.

"She birthed," I sobbed. "She birthed, and *ba'al*, I did it—with Rivka's help. We midwifed. Shifra was birthing Yael's baby who was coming the wrong way." I was babbling and I knew it, but I couldn't stop the flood of incoherent words any more than I could stop my tears.

"Then what's wrong? Is the woman all right? Is it Yael?" I could feel my husband's strong hands pressing me close to him, and I buried my face in the rough cloth covering his chest.

"No, Yael is fine—she birthed a daughter and they're going to name her Elisheva. But. . . ."

I stopped as a fit of coughing shook me.

"The woman?" my husband asked. "In the stable?"

"Yes, Miriam. She birthed the most beautiful *ben*, and he's healthy and strong. But. . . ."

I stopped and took a deep breath to calm myself, while strong hands caressed my hair.

"Her husband thinks the *yeled* is the Moshiach. He's going to name him Yeshua."

I surrendered to my sobs as my husband rocked me.

"Oh *isha*," he murmured into my hair. "Shhhh. Maybe he will change his mind. If he loves his wife, he won't want to see her stoned."

"They don't even have an excuse!" I pushed him away so I could look at him. "That last woman who claimed her son was the Moshiach was crazy, we all knew it. And the council of Sanhedrin priests *still* stoned her! She was stoned in the streets, crying piteously for her baby to come and save her, not knowing he'd been strangled earlier that day and tossed on a rubbish heap like a small dead animal. *Ba'al*, I couldn't bear it if that happened to the baby I just midwifed!"

My husband said nothing, just held me and let me grieve.

"Yosef, her husband, talks like he believes the claim. He told me he's been married to her all this time and hasn't touched her."

A hearty laugh startled me.

"Now *isha*," my husband said, looking at me and wiping tears from my face and smoothing my hair, "that one I don't believe. No man could live with his wife for that many moons and not touch her. If he takes that story before the Sanhedrin they'll *know* he's insane."

He looked at me and let his hands slip down over my shoulders.

"No man is going to believe that story," he repeated. "I'd believe a moshiach before I'd believe that."

"But will that save them? If he's crazy, will it save the child? Last time, the Sanhedrin didn't even care!"

"I don't know, *isha*." His hands slid down to cover my belly. "Always a mother," he whispered to me tenderly. "I will pray the father repents before anyone else hears the story."

Held in his arms, suddenly I realized how exhausting the night had been. I closed my eyes and sleep suffused me.

When I awoke it was to a loud banging at the door of the inn.

"No room!" chorused the people on the floor, their practiced response grown unified. I was lying on the pallet, my sandals had been removed, and I was wrapped in an extra blanket. Where had my husband found it amongst all the people?

From the blurred edges I could just make out in the room, I knew the pre-dawn light was slinking across the sky and the last stars were fading from view. I thought back to the night before, to Miriam, Rivka, and Yosef. Had it all been a dream? Gruff voices outside called back to the travelers.

"We don't want to stay in your inn! We want to see the innkeeper."

My husband was climbing slowly out of bed, and on impulse I followed him to the door. As he opened it, I saw a ragtag band of shepherds shuffling about in front of our inn. I was overwhelmed by the cold air and the smell of sheep. I thought of my son.

"Go on, then," said one of the older shepherds, pushing a younger shepherd still in his first beard toward the door. He reminded me of my boy—his healthy, robust air now denying the tiny child he once was. I thought of the baby in the stable.

The young shepherd coughed.

"Please," he asked. "May we look in your stable? We want to see the baby." My husband looked at me, then turned back to the motley assortment of shepherds.

"What baby?" he asked.

"The one . . . " the fuzz-bearded shepherd hesitated. "The one we were told would be under the star." He pointed to a gleaming star that seemed to hover just over our stable, still visible in the growing light.

"I don't know what you're talking about," my husband replied, running his hands through his hair. "But you may look in my stable."

He pushed the door closed on the shepherds and turned to me.

"How on earth did they get here? Did your Yosef go running all over the country already, proclaiming his blasphemous news?" He paused, leaning against the door.

"He would have had to run all the way there the moment you left him, to make it to the hills where the sheep are. . . ." He stopped, shaking his head. "Even so I don't see how the shepherds would have made it back here by now. And how would Yosef know where to find a herd of sheep in Beit Lechem, if he's from Nazaret?"

He stretched, and then folded me into his arms. "I'm sorry. I was hoping this would all disappear with the dawn."

We paused for a minute, suspended in time, holding on to the last remnants of tranquility before the travelers awoke and taxes, tributes, Caesars, and moshiachs disrupted our peace.

"*Isha*, think of this," my husband said, smiling down at me. "If your stable baby really is the Moshiach we can probably get out of this tax, wouldn't you think?"

I gave a rueful smile. "I just don't want the miracle of last night's birth to be in vain."

"I know." He pulled away from me, put his hands on my

shoulders, and looked at me. "You've had a long and tiring night. Why don't you go back and rest—I'll send for Avigail to help me feed these hungry travelers."

I smiled gratefully and wrapped my arms around him, then turned to make my way back to our pallet.

"Get some sleep," he called behind me.

As the travelers began stirring, though, sleep would not come and my mind would not calm. *Why did Yosef have to say the baby was the Moshiach? Did he want his wife and child put to death?*

And then, impossibly, *but what if it's true? What if after all this time, the Moshiach is finally here?* I could feel my heartbeat quicken, my palms moisten as I tried to process this terrifying thought. We'd been stoning moshiachs for so long, could we recognize the real one when he came?

I rolled over and pulled the blanket above my head. *Oh Yahweh. Answer me when I call to you, oh my righteous God. Give me relief from my distress; be merciful to me and hear my prayer.* My breath steadied as I prayed the ancient Psalm. *For you are a shield around me, oh Lord. . . .* My thoughts drifted to the family in our stable, and then back to the Psalm. *I lie down and sleep; I wake again because the Lord sustains me. I will not fear the tens of thousands drawn up against me on every side.*

But what of the new little one? What of the tens of thousands that would draw up against him on every side? I took a deep breath, then willed myself to go to sleep, tumbling down into the unknown.

2

Constant Companions

It was day two of the journey home, and I missed Miriam. On the way to Yerushalayim for the Feast of the Passover our families had walked together, her friendship a welcome comfort on the dry, dusty road. But Yosef, her husband, had been eager to get back home to Nazerat, and my little ones were moving more slowly each day. "Go on ahead," I'd finally told Miriam, mid-morning on the first day after the Feast. "I'll bring Yeshua back when we get to Nazarat. Or whenever I run out of food."

Miriam had laughed. Her eldest son, Yeshua, was my eldest son David's constant companion. The boys were inseparable, so much so that when I looked at my family I either saw three children, or five. If Yeshua wasn't around, neither was David.

One, two, three, four, five, I counted in silent rhythm as we walked, *one, two, three, four, five.* Five children. All present, all accounted for.

I paused for a moment on the dusty trail. Thoughts of Miriam slipped from my mind as I realized my feet were tired, my arms sore, and my overnursed breasts like smoldering coals beneath my dusty robe. *One, two, three, four, five,* I counted again. *One, two, three, four, five.*

I arched my back, shifted my daughter's weight from one hip to the other. But as I moved her she awoke, instantly hungry, and began frantically searching for my breast. I sighed and called to my husband.

"*Ba'al,* we need to stop. Zahara needs to feed again."

He looked at me. "Why can't you just feed her as we walk?"

I closed my eyes and counted four breaths before I answered. It was useless getting angry with him, he'd never nursed a baby. He couldn't understand. Once again, I missed Miriam.

"I've been feeding her as we walk since the passing of the last moon," I finally replied. "My breasts are raw. I cannot nurse her if I cannot pause to rest."

Zahara's rosy lips rooted against my robe. My husband sighed, moved to the side of the path, and sat down in the dirt before motioning me to join him.

"*Banim,*" he called to the children, "we'll stop for a moment and rest now. Zahara needs to eat."

My children were unfazed by the rest; they were young enough to be unaware of the passage of time and would blissfully walk forever as long as they had friends on the path. As Zahara suckled, her older brother Harel came up to me and began patting my chest.

"*Em,*" he sighed, his voice a silky whisper against my skin. "*Em. . . .*"

I put my hand on his chest and pushed him away, more roughly than I intended, and his brown eyes welled with tears that spilled on to his dusty tunic.

"Oh Harel, I'm sorry," I said. "*Em*'s sorry. But I need to nurse Zahara now, just Zahara. Ask Liat for a drink from her water skin."

He sniffed and toddled off obediently to find his sister Liat, and I felt a pang as I watched him. He had been so young when Zahara was born—scarcely more than a baby himself.

I watched the hot sun turn to golden flecks in his hair as he stopped to pick up a small rock from the path. *One, two, three,* I started to breathe as Zahara nursed and the tension drained from my shoulders. *One, two, three.*

Liat unslung a small water skin from her shoulder and tilted it gently to Harel's lips. Zahara patted my chest as she nursed.

"Liat?" I called. "Have you seen David and Yeshua?" The names rolled off my tongue as one, DavidandYeshua. She looked up at me and shook her head. But I knew they were to-gether, wherever they were, and they'd pop up soon enough when they got hungry. I rolled my head from side to side, taking advantage of the calm of nursing to stretch my aching muscles.

I glanced over at my husband, bending down to talk to Harel. The glints running through Harel's dusty locks were magnified in his father's rumpled brown hair; the resemblance between father and toddling son was keen. I heard them laughing as they held hands and examined a picture Liat was drawing with a stick. My husband traced a strong finger around the impressions she'd left in the dust, smiling, almost caressing her work. Anything could be made beautiful in his eyes.

He was a struggling carpenter before we married, making beautiful things that he sold for a fraction of the cost of his labor. As a bride I would lie beside him at night, pleading with him: make a chair, a workbench. Make something people will use. But my husband had to create beauty. Everywhere he went, everything he touched, became beautiful.

The partnership with Miriam's husband Yosef was our deliverance. I knew the rumors, of course, that Yosef wasn't Yeshua's father, that Yeshua's father was known only to Miriam. But I never paid them any heed. Yosef was a good carpenter, and his partnership with my husband had been our salvation. Yosef did all the practical work, faster than my husband ever could; my husband ornamented, decorated, and embellished to his heart's content. Then Yosef, a shrewd businessman, sold my husband's creations for what they were actually worth. Now the eldest sons of our two families were nearing the age of apprenticeship, and both would be apprenticed as carpenters.

My son David was going to be a good carpenter. He didn't have Yosef's dedication to his work, but neither did he have my husband's artistic bent, and for that I was grateful. My husband would never be a man of great respect in Nazerat, but David could make something of himself. David could grow to be an important man. I sighed as I nursed. That was my prayer for my eldest son.

The sound of running feet interrupted my reverie, and David stood in front of me in all his half-boy, half-man gangliness.

"I'm hungry," he panted, flopping down in the dust beside me. I reached a hand toward his tangled hair but he knocked it away, and I had to content myself with stroking Zahara's fat cheek instead.

"Where's Yeshua?" I asked. David shrugged.

"Answer me when I speak to you. Where's Yeshua?"

"I don't know," he replied, glancing around as if expecting to see him suddenly springing up out of the ground.

"Wasn't he with you?" The merest note of concern colored my voice.

"He was," David said, "but I think he turned back. What's there to eat?"

I ignored his question. "He turned back?" I asked. "What do you mean, he turned back?"

"I don't know," David said again, scratching his foot. "He said there was something he had to do. I think he went back to Yerushalayim."

"To Yerushalayim?" The note of concern was morphing into panic. "David, when? Why?"

"Yesterday sometime. After we ate. No, maybe before. *Em,* I'm really hungry."

"Why didn't you say something to me then?" I pulled Zahara off my breast. She began to fuss as I looked for my husband, still engrossed in Liat's picture, Harel hanging on his leg. I lifted Zahara up on to my shoulder and began to pat her back.

"I don't know, *Em,*" David answered, a deep sigh rising from his chest. "He just said he had something to do. I figured maybe he was going to walk with his parents. He told me not to come, so I didn't."

"But Yosef and Miriam left before we did," I said. "Why would he be turning back if he was going to find them?" The panic was stronger, nearly full-fledged. Two children wandering out of sight for a bit was one thing, one small boy going back to the city alone was another. An image of Miriam came to my mind, but I closed my eyes and willed it away.

David looked at me expectantly. "Can I have something to eat now? Talmor and Reut found an asp. We're going to see if we can teach it to do tricks."

I gave him a small cake of bread, and let him go back to his friends and their snake. "You boys stay where someone can see you," I called after his retreating back. I moved Zahara to my other shoulder and hurried over to my husband.

"*Ba'al*, Yeshua's missing." I could hear my voice beginning to tremble.

"Missing?" He looked up at me, unconcerned. "I'm sure he's around here somewhere. Wasn't he with David?"

I told him what David had told me. My husband was as unconcerned as my son. "I wouldn't worry about it," he said. "He'll turn up."

Liat looked up at me, tugging my robe. "Look what I drew, *Em!*"

"That's beautiful," I told her, absentmindedly. I didn't even look at it.

◆

It was day three of the journey home, and we were now walking back to Yerushalayim.

"Have you seen a young boy? About this tall? His name is Yeshua." The old man I was questioning shook his head, and I clutched Zahara tightly to my chest. Ahead of me I could see Miriam and Yosef, stopping another family with small children. I saw Miriam's anxious face, the woman's sorrowful shake. No one had seen or heard anything of the boy.

I glanced behind me to where my husband was walking, carrying Harel and hurrying Liat and David along beside him. David was carrying the snake. I'd suggested to him that if he was so interested in taking on extra weight he could carry Zahara instead, but my suggestion was met with scorn. Talmor and Reut trusted him with the snake, he said, and he was responsible for bringing it safely back to Nazerat. Back to Nazarat, now by way of Yerushalayim.

We'd questioned David endlessly, but the only thing he thought he remembered was that maybe Yeshua had said something about going back to the temple. All of the boys in his group of friends were shifty on the details; the story seemed to run something along the lines of: "Yeshua was here, and then we saw the snake, and I think he went back. But it was a really big snake! He might have said something about the temple? But Reut caught the snake, and it's huge!"

I ran to catch up with Miriam, Zahara fussing as I jostled her.

"Any news?" Miriam asked. I shook my head. "It wasn't your fault," she continued, her voice soft as the dust whispering against our feet.

"I know," I answered, then stopped. I had no right to let her comfort me.

"I'm so sorry . . . " I began, but broke off and buried my face into Zahara's moist head. I counted my children, scattered along the path. *One, two, three, four.* It was an anomalous number, underscoring my guilt.

"I'm so sorry," I whispered again. Why hadn't I noticed he was missing?

Who does Yeshua think he is? The thought sprang unbidden to my mind as we walked, our rapid footsteps now in rhythm, now not. *David would never dream of leaving the group and wandering back alone toward the city. And every step we take is a step we'll take again before we reach home.*

The gates of the city loomed open in front of us, travelers passing through them on their way home from the feast. Miriam and Yosef ran ahead of my family, in and out among the travelers, asking for Yeshua.

"You go on ahead," my husband said. "We'll wait for you here." He lifted Zahara out of my arms. "I'm sure you'll find him in no time."

Gratefully surrendering Zahara's weight, I ran toward Yosef

and Miriam, toward the bright white temple glistening so fiercely in the hot midday sun that I had to shield my eyes as we approached it.

We pounded through the empty outer court, into the women's court. My arms felt empty without Zahara, and I reached out and took Miriam's hand as we ran. An elderly woman was standing alone in the far corner, and as Yosef sprinted up the steps to the men's court we made our way over to her.

"Have you seen a boy?" Miriam asked breathlessly. "A young boy, traveling alone?" The woman turned her head, deep lines creasing her face. She shook her head. Miriam looked around. There was no one left to ask.

High above us in the men's court sat a knot of priests, their deep voices ringing out over the white stone in debate. As I listened, a clear treble voice punctuated their arguments, and I knew the voice at once: Yeshua. I caught my breath and loosed my hold on Miriam's hands. Yeshua was safe.

Yosef's footsteps slowed as he approached the clump of elders. He bowed his head, waited for one to finish speaking, and then looked directly at his son.

"Yeshua," he said, his quiet voice full of authority. "It's time to go home now."

Without a word, the boy stood up and followed his father. There was a lull in the priests' conversation as Yosef and Yeshua descended the steps, their worn sandals slapping in time against the glistening stone. When they reached the bottom, the priests resumed their discussions.

Miriam threw herself at Yeshua.

"Son, why have you treated us like this?" she cried, her voice ricocheting off the walls. In all the years we'd been friends, I'd never heard her yell. She grabbed him tightly by the shoulders, her face so close to his they were almost touching, her knuckles white. The elders glanced over at us again as Miriam continued to shout, until Yosef took one of her arms in his, the other hand still clutching Yeshua, and led them out of the temple.

Miriam's anger seemed to soften in the heat of the sun. When we got outside, she threw herself at her son. "Your father and I have been anxiously searching for you!" she cried, trying to embrace, kiss, and shake Yeshua all at once. He gazed at her, his expression unreadable.

I wanted to add my voice to her tirade, but I held my tongue. He wasn't my son.

Yeshua looked from Miriam to Yosef. "Why were you searching for me?" he asked. "Didn't you know I had to be in my Father's house?"

Miriam pulled her son back into her arms. I glanced toward the city gates and saw my family, waiting for me. The guilt and grief I'd felt over losing Yeshua was hardening into annoyance.

As Yosef placed his large, calloused hand on top of the boy's head and rustled his hair, I realized: Miriam and Yosef weren't going to be upset with Yeshua, not in the way I'd be upset if he were my son. They'd been angry, but now that he'd been found their anger was giving way to relief. That was as far as it went. I felt my annoyance deepening to resentment.

I watched their family walking together as we caught up with my own, and suddenly my own anger was so great I snatched Zahara back too quickly from her father, and she began to cry.

What did Yeshua mean, in his "father's house?" I fumed to myself as I prepared to nurse. He was in the middle of the temple, not someone's house, and his father was Yosef of Nazerat. Wasn't he?

"Would David like to walk with us?"

Miriam's small form appeared at my elbow, startling me out of my thoughts.

"Yosef would still like to try and get home quickly," she continued apologetically when I didn't answer. "But David is more than welcome to walk with us." She paused, then smiled up at me. "I promise not to lose him."

I smiled back at her, but my face felt tight. It was far too soon for me to make light of what had happened, what could have happened.

"No, you go on ahead," I finally managed, in a tone that sounded falsely bright even to me. "We'll keep David with us."

I looked at Miriam and suddenly I felt like I didn't even know her.

Liat came over and picked up Harel, who was trying to climb up into my arms while Zahara nursed. Her small feet followed mine, and I could feel her looking at me. Perhaps she'd understood more of our detour than I had given her credit for.

David plied us with ceaseless questions about the care and handling of snakes as the gates of the city grew smaller behind us, and wondered if we could catch up with Talmor and Reut on our journey back home. I assured him that Talmor and Reut were now days ahead of us, but held my tongue and kept myself from adding, *thanks to Yeshua*.

That night, we camped by the side of the road with another family from Nazerat. After lighting a small fire and cooking our evening meal, I found myself needing to talk about what had happened. As the children settled down to sleep, I stayed up into the night with a woman named Kefira. I'd known her in passing, having seen her at the city well, but we'd never really talked. I usually spent my trips to the well talking to Miriam.

"They didn't even scold him," I told her, pulling my knees into my chest as we sat together around the embers of our dying fire.

"I'm not surprised," Kefira replied. "You know how Miriam is."

"Miriam?" I repeated. "What do you mean?"

"She treats that boy as if he was a prophet," Kefira continued. "Most of us can't stand her."

I wondered who "us" was, and why I wasn't included in the group.

"I would never let my son hang around with Yeshua," Kefira said bluntly.

"Why?" I asked. "David plays with him all the time. They're practically inseparable."

"We know," she said. *We* again. "But even if the rumors aren't true, they're not doing the family's reputation any good, nor anyone who associates with them."

"You mean the rumors about his father?" I asked. "I thought that was just. . . . " My voice trailed off. I didn't know what I thought it was. Idle chatter? Spite? I looked at Kefira. "Why hasn't anybody ever talked to me about this before?" I wondered, aloud but to myself. Kefira answered me anyway.

"Everybody knows you're Miriam's best friend," she said. "We assumed you didn't care what people thought about your family."

She tucked a stray hair behind her ear, poked the last of the fire with a stick. "I'm sorry," she finally said. "Perhaps I've said too much."

My thoughts continued to torment me long after I'd lain down to sleep beside my husband, Zahara tucked into the crook of one arm and my other arm slung around Harel. Surely she couldn't be right, surely the entire community couldn't feel the way she did about Yeshua? The moon had almost set by the time I fell asleep.

♦

The first morning back in Nazerat, I rejoiced that the journey was behind us. I didn't see Miriam on my way to the well to draw the day's water.

"Ravital!" I called to a woman on the dusty path. "*Boker tov.*" I fell into step beside her. "How are Talmor and Reut?"

She smiled at the mention of her sons. "They're fine," she replied, "and they think David is a hero."

I smiled in return. Amazingly, the snake christened Pinchas had survived the journey home, much to David's delight. I wondered if the story of Yeshua's temple disappearance was fading into the boys' all-encompassing story of the snake's journey from Yerushalayim, and I almost hated to bring up what I so desperately wanted to ask. I took a quick breath.

"Ravital," I said hurriedly, before I could change my mind.

"Have you ever doubted if Talmor and Reut should play with Yeshua?"

She was silent for a moment, fingering the rim of the earthenware jug she carried.

"Yes," she finally said. "I've actually been thinking about it a lot lately."

"But why?" I asked. "Just because of the rumor? It hardly seems fair." The sun beat hot upon my covering, and I thought of the not-too-distant day when Liat would be old enough to help me carry water. My children were growing up so fast. "Yeshua is David's closest friend," I said softly.

"I know," Ravital continued. "But if you talk to some of the other women. . . . " She made a gesture with her free hand, taking in the knot of women gathered at the well now visible in the distance. "They think the rumors are true," she said. "And our boys are growing up now. Whom they call their friends is going to matter, very soon."

I mulled over her words and we walked in silence the rest of the way to the well. I had been so angry with Yeshua when we found him in the temple, but not angry enough to cast him out of our lives.

I looked at the women loosely grouped around the well, talking. Part of me was still amazed that these women believed the rumors about Yeshua's father, and part of me was thinking about my friendship with Miriam. Could I let her go? I glanced around me. I could make new friends, but Miriam and I were so close. I didn't want to give her up.

Walking home, I noticed again how the women traveled in small groups. Ravital had found another friend to walk with, and I was walking alone. Without Miriam, I had no one. It was no wonder I'd lost my place in the circles of friendship now spread out around me; I'd given all my time to Miriam.

And Yeshua. I thought of the boy, pictured him as he so often sat around our dinner table laughing with David. I couldn't ask David to give that up.

He's practically my son, I mused as I set my water jug down just inside the door to my home. Instantly in the wake of that thought was another thought, drowning out the first. *But he's not my son. And David is. I have to do this. For David.*

That night after the evening meal I left Liat rocking Zahara while my husband sang to Harel, and took David outside to sit beside me by the last of the dying fire in our small courtyard. I covered the fire with surrounding ash, damping it, while I worked out how to tell my son what I wanted to say. Finally, I turned to him.

"I don't want you to see Yeshua anymore," I told him abruptly. Too abruptly.

"What?"

"I don't want you to see Yeshua anymore," I repeated, softer this time.

"But *Em*, what do you mean? I see him all the time."

"I know, David, I know," I said, trying to convey to him with my tone that this was serious. "But. . . . " I let my voice fade into the growing darkness.

"*Abba* works with Yosef," David continued. "And Yeshua and I go to temple school together. How am I not supposed to see him?"

I sighed. "I mean I don't want you to associate with him anymore. I don't want you to sit next to him in temple school, I don't want you to walk home with him, I don't want you to speak to him if you can avoid it. It's important, David. For your reputation."

I thought of the circles of women at the well.

My son's brows knit together; I found myself praying that he would understand, praying that he would hold his tongue and not alert our neighbors to the conversation we were having.

"David, please," I said, reaching for his hand, "try to understand." I wound my fingers around his own, amazed that his hands seemed stronger, rougher, every time I held them. I looked into his eyes, just below my gaze, and realized that soon, my son would reach my height. Soon after, he would surpass it. But for now he was still a child, my child.

"Yeshua . . . " I began tentatively, then paused. "Yosef might not be his father," I said gently. "That's why I don't want you to be as close to him anymore."

"What does that matter?" David asked. "I don't care who his father is!"

"But other people do." I paused. "And you're growing so fast. Soon you will be a man, and the people with whom you associate will have an influence." David's eyes were murky. "On your reputation," I continued. "On who others think you are." I squeezed his hand.

He didn't answer me.

"I want you to have a good reputation, a strong name." I held his hands tightly, looked into his brown eyes. "I want you to marry a woman with a good name, and Yahweh will bless you with many children. And if we have to stop seeing Miriam and Yeshua for that to happen, then so be it. We need to care what people think about us, about our family."

"*Abba* doesn't care what anybody says," David finally replied, looking away.

"I know," I said, searching for words into which I could fit my thoughts. "But your father. . . . " I stopped. How could I explain to David what I meant, without dishonoring my tender, beauty-loving husband? I swallowed the thought and gripped my son's hands tighter.

"You have strong hands and a good heart," I said. "You can grow up to be respected. But continuing to be friends with Yeshua is not going to gain you respect." I sighed. "Yeshua is not the kind of boy who grows up to be the man you can be."

David looked at me, and I was stung to see tears in the corners of his eyes.

"But he's my best friend," he said.

◆

Lying awake that night, nursing Zahara on our pallet, I thought over my conversation with David. He'd barely spoken to me the rest of the evening, and I could see the anger burning beneath his smoldering eyes. I avoided my husband's questions as to what was wrong, and took Zahara to bed with me early. When my husband joined me later with a sleeping Harel, I kept my eyes closed and let him assume I was dreaming. But I wasn't dreaming; the visions in my mind were more like nightmares.

I could try to get my husband to talk to our son, but David was right: my husband cared as little for the respect of peers as he did. I couldn't explain to him, any more than I could explain to David, that our son had the potential to be what my husband never could. David wasn't a dreamer; he was strong and clever, and good with his mind and his hands. He could make a good match, perhaps the daughter of someone highly respected, and he and his family would have opportunities my husband and I could only dream of.

But David had to learn to guard his reputation. I knew that, even without talking to Kefira or Ravital, even if I didn't want to admit it to myself. David had to learn to guard his reputation, and so did I.

I sighed as Zahara let go of my breast, and I rolled over to where Harel was stretched out in between my husband and me. He wriggled his small body around in his sleep, impossibly taking up even more of our small pallet, then reached out a chubby hand and laid it on my arm. I saw his other hand was similarly holding on to my husband, and I laughed ruefully. Memories of David at his age came flooding back to me, back in the days when he was our only child, when friends and neighbor boys and their fathers didn't matter, when all he needed to be content was the ability to hold on to both of his parents while he slept.

David was growing so fast, and soon Liat would start to look like a woman, and then even little Harel would approach manhood. I pulled Zahara in closer to me and breathed into the folds of her baby neck, loving her for being so small, so innocent and new. I had to make David see how important this was. He could not continue his friendship with Yeshua, and jeopardize his entire future. I was not going to let that happen, even if it meant giving up my friendship with Miriam.

◆

The morning sun was still new enough to be pale when I opened my eyes and slipped from my pallet. Zahara was curled against Harel, their two bodies rising and falling in a mesmerizing rhythm. I watched them for a moment, then pressed my fists against my eyelids. My head hurt from a night spent lying awake, pounding over thoughts in my head as if they were grain I was beating into flour: each thought a kernel shattered with the strike of a rock. David's reputation. My friendship with Miriam. Strike, turn. David's reputation.

Preoccupation made me clumsy, and I fumbled with the ties on my sandals. But if I hurried to the well this morning, perhaps I could avoid seeing Miriam. Perhaps I could put off what I knew I had to do. It wasn't a solution, but it bought me one more day. I grabbed the water jug and made my way toward the door.

As I lifted the latch, I looked behind me. In the corner of the room I could see David sleeping on his pallet, the anger he'd taken to bed with him now quiet as he slept. I mentally traced the curve of his cheekbone, savored the feel of his skin as I gripped my jug. Nothing was going to stand in the way of my son. Nothing. I turned to go.

Perhaps if he made a good match, I thought, the bride-price would be enough that my husband could end his partnership with Yosef. This thought was a new one, and the incessant striking of rocks in my head was momentarily stilled. If I let Miriam go, David could grow up to be important. His marriage could raise our family's esteem. We wouldn't need Yeshua's father, wouldn't need anyone. I started down the path to the well.

"*Boker tov!*" Miriam's voice halted my footsteps. "You're up early."

I turned to see her standing in her doorway, one hand over her eyes to shield them from the light of the sun as it grew stronger. I smiled, but didn't say anything in return.

"Let me get my jug," Miriam continued, turning. "You won't believe what Yeshua said yesterday!" She disappeared from the doorway, then was back with her jug. "We were almost ready to eat, and he said. . . . "

"Actually, Miriam, I'm in a bit of a hurry," I said, giving what I hoped was an apologetic grin. I started to walk away.

I heard her laughing behind me. "It's all right, I can keep up!" Her footsteps were quick behind me. "Anyway, so Yeshua said—"

I turned and looked at her. "Miriam, I don't really want to hear it."

For a moment, it was absolutely silent.

Just then, I saw Ravital step out on to the path a few houses down.

"Ravital!" I called out, in sheer relief. She lifted a hand and waved to me, and I ran to catch up with her.

"*Boker tov!*" I called. "May I walk with you?"

"Of course," she replied, then paused, as she looked toward Miriam. Almost against my will, I followed her gaze. Miriam was standing in the middle of the path, her hands clutching her jug, her eyes taking in the scene in that quiet way she had. Her mouth parted as if to say something, and closed again, the story she had been telling now frozen on her lips. She dropped her gaze, then looked up at me. I could see the understanding in her eyes, and as I watched they filled with tears.

I wanted to run back to her, throw my arms around her and apologize, beg to hear the story she was trying to tell me about Yeshua. But I didn't.

David, I said to myself as I turned back to Ravital. *This is all for David.* Ravital reached out and linked an arm through my own, and together we turned our backs on Miriam. My shoulders ached and my throat felt choked with thick, hot dust.

David, I told myself again, against the tears now smarting in my own eyes. *David's future. David's bride.*

As Ravital and I walked on together toward the well I snuck one last glance behind me at Miriam, still standing in the middle of the path, hugging her water jar to her chest. She seemed so small. I looked away.

David's reputation. My footsteps fell into an awkward rhythm with Ravital's, the dusty path blurred through my tears. But I forced myself to keep walking. Because if I didn't save my son, who would?

3

When the Light was Still New

The light was fading as I slipped past an ancient, gnarled olive tree that had stood sentry at the edge of the vineyard for as long as I could remember. I paused a moment to press my hand against the rough trunk. Twisting branches reached out over my head, covering me in a canopy of gray-green leaves. From my spot under the tree I could just make out the twinkling lights of the homes closer to the city as well as the sounds of the villagers making their preparations for night. The last strains of daylight colored the sky, and I turned toward the city, imagining fathers returning from work, mothers calling to their little ones.

I imagined Gibbor walking toward the vineyard, walking toward me.

I heard him rustling through the branches before I saw him—and held my breath. The night air was warm and smooth on my skin; the heady bouquet of just-budding grape blossoms mingled with the welcome scent of damp earth. As I slipped away from the olive tree, I marveled at the delicate flowers clinging tenaciously to the vines around me. It had been a good year, and now as the rainy season approached its end, my father was beginning to speak of the grapes we would harvest in time.

The muted sound of footsteps on the well-tilled earth made my heart thump loudly. I stood, conscious of every breath, waiting for the voice I'd been longing to hear all day. My fingers pleated the soft fabric of my robe, my feet wriggled in my sandals.

He was almost here.

"My dove in the clefts of the rock," I heard a deep voice say, hushed in the stillness. It enfolded me, and a shiver ran down the length of my arms as I wrapped them around my body. I didn't answer.

"In the hiding places on the mountainside," the strong timbre rang out, "show me your face; let me hear your voice."

Gibbor stepped into the row where I was waiting, just wide enough for two people to stand together, just narrow enough to make them stand closely.

"For your voice is sweet, and your face is lovely," he continued, and grabbed my hands in his.

"Lovely," he repeated. He was grinning.

"Mithka told me I would find you here again tonight," I replied, looking up at him. A slight breeze murmured through the vineyard and gently played with a lock of his dark hair. I felt the breeze on the back of my neck as my own hair was blown to the side, sending tiny prickles rushing over my body.

"Did you have a good day?" I asked.

"Busy. Uriya stopped by today to see how my work was progressing on the earrings for his bride-to-be." He winked at me, and I blushed. "The wedding isn't for a full moon; I haven't even started."

I laughed. "Never one to rush things."

"Never. But, look what I have."

He dropped my hands and unslung a small satchel from his shoulder. I looked at his arms in the dying light, the defined muscles beneath the rough brown cloth of his plain tunic. We were so close the fabric of my robe whispered against the fabric of his. Peering inside his satchel, he drew out a small scroll.

"You finished it?" I asked.

"Not yet. Uriya is helping me . . . but I'm almost done. Look!"

He fumbled to unroll the papyrus without dropping it.

"Gibbor," I said, "Come and sit by the tree with me."

I took his hand, and we walked along the furrowed earth running straight between the rows of vines, our footsteps falling softly against the rich, well-tilled loam. We walked back to my favorite olive tree, ever standing guard in its ancient place in the middle of the path. I sat under the tree and leaned back against the rough old bark. Then I patted the ground beside me. Overhead, the night sky grew darker until I could just begin to glimpse the first stars.

"Look, *ahavah*," he said again, sitting down beside me and unrolling the scroll with alacrity. "I have almost the entire book. It takes ages, and I don't write well. . . . " His fingers skimmed the wobbly markings on the parchment.

I reached for the scroll and glanced up at him sideways. "It doesn't look much like the Torah in the synagogue—all of those lines are straight."

"You try copying these lines someday," he told me. "You'll see."

"Maybe I will."

I held the two ends of the scroll at arm's length apart, the papyrus crinkling over my lap.

"Read to me."

"Here, toward the end. . . . " He took a side of the scroll with one hand and with the other took my hand and placed it gently on a line of markings. "This is where I stopped tonight: 'Come, my lover, let us go early to the vineyards.'"

He paused to smile at me.

"'See if the vines have budded, if their blossoms have opened, and if the pomegranates are in bloom—there I will give you my love.' That's all I have for now."

He stopped my hand at the end of the last mark.

"It's beautiful. What happens next?"

"Next the friends of the lovers speak. They have a younger sister, and they ask how to protect her until it is her time."

"And then?"

"And then the lover takes his beloved away with him."

I squeezed his hand.

"And then?" I couldn't resist teasing him.

"And then I finish copying the scroll and set the most beautiful passages to music, for our *chassuna*." He pulled the scroll away from me, laughing, and began to roll it back up tightly.

I sighed and settled my back more firmly into the tree trunk. "I wish it was now. I wish you would talk to my father and ask him if we can be *airusin*." I tucked a stray piece of hair behind my ear and looked at Gibbor. "I wish I was a little fox and we could run into the vineyard and hide and never be found again."

He laughed.

"*Ahavah*, if we were little foxes your father would definitely chase us out of his vineyard. Even Solomon chased out the foxes." He gestured toward the scroll.

"I know. I just want to stay here with you."

Placing the scroll back in his leather satchel, he turned toward me and leaned down until his forehead rested lightly on mine. I closed my eyes and let my skin feel the nearness of his body.

"In time, my little fox," he murmured.

Outside the vineyard, I could hear the city noises settling down into slumber and stillness. I needed to get home soon. In the daylight, I could see the house from my spot beneath the tree, but now the darkness was gathering like a storm, and Mithka would soon be worrying.

"I am going to speak to your father before the next moon." With his forehead still pressed against mine, the words fell from his lips and washed over my face with the warmth of his breath. I kept my eyes closed, holding onto the moment.

"Are you sure?"

"Yes. I want to finish the earrings for Uriya—then I will bring them to show your father, and tell him the price I was promised, and he will see that his daughter will do quite well if she is *airusin* to the city's youngest, strongest metalworker."

I bit my lip. I desperately wanted him to be right, but I knew my father might have his own ides about whom I would marry.

"Don't worry." Dropping my hand, he touched my cheek with one finger, and then slid his hand down to the curve of my neck, running his fingers underneath my hair.

"Don't worry," he repeated. "You'll see."

He dropped his voice to a mere whisper.

"Goodnight, my love."

◆

"Is he really going to ask?" Mithka dropped her mending into her lap and stared at me with eyes like a fawn. She was sitting on the soft rug next to my bed, the light from a small oil lamp casting circles and shadows over her work. I sank down beside her on my knees and took her mending.

"Mithka, you shouldn't work so late. It's bad for your eyes." I took the lamp and moved it off of the rug, onto the white limestone floor and further away from my bed. "And one of these days you're going to set fire to my bedroom."

Mithka laughed and reached for her mending. "But if I don't work late into the night, how can I keep my lady's clothing beautiful and ready for her *chassuna*? And I need something to do while you are out with Gibbor."

"There isn't going to be any *chassuna* if he doesn't ask my father soon. Or if my father . . . " I stopped and looked at Mithka.

"Who do you think my father intends for me to marry?"

The silence was palpable as Mithka looked at me and considered. Lamplight flickered around the room, and she drew her knees into her chest and wrapped her arms around them. I clenched my hands into fists and steadied my breath. If my father had finally picked a man for me, Mithka would probably know about it before I did. Servants knew everything.

I waited.

Finally, Mithka looked at me and smiled. "I don't know what my master's plans are, but if the decision were mine, I would have to say Amnon, the old Torah school master. That hunched back of his is *marvelous* . . . and the way he spits whenever he talks is so enchanting. The schoolboys just love him."

I grabbed a small cushion from the bed behind me and threw it at her. "You are not funny. You know that Father would marry me off to anyone if it made him look respectable to the elders or made him money."

Mithka threw the cushion back at me. "Then Amnon it is!"

I lunged at her but she simultaneously leapt to her feet and snatched the cushion again. I reached for another cushion, and she dodged away from me, laughing.

"You are not funny," I repeated. Although a year older than I, Mithka had always been smaller, and she looked catlike now, crouching in the dim light behind her cushion, her playful eyes just peeking over the top. I lunged at her, and she squealed like a child, whirled around and hit me flat across the back with the cushion. She was small but surprisingly strong, and I stumbled back and knocked over the lamp. It went out with a small sputter, and the room was completely dark.

Beside me, I could hear Mithka struggling to muffle her laughter.

"*Reia*, you need to go to sleep—if your father hears us up this late again he's not going to be pleased."

"We're never going to grow up, are we?" I asked her as I tossed the cushion onto my bed. "Both of us are ready for marriage and here we are, still playing around like children." I thought of Gibbor, and how he would laugh if he could see me and Mithka still fighting in my room, just as we did before we were old enough to cover our heads.

"Bring your mat up here! Please?" I fumbled for the lamp in the blackness, and then gave up. "Please—we can keep talking, and you can tell me about Yaacov. And Gibbor's almost finished the scroll—I have to tell you what he read me tonight."

Mithka's sigh melded with the darkness. "I'm not supposed to sleep up here; you know that." She paused for a minute. "Only for tonight."

I laughed as she went to get her mat. Mithka had been saying "only for tonight" since she was old enough to talk, but I always won. I slipped out of my mantle and untied the thongs of my sandals, then I climbed into bed and tucked my feet up under my tunic. As my eyes adjusted to the starlight streaming in from my two windows, I ran a fingernail over the ivory inlaid stripe at the top of my bed and thought about Mithka.

She had been my closest friend since before I could remember. Mithka's mother, one of our housemaids, had nursed me after my mother died in childbirth, and Mithka and I had played together as infants. When Mithka's mother later died giving birth to a stillborn boy, my father decided to keep Mithka because he couldn't bear the thought of taking someone else away from his baby daughter. I never missed my mother—having been only a day old when she died—but I missed the idea of an older woman living in our house. Mithka was my female ally in a largely male house, and as I contemplated being old enough to marry, I realized I couldn't imagine living without her.

A small sound interrupted my thoughts and Mithka was back, dragging a rolled-up mat. She unfurled it on the floor beside my bed, took off her robe, laid down on the mat and covered herself with her robe. I handed her one of my bed covers.

"Here," I said.

I knew Mithka was my servant, and that she washed and mended my things and did small chores around the household. But she always seemed like more of a friend.

"Tell me about Gibbor," she said.

"No, you first. Tell me about Yaacov."

"If we had our freedom he would ask me to be *airusin*, I just know it. But now. . . . "

"Why don't you marry? Other servants do. Yaacov is my father's best wine steward—it would be perfect!"

"Oh *reia*, you don't understand. After you marry and leave this household there's no reason for your father to keep me here. I don't do nearly as much work as the rest of the servants anyway . . . he only keeps me because you like me."

I didn't answer. I'd never thought about that before. Suddenly an idea seized me.

"Mithka, when I am *airusin*, I will have Gibbor ask for you as a part of my dowry! Then you can marry Yaacov!"

I could sense, rather than see, her face as she pondered my suggestion. Mithka took things seriously, and tended to think before she gave an answer.

"He might be willing to consider that," she finally replied. "But I don't even want to let myself think about it. . . . "

"Consider it done," I said, confident for the moment that my father would listen to Gibbor's proposal. I wriggled my toes in the darkness under my covers.

"And now what about the scroll?" Mithka prompted. "You said he was almost finished?"

"He is—Solomon's songs are so beautiful, and when Gibbor reads them to me. . . . " I stopped talking. Some things I didn't want to share, even with Mithka. As I thought of Gibbor, I hugged my arms to my body just as I had in the vineyard. He made me feel like I needed to hold myself tightly or else something inside of me would fall out and spill onto the floor, running like the rushing of wind through the vines.

"I want to hear them," Mithka said softly.

"I'm going to memorize some of them, and then I will tell them to you. The one he read to me tonight was about a vineyard."

I heard Mithka yawn, and knowing she'd have to get up long before I would, I whispered goodnight. Still hugging my arms around myself, I abandoned my thoughts to waking dreams of Gibbor. He was going to ask my father if I could be promised to him, and then Mithka would be part of my dowry and could marry Yaacov. I couldn't wait to tell Gibbor my idea. He would smile the smile that made my lips go numb, and slide his fingers through the hair at the nape of my neck. I shivered in the warmth of my bed.

♦

As the moon slipped into waning, Mithka woke me one morning when the light peeking into my room was still new.

"*Reia*! Wake up, quickly!" I opened my sleep-suffused eyes to see her wide awake and ready to shake me.

"Your father sent for you, and he told me to dress you in one of your finest robes!"

Instantly I was fully awake, my dream about Gibbor sharpening to reality—had he finally talked to my father? Was this it? Was I about to be betrothed? I hadn't seen Gibbor in so long; it seemed like a whole moon had passed since the night he played his lyre for me in the vineyard. I knew he was busy, and our household had recently been turned upside-down by the arrival of my father's distant cousin, Menashe. He had come to announce that he would be moving to our part of the city to cultivate his own father's adjoining lands, and my father was now spending interminable amounts of time with his cousin, giving him advice on planting, walking him through the vineyards, introducing him to stonecutters and builders and all the prominent men of our town. I felt like I hadn't seen much of my father recently, either. He'd taken to lunching alone with Menashe, and I ate my meals in my room with Mithka. But now he wanted to see me.

"Mithka, do you think this is it?" I jumped out of bed and threw on the robe she handed to me. As she gathered up my hair under my covering I could feel her fingers shaking.

"I don't know, but I can't imagine why else he would want to talk to you so early."

"It has to be. Gibbor finished the earrings he wanted to show him, and he said he was going to talk to him before the passing of this moon. Ahhh!"

I'd been reduced to incoherent noises. I jumped away from Mithka and spun around, my hair spilling out and over my shoulders.

Mithka threw up her hands in exasperation. "I have to get you ready!" She protested.

"He can wait! Dance with me!" We'd been waiting for this moment since we were little girls. I grabbed her hands and whirled around until I was dizzy. When I couldn't spin anymore,

I collapsed on my bed, laughing until tears welled in my eyes. Through my wet lashes, I looked deep into Mithka's eyes as she sat on the bed beside me, and held her gaze in silence.

"I wonder if I can go see Gibbor today, as soon as father tells me," I finally said. "I wonder if he's already here!"

Mithka grabbed my hand and pulled me up off the bed. As she bound up my hair again, I shifted my weight impatiently from one foot to the other. I could just picture Gibbor's face—the slow smile, the way his eyes would mist, the way he would lift me and whirl me around and around in his arms. I couldn't wait.

Mithka finished my hair and spritzed me with perfume from a bottle I hadn't seen before.

"Where'd you get that?"

"It was my mother's. She wore it on her wedding day. Your father saved the bottle for me."

I turned to face Mithka and grabbed her hands in mine again. Silently, she was crying.

"Don't start, or I'll be crying, and I can't look like a mess on the day of my *airusin*." I pulled her into my arms and hugged her tightly.

"Thank you," I finally said. I didn't know how else I could convey what I was feeling. We held each other for another moment before I slowly let her go, and then turned to race downstairs to find my father.

He was sitting at our big table, alone, and smiling. I ran to him, and then stopped myself, lowering my eyes.

"Come here, *biti*," I heard him say softly. As I looked up, I saw him rise from his chair, and I threw my arms around him and buried my face in his chest.

"My little *yeled* today is all grown," he said as he held me. My chest heaved with such excitement I was sure he could feel it. This was it.

I pulled back from him enough to look up at his face. His eyes were moist, his face full of emotion.

"I only wish your mother could have lived to see this day.

How happy she would have been!"

I didn't say anything. I felt for him, but I couldn't truly share in the depth of his grief. I tried to imagine how I would feel if Gibbor died shortly after our wedding, and stopped myself. The thought was too painful. I couldn't imagine going through life without him.

"*Biti*," my father finally spoke. "You are going to be *airusin*. I had a fine young man come and speak to me on your behalf, and I have agreed."

I could feel myself starting to cry.

My father folded my small hands into his big ones, and held them tightly.

"I have pledged you to be married to Menashe," he said. "You can live with him in the beautiful house he will build, on the land adjoining our vineyard."

Menashe? His cousin? What was my father talking about?

He lifted my hands to his lips, closed his eyes, and began to murmur a blessing over my palms. He looked up at me with joy.

As he beamed at me, I felt as if something horrible had started to grow in my stomach. The tears already in my eyes changed consistency; instead of being sweet, now they hurt and stung. What was he saying? I pulled away from him.

"No . . . no," I heard myself say. The tears were still falling.

"*Abba*, I don't love him," I tried to say. "I love someone else. I can't be *airusin* to Menashe; I don't even know him!" I was starting to panic. This couldn't be real. It had to be a dream.

My father was still looking down at me, beaming.

"My *biti*," he said. "Your mother and I barely knew each other at our *chassuna*, yet for the brief time I had her, she made me happier than I can express. You will grow to love Menashe. In time."

"No!" I was almost screaming now. Something black was wrapping itself around me, squeezing tighter and tighter until I could barely breathe. The horrible growing thing inside me threatened to spill out of my mouth.

"No," I said again.

And without looking at my father, I turned and ran.

The workers in the vineyard stared at me as I ran past them, sobbing, my hair covering loose and tears streaming down my face. I didn't care. I stumbled on a rock and twisted my ankle, but I didn't feel pain. I kept running. Finally, I made it to the edge of the vineyard and collapsed underneath my tree. Our tree. I couldn't stop crying. I felt as if I might retch or break in two from the pain of my sobs.

I couldn't even think. I kept trying to calm myself, force myself to stop crying, formulate a plan—any plan. I would be fine, I told myself, if only I could think of a plan, some course of action other than crying uselessly under a tree. But I couldn't think. Every time I tried to quell my sobs I pictured Gibbor, his slow smile, his strong hands. I felt as if I was breaking apart.

When the sun slipped slowly beneath the horizon, I was still sitting with my back against the tree. I had been there since early light, and had reached a point beyond which I couldn't cry. But I felt as if getting up from my spot would only seal the horror into reality, so I stayed there. Night fell.

"*Reia?*" A soft voice startled me, and I looked up.

"Mithka! What are you doing here? How did you know where to find me?" As I struggled to move, I found my limbs had grown numb. Mithka sat beside me.

"I know more about you than you think," she replied. She was smiling, though her eyes were full of sorrow. "Gibbor couldn't come, so I did."

"Oh Mithka . . . Gibbor. . . . " The tears found their way to my eyes again.

"No, shhhh. Don't cry. Gibbor knows. I had Yaacov send a message to him by way of one of the errand boys. Here," she continued, pulling a small flagon out of the knapsack she was carrying. "Drink this."

"I'm not thirsty," I said, through the tears that were falling again.

"I don't care," she answered. Drink it. You can't cry while you're swallowing."

This statement surprised me, and I reached for the flagon. It was filled with cold water, which felt wonderful as it touched my salty lips. As I swallowed, I realized with surprise that she was right—I couldn't cry and swallow at the same time.

"Mithka," I started to say as I lowered the flagon.

"No. Eat this first."

From her knapsack she took out a few of the small lentil and olive cakes I loved. Breaking one in two, she handed it to me. I took it and made an effort to eat, though the grains seemed dry in my mouth.

Time slipped on as we sat together, eating and drinking in silence. The night had grown so dark that I could barely see her face. When we'd finished the contents of the knapsack Mithka took my hand in hers.

"What do you want to know?" she asked simply.

"Tell me about my father." I closed my eyes.

"He was angry—and justly so. No, don't cry," I felt her small fingers brush against my cheek before she took my hand again. "He feels like you've gone against his word by not agreeing to the *airusin*. The entire household is feeling it."

I squeezed her hand. I didn't want my actions to cause grief for anyone else, but what was I supposed to do? I loved Gibbor. He loved me. I forced myself to breathe evenly and tried not to cry.

"Do you think. . . . " My voice trailed off. I couldn't bring myself to finish, but Mithka knew what I wanted to ask.

"*Reia*, I don't know. It isn't often heard of. But there's a chance." She paused, chewing on her lower lip. "I think Gibbor should talk to him."

For a moment, we were quiet again together.

"But I think the person we need to think about the most, the one who could potentially be dangerous, is Menashe," Mithka continued. I opened my eyes.

"Menashe?" I hadn't even thought of him. "Why?"

"He was promised a bride. If your father should change his mind, he will owe Menashe—and Menashe could be very angry.

Several of the servants say the rumor is he's not nice, especially after he's had too much wine. He puts on a good face for the public, but in private. . . . "

She looked at me significantly with her clear, brown eyes.

A shiver ran down the length of my arms.

"He's always seemed cordial to me," I offered.

"He's had your father to impress. I've heard that he's quite temperamental, though. He doesn't like to be crossed." She paused for a moment, looking out over the vineyard.

"I only hope, if your father will change his mind, he doesn't offer me to Menashe instead."

"Oh Mithka, no!" I said, suddenly alert. "He couldn't do that!"

"He could quite easily. But I think I'm safe, since I doubt Menashe would settle for a servant girl instead of the daughter of *Baal HaKerem*. . . . "

"Mithka." I placed my hands on her shoulders. "I won't let that happen. I promise."

Although we both knew I was powerless to make that promise, neither Mithka nor I said anything.

◆

After that night, I didn't leave my room again until the moon had reached her fullness and passed on. As the days wore on, a sickness overtook me, a sickness not of body but of spirit. I lay on my bed, holding a cushion tightly to my chest, singing the song Gibbor had played for me.

"Show me your face, let me hear your voice. . . . " My own voice sounded strange in my ears now, closeted within my room instead of running free with Gibbor in the vineyard. "My beautiful one," I sang on, "arise and come with me."

A gentle scuffling sound made me turn my head. It was Mithka. She came to visit me every day, bringing food and wine and what little hope she had to offer. Today she sat beside me and didn't speak for a moment. Then, she stroked my hair and looked at me, a curious expression in her eyes.

"I have news for you," she said.

"My father?" I sat up faster than I intended, and the room spun crazily around me.

"No. But Gibbor—Gibbor would like to meet you tonight in the vineyard."

Longing and fear chased each other through my mind in rapid succession.

"Oh Mithka, I can't. If my father found me. . . . "

"He won't." She paused for a moment. "Yaacov is watching the vineyard from the tower, and he will make sure."

I looked at her face, earnest, entreating. She wanted me to go. And from the small wooden box built high above the vineyard where Yaacov sat on the lookout for thieves, he'd be able to see anything and alert us.

"Do you think I should?"

"*Reia*, I haven't seen you smile in so long I've forgotten what you look like when you're happy. Go and see Gibbor."

♦

As the last colors of the setting sun filtered through the vines, I waited in the vineyard, shifting nervously from foot to foot. I was scared. I hadn't seen or spoken to Gibbor since my father's announcement; what if he didn't feel the same way about me anymore? I knew he loved me, but maybe he wanted to be with a woman he knew he could have for his bride. I cupped my hands around the white flowers now in full bloom on the thickly growing vines. What if I was too much trouble for him? My father had given his word—for Gibbor to try to challenge that would be foolish, and probably painful. I buried my face in the delicate white blossoms. I was more afraid of losing Gibbor than of my father, or even Menashe.

"'Who is this that appears like the dawn?'" The voice startled me. My thoughts had been so loud I hadn't heard Gibbor coming.

"'Fair as the moon, bright as the sun,'" he continued, and wrapped his arms around me.

"Gibbor," I started to cry. "I'm so sorry."

"Hush, my little fox," he said. "Shhhh."

He held me, and I cried, soaking his tunic, releasing all the fears I'd been building up in my mind since I last saw him.

"I thought maybe you wouldn't want me anymore," I said. "I thought it would be too much trouble . . ."

He pressed his fingers to my lips. "Don't talk. Just let me hold you."

Time seemed to stop, and as he supported me in his strong arms, I wondered if this was what is was like to be held by a mother, enveloped in a mother's love. I wanted to be rocked like a baby, held tight against a comforting chest. I thought of Yaacov up in the watchtower, looking over us, and I felt safe.

"I've transcribed another song," Gibbor finally said, releasing me. "Would you like me to read it to you?"

I nodded and sniffed, feeling like a little girl again, being comforted. I sat down on the ground right where we were, in the furrows between the vines. Gibbor laughed and sat down beside me.

"You don't want to go to your tree tonight, *ahavah*?"

I shook my head. The last time I was there . . . I didn't want to think about it.

"Then we will read here."

Gibbor unslung his satchel and pulled out the scroll. I ran my finger over it hesitantly, feeling the roughness of the stretched skin. I hadn't seen it in so long.

"Listen." Gibbor unrolled the scroll and pointed to where he was reading.

"'My dove, my perfect one, is unique,'" he read. "'The only daughter of her mother, the favorite of the one who bore her.'" He stopped reading and looked at me.

"*Ahavah*, that's the answer."

I sniffed again. My nose was running, and I didn't want him to see it.

"What do you mean?" I asked.

"'The favorite of the one who bore her.'" You are your father's favorite; his only daughter and his only child. I'm going to speak with him. I believe if he truly loves you, he will see how much I love you, as well.

I hiccupped and leaned against him. I wanted to stay quiet, right there beside him. He made me feel as if everything would be all right. I nestled my head against his shoulder, into the spot I called my own. Listening to his voice echo deeply through his chest, eventually I fell asleep.

◆

After my meeting with Gibbor, I tried to resume life as it had been before the day my father announced I was promised to Menashe. I still spent most of my time in my room, but that was largely because I wanted to avoid meeting Menashe, who was often with my father. The plans for his house grew more elaborate with each passing day, and I'm sure my father thought I was a fool to spurn him. But all I could think of was Gibbor. One warm day when the sun had just passed its zenith, Mithka left me alone in my room to go help the other servants. I sat on my bed, staring up at my high windows and breathing the air, thinking about Gibbor. I slid my fingers through the hair on the nape of my neck and shivered, recalling his touch. Suddenly, I heard a small noise, and turning, saw the heavily embroidered curtain that covered the doorway of my room being drawn back. I tensed.

It was my father. I jumped up off my bed in shock.

"*Abba*! What are you doing in my room?" He never came into the girls' part of the house.

"*Biti*, I want to talk to you. And I wanted to make sure we were alone."

He sat down on the foot of my bed. I sat down again as well, slowly, pushing myself back against the wall at the head of my bed and pulling my knees in toward my chest. I curled my toes so hard they hurt.

"Gibbor came to talk to me." He paused. I held my breath and looked at him. I wasn't sure what to say, or even how to feel.

"Gibbor came to talk to me several times, actually."
I waited.

"I can see that he loves you, *biti*. And I'm sure you feel as if you love him."

"I *do* . . . " I started to speak, and then changed my mind. I looked at him to continue.

"It's just not how it's done. I made a match for you, and as my daughter, it's your responsibility to accept it, and to thank me for the match."

He paused again, and I tensed even further to keep from crying.

"Menashe is going to make a fine *Baal HaKerem* with his vineyard, and he would make you a fine husband. I'm not sure Gibbor is going to do that."

I wanted to scream, wanted to ask him why. I wanted to see him justify his claims. But I~~   ~~ nothing.

"Gibbor is not my idea of a good match. He's a fine young man, I'm sure, but he's not what I wanted for you."

A breeze floated in from my window, smelling of white blossoms and fresh earth. It seemed cruel.

"However." My father swallowed, and looked at me keenly.

"Menashe is less than enthused about entering into an *airusin* agreement with an unwilling bride. He has agreed to let me break my word."

I wanted to hold my breath, but I realized I'd been holding it for too long already. I let it out slowly, and looked at my father.

He looked away from me. "I have decided to allow you to become *airusin* to Gibbor, if that is what you still desire. I can't force you to marry Menashe, even if it is my right. So that is what I wanted to tell you." He stood stiffly, and turned to go.

"Wait!" I leapt up off the bed and followed him. I wanted to thank him, to tell him how much his words meant to me, to pour out my heart and show him everything I was feeling. But I couldn't. So I put my arms around him for a fleeting moment before he turned again and left.

◆

The joy of wedding preparation was tainted by the knowledge that my father still wanted me to marry Menashe, and my fears of a reprisal on Menashe's part. As the moon waned, however, my father seemed to warm to the idea. I didn't know how or why, but the smiles he gave me grew more frequent, and he began to inquire about my planning. I was going to marry Gibbor in my mother's wedding garment, which my father had saved for me. Mithka and I pulled it from the crisp sheet it had been wrapped in, and I tried it on shortly before the day of the wedding.

"You look beautiful," Mithka breathed as the soft fabric slipped over my head and fell gently to my feet. It was embroidered more intricately than anything I'd ever seen, and as I looked at the delicate work I recognized symbols from Solomon's songs.

"Look, Mithka!" I said, pointing. "That's the dove in the cleft of the rock. And that's the rose of Sharon." I twirled slowly for her. "Gibbor is going to love this."

Mithka ran her hands through my hair, pulling it up and off my neck.

"I can't believe this day is almost here—we've been talking about this for so long."

"Most of our lives," I agreed. I turned back to face her and wrapped my arms around her. "Gibbor asked for you as a part of my dowry."

"Oh *reia*!"

"I don't know what my father said, but I can't imagine it was anything but yes. He knows how I love you."

"Tell him *todah*, thank him for me. That was the kindest thing to do."

"Actually, you were the only thing he asked for as dowry."

Mithka laughed. "With all he could have asked for?" Her fingers were working my hair again, braiding it into thick ropes. "Sometimes I think men are foolish."

"I'll make sure Yaacov hears that," I teased her.

"You stop; I can't tease you when you're wearing your wedding dress."

"Mithka, I'm so afraid something's going to go wrong."

She ignored me, her fingers combing through my hair. Finally satisfied with her preparations, she let go of my hair, and it fell around my shoulders again. Carefully she helped me out of my wedding garment, and I put my robe back on. It felt plain. I watched as she carefully wrapped the embroidered wedding garment back in the sheet, and turned to go.

"Wait," I said. I crossed the room and sat on the bed, up against the inlaid wood.

"I'm really afraid. What if something happens?"

"What are you afraid of?" she questioned me in return. "What could go wrong?" She laid the garment out carefully on the floor and walked over to the bed.

"Is it Menashe?" she asked.

I nodded.

"Oh *reia*," she said. "Don't let him ruin this for you. Put it out of your mind." She took my hand in hers and held it tightly.

"What are the servants saying?" I asked her.

She paused for a moment before answering. "He's not happy," she finally said. "He's been making some threats, but. . . ." Her voice trailed off.

"Threats?" I felt my shoulders tense.

"It's nothing," she assured me. "He just likes to talk big. He can't do anything; your father will see to that." She looked me full in the face.

"*Reia*, you've gotten everything you wanted."

"I know, and Mithka, I thank you so much." She pressed my hand. She understood me. "I'm just worrying," I continued. "I don't want Menashe to ruin things, and I want everyone to be pleased—both Gibbor and my father."

She smoothed my hair. "Your father will be happy. You see how much he's changed since we started preparations? He will be happy to see his daughter so loved."

"I wish I could talk to him about Menashe," I said quietly.

"Don't," Mithka said instantly. "He wouldn't believe a word you say. The man he thinks Menashe is differs so much from the real Menashe, it would be hard to make your father understand your fears. All it would do is bring back the broken engagement. Don't do it, *reia*."

I looked at her earnest face, chewed the side of my thumb, and was silent.

"Besides," she continued in a different tone as she stood, laughing. "The worst thing that could happen to a bride would be running out of wine at her nuptial feast. And as the daughter of a vineyard owner, at least you don't have to worry about that."

I laughed with her. Fathers started putting away their best wines as soon as a daughter was born, in preparation for her wedding feast. To run out of wine was the greatest shame a bride's family could endure. Mithka and I were both raised on the stories: the wine bearer scraping the empty cask, the young bride shamed, the families calling off the wedding in their anger. Mithka was right: at least I didn't need to fear that.

On the eve of the wedding, I met with Gibbor one last time in the vineyard. The grapes were beginning to bud, and the entire night was filled with their heady scent. Fingers loosely entwined with mine, he led me to the foot of our olive tree. We sat down together, resting against the ancient trunk.

"This tree has seen a lot of my emotions," I told Gibbor. "It will be hard to leave."

"You don't have to leave, *ahavah*. I barely live a moment's walk from here. Wait until you see my home. I've been getting it ready for you!"

I smiled and curled my body against his, warmth suffusing me as I wriggled my toes in my sandals. He wrapped his arms around me and held me there.

"Gibbor, I'm feeling so many things," I told him. "I'm sad about leaving Mithka, and worried about my father, and afraid something's going to go wrong at our *chassuna*, and Menashe. . . ."

"You worry too much." His voice rumbled deeply through his chest.

I lifted my head and looked at him.

"And I'm happy to be *airusin* to you," I said quickly. I don't want you to think I'm not happy. I can't wait to be your bride."

He held me more tightly. "I understand," he replied. "It's the biggest day of your life. Of course you're worrying."

I nestled closer to him and silently thanked him for understanding.

"Everything will be all right, you know," he said finally. "We'll be like the little foxes, running through the vineyard."

I laughed and sat up. "Tell me another song."

"I finished the scroll," he said, retrieving it from his satchel and unrolling it. "This is my wedding present to you." Running his finger lightly through the waving lines, he found the place he was looking for and began to read:

"'Arise, my darling, my beautiful one, and come with me. See! The winter is past; the rains are over and gone. Flowers appear on the earth; the season of singing has come. The cooing of doves is heard in our land.'"

He looked up at me. I held his gaze within my own and couldn't speak for a long moment. Finally I found my voice.

"Tomorrow I will be your bride."

"My beloved. 'Until the day breaks and the shadows flee,'" he read again, "'Come away with me, my bride.'"

The warmth flowing through my body made me tremble, and tears whispered against my lashes.

◆

On the day of the wedding, Mithka woke me before the sun even began to creep into the sky. She helped me dress, perfuming my body as she worked. My father had sent her with a beautiful carved wooden box, and opening it we found my mother's wedding jewels. As I adorned myself, the stones more precious than I had ever dreamed of wearing, I turned to Mithka.

"I can't say *todah* too many times." I clutched her hands in mine, fighting tears. "You have been a sister to me, and my dearest friend."

Mithka gazed at me. "It seems like only a moon ago we were girls in this room, fighting each other with bed cushions." She was crying in earnest, but her words made me laugh.

"It *was* only a moon ago. Mithka, don't let my *chassuna* change our friendship."

"I won't," she promised me.

"And before you know, the time will come for you to be *airusin* to Yaacov!"

She laughed through her tears, and hugged me closely.

"I have to take you downstairs now," she said, pulling away. "Your father wants to see you."

Descending the narrow staircase, I felt as if I'd never walked the steps before. The bridal garment was like nothing I'd ever worn, and beneath all the jewels, I didn't feel like myself. Coming into our large common room, I saw my father. He stood when I walked into the room.

"Little *biti*," he said, crossing to where I stood. He picked up my hands and held them tightly.

"I wanted you to know that you are loved, on this the day of your *chassuna*. Today, and always." His eyes were wet. Looking at me, he didn't need to say anything else. It was enough, and I understood.

"Thank you, *abba*." I whispered.

Outside, I heard the noise of the wedding guests; the entire community had come to share in the feast. Through the sound of their laughter I heard the strains of Solomon's song that Gibbor had set to the lyre. I fought the wild desire to scream and run outside like a child. Today, I was marrying my love.

The wedding feast was held on the edge of the vineyard. As I was led outside by my father, I saw Gibbor, standing with a group of young men close to the vineyard. They were playing his song. For me. For us. When Gibbor saw me, he trembled ever so slightly. I looked at him, and couldn't wait until the feasting and the crowds melted away, and we could finally be alone.

We were seated together at one end of the high table, my father at the other. I looked around at the guests as I sat next to Gibbor, faces I knew, faces I recognized. And a few that I didn't.

"Gibbor?" I asked.

"Yes, my love?"

"Do you know who that man is?"

Gibbor turned to see where I was looking.

"No, I don't," he answered. "Why?"

"I was just wondering. I don't remember ever seeing him before." I peered at the man again. "I thought he looked like he was watching me," I said.

"Everyone is watching you," Gibbor said, his voice suddenly husky. "There isn't a soul at this feast who can keep his eyes off of you."

I felt myself warming all the way down to my toes.

Servants brought us wine and dates, but I couldn't eat. I pressed Gibbor's hand tightly under the table.

"My beloved," he whispered to me. "You smell like honey and grapes."

I laughed. "I wasn't sure you'd recognize me, looking so different."

He smiled at me. "I will always know my *ahavah*."

I held his hand in mine. I could see my father at the far end of the table, laughing with a friend and beaming at Gibbor and me. The strains of music floated gently over us, and all around people were laughing, talking, eating. It was our wedding day, and it was perfect. All my fears had been unfounded. I rested my head gently against Gibbor's shoulder.

"*Reia!*" An urgent whisper shattered my peace.

"Mithka? Where are you?"

"I'm under the table!"

"What is she doing?" I asked Gibbor, confused. He looked equally bewildered, so I cautiously pushed aside the heavy table cover, to reveal Mithka crouching underneath. Her eyes were wild.

"*Reia*, I have to tell you something." She looked terrified.

"Mithka, what? What's wrong with you?" Gibbor held my hand as I peered down to talk to my friend.

"There's no more wine."

A cold wind swept over me and I shuddered. It was a joke, it had to be.

"Mithka. Don't tease me."

"I'm not teasing!" she hissed, urgently. "It's gone—your father doesn't know yet. When the servants went to the storerooms this morning, there were only a few barrels. The rest were gone."

I didn't know how to react to her words. It was every bride's worst fear. It couldn't be happening at my own wedding.

"But Mithka, my father's been saving my entire life! This can't be true." I felt like I was slipping out of reality, into some strange and otherworldly place. I felt as if the torment I went through when my father said I couldn't be promised to Gibbor was back to haunt me.

"Come out from under the table."

"No—I shouldn't be seen at this table, talking to you."

Without a thought, I slid out of my chair and joined her. She motioned wildly for me to remain where I was, but it was too late. Gibbor let the heavy cloth drop and cover us.

"Mithka, this can't be happening." I scrunched my jeweled fingers into tight fists as I crouched beside her. "It can't be happening on our *chassuna*! Not after everything we went through." Above us, I could hear feasting and merrymaking. What was going to happen when the guests found out we ran out of wine? They would mock my father. I would be shamed. He might even call off the wedding.

"Mithka, I have to go talk to him." I was panicking. "How did this happen?"

She took a deep breath. "The servants say Menashe and some of his friends stole into the storerooms in the middle of the night. Your father gave him a key ages ago so he could have access to the cellars."

I stopped trying to keep my beautiful garments clean and sat down hard in the dust. I leaned my back against Gibbor's shins. He dropped his hand underneath the table and rested it on my shoulder.

"Once he and his friends got drunk on the wine, they must have stolen the rest," Mithka continued. "This was their revenge for Menashe's being wronged."

She held me tightly. I shut my eyes, trying to drown out the image of Menashe drunk on my wedding wine. It was more than I could bear.

"I have to go talk to my father," I repeated. I struggled to get up.

"Before you go you should know . . . " Mithka hesitated. "There's a man here who claims to be a magician. I think he's a friend of Menashe's. He was talking about sending a cupbearer to your father with an offering of water, to show him there's no more wine. The cupbearer tried to say no, but some woman told him to do whatever the magician told him to. And so he did."

I couldn't stand the thought of that final disgrace. With a desperate glance at Mithka, I found my way back out from under the table and quickly told Gibbor what had happened.

"Shall I come with you?" he asked.

"No," I said, as I smoothed my hair and my rumpled garment. "I think this is something I have to do alone."

The short walk to the far end of the table seemed to last the cycle of a moon. As I passed, guests congratulated me, smiling and wishing me well. I couldn't meet their eyes. This was my wedding, and now everything was ruined.

I reached my father just as the cupbearer did. I saw a group of men standing nearby, watching him, and wondered which one was the trickster. Looking into the cup as it was handed to my father I saw the clear water he would soon taste. I was too late. It was over. I held my breath and watched him raise the cup to his lips. He gestured with it toward me before he drank, a toast to the bride. I couldn't bear the shame.

As the cup tipped toward my father's lips I saw him swallow, and then lower it in surprise. I cringed and shut my eyes.

"This wine is amazing!" I heard him exclaim. My eyes flew open, startled.

"Which barrel was this?" he questioned the cupbearer. The young man stammered and turned away. I wondered if my father had lost his mind.

"Refill everyone's cup!" my father called. He smiled at me. "I didn't know I was this talented," he laughed, as he swirled the cup. I peered within. Inside, a dark red wine splashed against the rim, breaking into a heady fragrance I could smell from where I stood. One of my father's friends leaned closer to him, and my father gestured for the cupbearer to return and fill the glasses. My father's friend drank deeply then lowered the cup quickly as his eyebrows arched in surprise.

"Everyone brings out the choice wine first and then the cheaper wine after the guests have had too much to drink," he said, "but you have saved the best till now."

My father beamed, and the cupbearer again refilled his cup.

I didn't know what to think. Had the magician done this? I looked back over at the cluster of men. There was the one I was sure I'd never seen before—maybe this was him. I attempted a smile as I walked over to him.

"Are you the one who turned the water into wine?" I asked. He was young, about Gibbor's age, with thick hair and a firm set to his jaw. His robes were simple but clean, and his brown eyes were gentle and seemed full of laughter.

"My blessings on your *chassuna*." He smiled and then intoned quietly: "'Eat, O friends, and drink; drink your fill, O lovers.'" It was a passage from one of Solomon's songs. Who was this man? Suddenly I felt a strong hand around my waist, and Gibbor was next to me.

"Is everything all right?" He looked at me with concern, and curiosity.

"Yes," I said. "This man—" But I was interrupted.

"The procession! To the groom's chamber!" The guests were preparing to escort us to our bridal bed. We were caught up in the press, and I lost site of the man. But as we were swept by, I heard him softly singing:

"'We rejoice and delight in you; we will praise your love more than wine.'"

It was a line from the song Gibbor had set to music. It was even his tune.

"Who was that man?" I asked Gibbor, bewildered but happy. "He saved our *chassuna*. He saved us!"

Gibbor laughed, and I began to laugh too.

"Oh Gibbor, I'm so happy. I love you so much."

The assembled guests swirled around as we began our processional, away from my home and the vineyard, to Gibbor's house where I would be his wife. Tears brushed against my lashes but didn't fall, caught between sorrow and joy. I turned to take one last look at the vineyard and caught site of Mithka, beaming at me as she reached for Yaacov's hand. Standing not too far away from her was my father, and as he joined the wedding processional, he raised his hand to me in blessing.

I looked at Gibbor, wanting to share with him all that was in my heart. I couldn't find the words, but as I held his gaze I felt he understood.

"Come away with me, my beloved, my bride."

Gibbor's deep voice whispering in my ear sent little thrills through my body, and I squeezed his hand as we began our procession to his home, and to our wedding bed.

4

Sounds of Them

I used to be a mother. I used to have a son. I used to toss him in the air when he was little and thrill at his tiny cries. I used to have a daughter I would cradle to my chest and a husband who would cradle me to his.

But now I am old. I am old, I am useless, and I cannot walk. I lie here in this bed, all day long, and listen to Them. The wind blows hot outside my narrow room and I remember my daughter who used to dance in that wind. But now I fear the wind for it brings me, always, sounds of Them.

They came when he died—the voices—they came when he died and I sponged off his body and anointed him with oils. Such oils they were, so lavish, rare. Oils such as our neighbors had never before seen. I spent all I had, because I had to. He was my husband, my love, and it was the only thing I could do.

My sister told me God frowns upon such waste. I laughed and told her I believed in a God of love. She laughed, and said only time would tell.

And then the voices.

They were soft at first, so I almost didn't hear Them. My perfumed hands slipped down his body, down the arms that used to hold me and the body I used to love. I grasped his hands—almost warm in the arid summer, almost filled with the life I couldn't live without. *Speak to me*, I keened, as I ripped the soft white cloths into strips to wrap him. *Speak to me just one more time.* I knew it was wrong to have this wish. But I breathed this cry as I wrapped him, laying before me, the shell of my memory. The man I used to love. I wrapped him and wrapped him as I'd swaddled my daughter, swaddled my son.

But no resistance met my efforts. This was not my daughter or my son. This was the man who gave them to me and now he had nothing left to give. No daughter. No son. No strong, healthy legs to kick as theirs had, no fists to punch at the cloths. How he used to laugh at my first swaddlings! Inept, I was unable to swaddle my son as he moved and breathed—a living, tiny person. A gift. A squirming, impossible, precious gift. In frustration I threw his cloths to the floor and declared he'd live naked until the day he was circumcised, as I'm sure the heathen babies do. And my husband laughed. Laughed, and held me, murmuring in my ear.

Now he cannot murmur. He cannot hold me, he cannot laugh, he cannot love. He is gone and I am alone.

I leaned into him as I once did, covering the strong chest with white cloths. *Speak to me*, I moaned. *Just one word and I can let you go.*

And then the voices started. So subtly, I almost didn't notice. It seemed natural, seemed right. He was there; he was speaking to me. *My love,* he said—They said—and I wept, my tears falling hot on the cloths. *My love!* I called back, and then I knew. Too late. I knew, with all the anguish of knowing in a second that it wasn't him, it couldn't be. It was a demon. Many demons. The demons inhabited my body and I was possessed.

At first I fought Them. I knew I'd be shunned, locked up, cast out, if I ever admitted to the voices within. But fighting Them only made Them stronger. They were legion, not one; They were an army swirling through my head tormenting me with shouts and whispers. I tried to fight, I tried to hide, but the voices were far too strong. They'd command, and frighten, and scream, and I had to acknowledge Them, even to reply. Sometimes it was my own voice that answered; sometimes They spoke through my mouth. My mind was filled with unclean thoughts, and unclean words came pouring out of a mouth I no longer controlled. I lost my husband. I lost my life. And then I lost myself.

My sister tried to cover for me, though privately she told me it was my own fault. I invited Them in when I bought the perfume. I invited Them in when I spoke to his body. I invited Them in with the strength of my grief, overpowering every wish but to speak to him again. It is wrong to love the dead, she exhorted me, and that is why you now pay the price.

But I didn't love him *dead!* I wanted to scream. He was once a living, breathing man and it was *him* I loved! *Him* I mourned! *Him* I keened for! Can't our God understand what it means to love?

Eventually even my sister had to give me up for lost. The words that came pouring out of me were never my own. I couldn't be around children, animals. The small ones were terrified of me, and They made me fear small things. When I saw them I screamed as if I were insane.

I wasn't insane. I was possessed. Insanity hopes for a cure that doesn't exist; possession flees any cure that does.

I went to live with my son-in-law, Shimon. He was a man of God and unafraid of the voices I'd grown accustomed to hearing. I gave up fighting—it was easier not to struggle. I acquiesced until each voice that sounded pierced me a little less that the one before. *Just give in,* They said, to the little bit of me that was still fighting Them in the murky darkness of my mind. *Just give in,* I echoed. *Just give in and They will hurt me far less.*

The Galilean sea had been good to Shimon; his house was spacious, and he welcomed me into my own little room in a corner. I lay on the bed and watched him move. He reminded me of my husband at times, but other times he was so different. He came home with the smell of fish clinging to his clothes, and I longed to take those clothes and hold them to my face and bury myself again in the scent of men.

But the voices now occupied so much of my mind there was no room left for movement. I forgot how to walk, how to stand, how to eat. I was bathed and dressed like a child, like the son and the daughter I used to swaddle. I forgot my name. I forgot my place. I forgot the man I loved.

Shimon often had friends over—men of God—and if I had my strength the voices would have made me kill them. I wanted to love these men, love them with the little bits of me that were left, floating suspended in my world of Them, but the voices hated. *Kill!* They would scream, and the part of me still aware of myself was grateful I'd lost the use of my worn-out body ages ago.

I was possessed with fever. Possessed with voices. Years I laid on the cot in the narrow room until I could barely hear, barely see. When the hot winds blew, my ears unclogged and I heard Them, in my head, always whispering, always there, so much a part of me I barely noticed. It was like breathing—every breath I took, I breathed Them.

One day when the hot winds blew up dust and sand until they covered my useless shell of a body, Shimon brought home a man. I was lying on my eternal cot wracked with fever and voices, and when the man entered They began to scream. *No!* The voices chorused in my head, pounding through my blood and into my fever. The screams were blinding and I felt my body arch and slam into the unwelcoming stench of my cot—again and again and again. They were screaming, we were screaming, my body was screaming, my fever was screaming, the air all around me was screaming. I knew for certain I was going to die; this was death and it had finally come to claim me. I would leave this day and join Them in whatever terrors They had planned for the afterlife of my soul.

Then he touched my hand.

And it was quiet.

Quiet.

My mind was so absent of familiar voices I screamed in panic-stricken terror. And then I did not recognize my voice. It was my voice, my own. They were gone—as surely as They had been a part of me. They were gone.

It was quiet.

I couldn't hear without the voices. I'd forgotten how to hear without Them. I laid on my cot while sobs wracked my body in place of the fever that left with Them. I howled until I could no longer hear myself, and wept for this new, stripped existence.

Then, without warning, I sat up. My body, so wasted, so torn, sat up on the bed. I looked at the man who had touched me. *Who are you?* I wondered, heard myself ask in a voice suddenly audible in my mind, a voice of words that I faintly remembered. But no sound passed my lips.

The man laughed. He was young, younger than Shimon, and his solid shoulders supported a dark head of thick brown hair. The air around him crackled with the intensity and vitality of youth. He didn't say anything to me, just reached over and helped me to stand. I could stand! His brown eyes twinkled and I looked away for fear I would look too deep and drown.

We walked outside, his footsteps steady, mine leaning against him for support. Outside I shied at the dust-filled wind, now strangely quiet and voiceless. I began to hear myself thinking again. My own voice, my solitary voice, ringing through the ears of my mind in jubilance. *They are gone?* I wondered, scarcely dared to ask. And They were gone. They were gone and I had lived so long without myself I didn't remember me.

Outside a young child played in the dirt, scratching houses and trees in straight lines with a stick. I watched her step back to survey her work, and then, with a critical frown, she scratched the entire set out. A strange bubbling, a croaking, was forming at the base of my throat. When it reached my parched lips I realized it was laughter. Laughter for the child, not screaming, not voices. I laughed and I laughed and I laughed.

The man laughed with me.

With my laughter I found my spoken voice—my own voice, dead all these years in the legions of Them. I turned to the man and asked my question.

"Who are you?" I asked of those brown, lilting eyes.

He smiled and once again touched my hand.

"I am one who understands about love," he said.

5

A Broken Melody

Screams shattered my sleep as I jolted awake and clenched my hands into fists. My breath seemed loud, so I held it, checking to see if I could still hear my brother and sister asleep on the floor beside me. In the darkness I could hear Asher rolling over on his mat, and Naamah coughed and then whimpered in her sleep. She cried out again and I pushed myself up off my mat and reached out my hand to touch her back. She shuddered, drew in a sucking, mucous-clogged breath, then breathed a deep sigh and was quiet. I heard her find her thumb and begin sucking it in her sleep.

I lay back down and waited, tense. Another scream from the adjoining room and I felt Asher sit up, startled.

"Asher," I intoned quietly. "Shhh. It's all right."

Although I couldn't see him, I could feel him looking at me, those dark brown eyes in his skinny, oddly pale face seeing right through me, not willing to believe my comforting lies.

"Shhh," I said again.

In the next room I could hear my mother crying, stifling her sobs on her mat, not wanting to wake us. My father's low growl threatened her again.

"I told you I wanted my family *up* and *waiting* for me, when I return home in the evenings!" he spat out, and though I shut my eyes as tightly as I could, I couldn't shut out the image of my mother cowering before him. "Why are the children in bed? Why is there no respect given to the father of this household?"

I heard a sickening thud and knew he'd kicked her. Hot liquid stung the back of my throat and I swallowed several times to keep from being sick.

"*Ba'al*, my mother whispered. "You were gone—we didn't know where. I kept them up for hours, and Naamah is sick. . . . " Her voice trailed off into silence.

"Liar," my father roared. "*Isha chotet!*" The hot liquid in my throat bubbled at the insult. "Don't lie to me. I know you, you and your kind; you pretend to be virtuous, but in truth. . . . "

Without realizing I'd gotten up, I found myself running into the next room. The oil lamp hanging on the wall threw circles of light over the scene, although I didn't need the light to be able to see. The scene was already etched in my mind from too many nights gone by. My mother lay on her mat, curled in on herself as if she were Naamah. My father stood over her, towering, huge. The smell of his goatskin cloak assailed my nostrils. He was drawing back his sandaled foot when I heard myself scream.

"Stop!" I yelled, frightening myself as the high voice settled upon my father. He turned to me.

"And *you!*" he bellowed, turning toward me and grabbing my upper arm in his strong hand until I felt myself bruise. I heard Asher beginning to cry softly in the next room. Any moment now Naamah's shrill screams would join the clamor and wake any neighbors not already listening. My father slid his hand down to my wrist and twisted my arm, bending it up and behind me until my chest pushed out at him to escape the pain. I heard Naamah begin to scream. I could see my mother rising to her knees behind my father, and heard Asher's quiet steps coming from our room. I forced my eyes to remain open, looked my father full in the face, and defiantly, didn't say a word.

◆

The next day as my mother was preparing the evening meal outside in our small courtyard, I sidled up beside her. I watched her long fingers working through flour and water, mixing them together into the flat cakes my father loved. I stared at her nails, broken and jagged, stained with work and worry. I didn't look at her face.

"*Em*," I whispered, still watching her hands. "*Em*, why— why is he like that sometimes? I don't understand."

From within the house I heard Naamah cough, then laugh, then cough again. Asher was playing with her, but I didn't know if his efforts were making her better or worse—even the smallest exertion was enough to send her off into spasms of coughing. My mother turned from her cakes and looked at me, her eyes reddened but firm.

"Go and watch Naamah," she replied quietly. "Asher will make her laugh too hard and her cough will settle more strongly in her chest." Her expression softened. "Be like the *chazakim*, little one."

I wasn't little anymore. But she had called me that for as long as I could remember, even though she'd had two other surviving children after me.

I heard the sound of footsteps approaching up the narrow, twisting path that ran between our close-packed houses, and in my mind the entire neighborhood seemed to still itself and listen. Inside, Asher was silent and even Naamah hushed her coughing. I ran away from the street toward the doorway. A shadow covered the door from behind me and the smell of goatskin invaded the room even before my father's voice. I closed my eyes before I turned around.

When I opened them, my father was standing there, smiling at me.

"Little *yaldah!*" he cried. "How was your day? Did you help your *em?*" He turned away from me to look at my mother, leaning down over our small brick oven, and rested his hand against the small of her back as his lips brushed the top of her head. "And where are my fine *banim?*"

"They're all inside, *ba'al*," my mother answered, not lifting her eyes from the backs of her hands, which looked like they were still immersed in the gluey flour and water. "You're home early today."

"How could I stay away with such a fine family to come home to?" my father boomed as he entered the house in search of my sister and brother. I heard Naamah whimper softly.

Moments later, my father was back just in time to see my mother placing the dinner cakes next to the fire. As usual, she had wrapped the cakes in the fig leaves that would both keep them from burning and provide them with a pungent flavor.

"We will have a good dinner tonight, *banim!*" he sang out as he walked over to my mother and again placed his lips on the top of her head. In his right hand he held Naamah's left, and she clung to him with shining eyes, her mouth working around some small, sticky sweet my father had given her. Asher stood just behind Naamah, straining to be tall and fierce-looking, just waiting for my father to notice him.

"*Ba'al*, do you really think that's good for her? She's been coughing all day," my mother said worriedly, frowning at Naamah's sweet.

"She'll be fine," my father boomed, then looked down at her. "Won't you?" He winked. Naamah laughed and a sticky trail of sweetness oozed out of her mouth and down her chin. She stuck out her tongue and tried to lick it off, and in the process the sweet fell out of her mouth. Instantly, she started to cry.

My father scooped her up in his big arms and held her tightly, shushing her as he smoothed her hair with a work-worn palm. Asher watched him quietly, and soon Naamah was also quiet. I hated the way she responded to him so well whenever he wasn't angry.

Finally my mother turned from our dinner cakes and looked at my father, reaching out her arms for Naamah. My father handed her over and my mother pressed her close to her breast, eyes searching my father's face. She didn't tell him how Naamah cried for him on the nights when he didn't come home. She didn't tell him how Asher slept fitfully last night after witnessing his anger. She didn't tell him about the bruise on my arm or the questions I'd asked her; she didn't say anything I wanted her to say. She just looked at him and smiled.

While we waited for dinner to cook, my father dandled Naamah on his knee and talked to Asher about his studies at synagogue school. Asher's words tumbled around like puppies until I was sure my father couldn't understand anything he said, but my father continued to smile and nod at him, rumpling Asher's hair with a free hand and encouraging him to go on. As I walked by my father's chair I let my fingertips brush Naamah's cheek and it felt hot to the touch. I ran my hand over her smooth skin and murmured prayers for her health.

Just as my mother announced that dinner was almost ready, my father set Naamah down next to me and reached up to the shelf on the wall where we kept the prayer shawls and my father's small wooden flute.

"Shall we have a little music?" he asked. Naamah clapped her hands, jumped up and began spinning around in small circles. I glanced over at my mother. Much as I loved to hear my father play, I knew that if he wanted to play right now, dinner would either be burned or cold by the time we got around to eating. And then he would beat my mother again. But she didn't say anything, merely went outside to move the cakes a little further away from the fire.

A strange, haunting melody snaked through the room as my father raised the flute to his lips. If the tune had words they would have been about shepherds, alone on the hills on the coldest of nights, beset by dreams until the dawn. Naamah abruptly stopped her spinning and plopped down next to me, burying her head in my lap. Then my father played a mournful tune, a melody of brokenness and death, until tears whispered against my eyelashes and I stayed my gaze on the top of Naamah's head.

And then my father played my tune. Glancing at me, he winked and took a deep breath before bringing the flute up to his lips, only to pause and look at it as if he had never seen it before. He held the flute, suspended for a moment in midair, and then turned it around and blew gently against the wrong end. When nothing happened he held the flute away from him in mock surprise, and tried again, blowing harder.

"What has happened to my flute?" he cried out, laughing. With one hand he gestured to my mother, returning from the courtyard. "*Isha*, can you make my flute play?" He held it out to her and with a tolerant smile she tapped on it with one finger. When my father brought it back to his lips, again he turned it the wrong way and blew until he was red in the face. Naamah sat up and began to laugh.

"Naamah?" he asked, waving the flute at her. She coughed and then gesticulated wildly at him.

"Turn 'round! Turn 'round!" she all but squeaked. I glanced at her eager face and sighed, wishing it could be like this all the time. Although she was old enough to speak a few words and phrases, she rarely ever did so. And when she did speak, it was almost always for my father.

He smiled at her, turned the flute the right way, looked at it as if confused, and turned it around again and blew.

"No no no!" Naamah giggled, collapsing into my lap once more.

"Asher?" My father looked over at him, sitting slightly away from our group at what I'm sure he thought was a respectful distance. Asher shrugged and spread his hands in a helpless gesture, his face betraying that although he felt too old for this game, he would play along to please my father.

Then my father turned his eyes to me. "What about you, my eldest child? Can you make my poor old flute play?"

As I reached for the flute, I could see my hand as it had reached so many times before, back into my memories further than I could go. I took the flute from my father and held it to my own lips, to play the tune he'd taught me before I was even old enough to help my mother bake. I shifted Naamah on my lap, positioned my fingers, and began to play.

The notes flew from the wooden cylinder. Naamah got up

and began spinning again. I played a sprightly tune, a dance, that spun itself and gamboled through the room like Naamah, who would soon be dizzy drunk from her whirling. As I played I looked at my father and saw the man who taught me to love music, the man who listened to his son's incoherent ramblings, the man who remembered sweets for Naamah. I saw my younger hand in his, and his hand on the small of my mother's back. And so I played my love for him, my love for all about him that was beautiful and good, and my hope that someday this love would drive out all that was fearful and bad and dangerous.

When I finished, my mother and Asher clapped and Naamah beat her fists against the ground and shrieked for more music. My father bent toward me and took the flute, brushing my hair away from my face with a rough but gentle hand.

"My firstborn," he said, looking me deep in the eyes. "Only my firstborn can teach the wooden flute to play." Then he brought it to his own lips and began to play my tune, only more intricate and diverse. As the melody swooped and dove around the room, my mother clapped and Naamah spun, and even Asher came over with a shy smile, grasped my hands in his and pulled me up from the floor to dance. We whirled and stomped in time to the music, while Naamah spun around us, crashing against us in succession. When the tune finally ended, Asher and I sat down hard on the floor, breathless and laughing, our bodies filled with the notes of the music. My father put the flute gently back on the shelf, and my mother announced dinner.

Although the cakes were both burned and slightly cold, my father didn't seem to notice. He regaled us with stories about his work and his day spent among the elders, and we choked down the burned morsels as if we, too, were oblivious to their state. I looked at the faces around our small table, at my mother, appearing so calm and relaxed; at Asher, so desperate to please; and at Naamah, almost as oblivious as my father, being too young to cling to fear. Then I looked at my father, laughing uproariously over some joke and pounding the table for emphasis. He could make us laugh just as easily as he could make us cry. I wondered if he knew how much we depended on him for our joy. I glanced around the table again, and wondered what my own face looked like.

♦

In a dream of shepherds and flutes I heard Asher's voice, calling to me from far away. His urgent treble grew more and more insistent, until I knew my music was a dream. I screwed my eyes up tighter and willed my dream to stay, filling my mind with music and song.

Bony fingers prodded my shoulder. "Wake up. Wake up—I think *em* needs us." The darkness of the room penetrated my unwilling mind and I slowly opened my eyes. Asher was looming over me, his eyes so wide and his face so close to mine that I inadvertently startled and pushed him away.

"Asher," I began.

"How many times do I have to tell you?" my father's voice crashed from the next room. Small sounds of protest melted into silence as I turned to my brother.

"You know we'll only make things worse. Lie down and go back to sleep. And thank Yahweh Naamah hasn't woken up yet."

"She *did* wake up." Asher's legs were crossed in front of him, his knees raised up to his armpits as he rocked himself back and forth. With one fingernail he picked at invisible scabs along the floor of our room. "She was coughing again, but I told her to go back to sleep and she did—I couldn't wake you. I was getting worried." Rocking back and forth like that he looked like a sick animal, a sick, frightened animal.

"Quit rocking like that," I said, more firmly than I intended. "It makes you look dim-witted."

He raised his eyes to mine, and I almost believed he could see through me, through the thin wall and into the other room. My mother was trying to reason with my father, and I hated her for it. Once he became incensed like this, there was no reasoning. I wished she'd save her breath and spare her dignity.

"*Isha chotet!*" Surely every person in the town heard that

scream. It was quiet for a moment, so quiet that Asher and I couldn't hear anything. Then the small sounds resumed. My mother sounded like she had stopped her reasoning and gone back to quietly sobbing.

"Why don't we do something? Why do you always tell me to go back to sleep? Why can't we help her?" Asher's words were accusing, and, as if in total defiance of me, he started rocking again.

"Stop that!" I said, throwing my arms around him in a cross between an embrace and a restraint. "Asher," I said, "you know we can't do anything. It only makes things worse. Lie back down and go to sleep; I don't want to hear you say another word until morning."

I could feel his shoulders heaving within my arms as if he were locking his grief deep down inside himself, away from my censure.

I pulled away from him and ran my fingers through his damp, sweaty hair. "It's going to be all right. I promise. One of these days something's bound to change. He'll yell himself dry, or. . . . " I couldn't think of what else might happen. But I attempted a smile in the darkness. "Now lay back down before Naamah wakes up again."

Asher's unforgiving stare lingered in front of my eyes even after he left off rocking and went back to lie down, pulling his mat as far away from me as possible. I listened to my father's voice reach a fervent pitch in the next room, heard his fists flying at anything he could find. I jumped when I heard them slamming down against unseen surfaces—even when I knew it was coming. I clenched my hands into fists until my fingernails dug into the skin on my palms.

My mother was crying harder now, begging him to stop. I hated it when she begged; it was worse than trying to reason with him. I heard my father kicking and punching, infuriated, and then there was a sound I couldn't identify. Something breaking with almost a thud. Instantly my mother was quiet.

"That'll teach you," my father roared, and then I heard him

throw back the curtain that hung over their doorway, cross the living room, and stomp out into the night. The ensuing stillness was tangible.

Asher sighed and rolled over, and together we listened to the noiseless house. Finally, I grabbed the robe I used as a night cover, wrapped it around myself, and began quietly rolling up my mat.

"Where are you going?" Asher sat up abruptly, without even a pretense of sleep.

"I'm taking my mat up to the roof. There's too many people breathing on me in here."

"I'm coming with you!" He jumped to his feet and began rolling his mat as well.

"No. You stay here with Naamah. I want to be alone." I picked up my mat. "Besides, it's too cold out there for you tonight."

"Then it's too cold for you, too!"

I could see he was angry, but I didn't feel like dealing with him. "Asher, quit being a stupid child. Lie down and go to sleep."

Tucking the mat under my arm, I turned and walked away from him without another word. To my surprise, he didn't try to follow me.

◆

The night air was cold on my skin as I climbed the staircase that snaked up the side of the house and led to our flat roof. In warmer months, rooftops all over the town would be filled with blankets, mats, and people, all trying to escape the stifling heat indoors. But tonight it was both cold and quiet, and though I shivered as I spread out my mat, it was good to be alone. I tucked my knees up under my chin and wrapped my robe more tightly around me, then sat listening to the town. The quiet murmurs of sleeping families seemed eerie, in contrast to what I'd just heard downstairs. I tried to push the thought out of my mind.

Finally, I laid down and pulled my feet up under my robe. I curled up in a ball and tried to abandon myself to sleep.

It must have been much later that I awoke to footsteps on the stairs next to me. The sky was covered with so many stars they looked like tears—Yahweh's tears falling down on the earth as He wept for the pain of His children. I was stiff from sleep and it took much effort to roll over and look toward the stairs.

"Asher?" I called hesitantly into the darkness. "Is that you?" Now that my anger had passed I looked forward to having him come find me, seeing his big eyes looming over the top of the roof at any moment.

But it wasn't Asher. At first, I didn't recognize the figure in the darkness, he was moving so slowly and softly. As he finished climbing and started walking over to me, though, I knew who it was.

"*Abba?*" I whispered, and then stopped, unsure of what to say. I propped my body up on one elbow to look up at my father.

He sank to his knees beside me, and as his body moved closer to mine I could see he was trembling all over. I sat up all the way.

"Are you all right?" I asked, reaching out my hand. He grabbed my hand with a desperate force and held it up to his cheek, rubbing his rough face against my arm. I flinched but didn't draw back.

"My firstborn," he murmured. "My darling. Such a beautiful baby." The air was cold and my arm hurt from the hair on his face. "Such a beautiful woman," I heard him whisper.

I tried to pull my hand away from his, but he wouldn't let me go. With his free hand he was reaching out to me, stroking the hair away from my face. I pulled my knees in tightly to my chest.

"Such beautiful hair." He pulled my hand, hard, and in the space of a breath he had me pinned against his chest and was burying his face in my hair. I could hear his heart pounding against mine and the smell of goatskin made me start to feel sick.

He was still murmuring, now running his hands through my hair. The night was cold, and I felt sick. I wanted to get away, but I couldn't. I was trapped. His hands were pushing against my face in what might have been a caress if he wasn't using enough force to hurt me.

"You were always beautiful to me," he said. "Even more beautiful than your mother."

His hands were on my body, seeking my skin. I felt new bruises rising under the force of his touch.

And then the night was all around me. I was lifted up from my body, floating. On a wisp of wind I traveled through the town, looking in through high, small windows and watching the sleeping people breathe. Unwittingly, I floated over my own house and saw myself pinned up on the roof. I vaguely wondered why I didn't cry out, and then I was leaping, soaring away from him, shooting up into the sky like stars, falling down like Yahweh's tears. When I hit the roof again I lay still. My father was gone, and I felt nothing but cold, and pain. I convulsed; my bones struck against each other and crashed into my mat. I closed my eyes and pushed my fists against them as hard as I could, forcing my mind to surrender to the darkness.

The first light of dawn woke me, and I lay in a crumpled heap on the rooftop. My mat was twisted and my robe lay in a heap out of arm's reach. I realized I was shaking all over. The memory turned my stomach and I retched until I was sobbing, tasting mucous and blood in my mouth. I wanted my mother.

As I crawled down the stairs, leaving my mat on the roof, I wondered why the house was still. Usually my mother would be up at this hour, preparing the morning meal and just about to wake us. I pulled myself to standing just long enough to make it around to the front door, and then pushing open the heavy door I collapsed on the threshold. I could hear my sister and brother in the next room, and from the sounds of their breathing I knew they were still asleep. I crawled past our room and toward the room at the back of the house. I wanted my mother.

In my parents' room the light from the one high window illuminated my mother's form lying still on the floor, her face turned away from me, pressed against the wall.

"*Em*, I croaked, recoiling at the way my own voice grated in the silence. There was no response.

"*Em*," I called again, louder, crawling along the floor to the side of the mat.

"*Em!*" My mind felt like it was slipping. I was half-screaming now. "Why don't you answer me?" Tears dripped into my mouth as I reached for her, crawling on to her mat and extending my hand toward her back. Sobbing, I put my hand on her and shook her. I needed her, needed her to wake up and hold me and make my memories of last night disappear. I was crying so hard I couldn't see and she wouldn't answer me, wouldn't respond to my pleas.

Finally I tugged her robe hard enough that she rolled over to me, and I saw her form, full in the light of the morning.

My mother was dead.

◆

The passage of time seemed interminable before the sun reached its zenith that day, burning a hole in the sky. My back ached as I carried a small bag of our belongings through the dusty streets.

"*Achot*," Asher called from behind me, his thirsty voice a growl.

"What," I bit back sharply. "Keep walking. Don't let go of Naamah's hand."

I felt, rather than saw, his skinny legs come to a standstill alongside the road.

"Naamah can't keep walking. And neither can I. We *have* to stop."

I whirled around to look at him, almost dropping the bag in my own exhaustion.

"Come on," I said. "I think I can see a city up ahead—if we make it there, we should be able to find a well and then we can rest." Without a word I turned around again and kept walking, leaving Asher no choice but to follow me. Naamah coughed but didn't cry; her small feet continued to patter on in the dust.

It had all happened so fast—somehow I'd gotten Asher and Naamah up and dressed, and we'd left the house before I had fully made sense of my mother's death. All I knew was that I had to get us out of there, and far away, before my father came back. We'd walked through the streets of our town, staying close to the houses and trying to avoid the curious gaze of passing men who wondered what three children were doing alone on the street that early in the morning, and in such a hurry. Many of the men worked with my father, and probably let us pass without inquiry because they knew him, knew what he could be like.

Around mid-morning we'd made it to the walls of our city, and after stopping to drink from the well, had passed on through the gates. I had never been outside the walls before, and yet there I was—leaving never to return again. The pain of my thoughts battled with the pain in my body, but I ignored both and pressed on. By midday we'd made it far from the only places I'd ever known, walking along the barren, dusty trails used by travelers who went from city to city. Fortunately, the day was hot and the path seemed to be abandoned.

When we reached the next city, I mused that it couldn't be that far from our own since we had walked there in less than the time it took the sun to make one bristling arc across the sky. It wasn't far enough. We needed to go much, much farther.

Just inside the city gate there was a well, and I bathed Naamah's face and then filled the bucket for her to drink. She drank, and I lowered the rope again to pull up a bucket of cold water for Asher. After he drank I brought the bucket to my own lips, but the water turned my stomach. I set it down and Naamah started playing in the cool water, splashing and singing to herself. I motioned Asher aside as she played.

"Why are you doing this to us?" he spat at me before I could even begin talking.

"Asher." I pulled him down to sit beside me, atop the city

wall. Naamah played nearby, just out of earshot. My body screamed in silent rebellion as we sank to the ground. "Asher, I have to tell you something."

"I want to go home," he said, turning to face away from me. "Whatever reason you're doing this for is stupid. I want to go back."

"Asher." I laid one hand on his shoulder and placed the other one beneath his chin, gently forcing him to look at me. "*Em* has gone to be with Yahweh."

The words coated my tongue and tasted like the dust off the streets. I wasn't even sure I'd said them right, or that Asher had heard me. His thin shoulder didn't stir beneath my hand, and although he made no move to turn his face away, he didn't say anything.

"Asher, I'm sorry. I wish it wasn't true, but it is. I saw her and then. . . . " My voice trailed off.

He lifted his gaze and locked on to my own. The look in his eyes hurt me more than my father's touch the night before. For a long time we sat looking at each other. The pain in my body paled in comparison to the pain of watching my little brother grow up, instantly, on a dry, hot afternoon in a foreign town.

"Naamah?" he finally asked.

I shook my head. "I didn't want her to know. I didn't say anything. I figured she's young enough. . . . "

Asher interrupted me. "She'll ask for her mother." His tone was almost accusing.

I sighed, heavily. "Today she will. Maybe tomorrow. When the moon has passed, and time moves on . . . eventually, she'll forget to even ask."

"Tomorrow we could be dead!" Asher yelled and startled Naamah. She dropped the bucket of water and began to cry. I glared at Asher as I ran to her and scooped her up in my arms.

"We certainly will be if you have that attitude," I began, smoothing Naamah's hair as her sobs settled into my shoulder.

"Why can't we just go home? he yelled again. "Why can't we just go back to Father?"

"Asher!" I grabbed him with my free hand while Naamah's wails grew louder. "He left. Do you understand me? He left, and he's never coming back. Your father is gone!" I was screaming at him, screaming the words I hadn't wanted Naamah to hear. "Your father is gone and your mother is dead, do you hear me? They are gone! You'll never see them again! Now are you going to quit acting like a child and help me keep Naamah alive, or do you want us to all die right here, right now?"

Something wild and fierce was burning inside me. I was yelling at Asher in a way I never had before. He was crying, I was crying, Naamah was hysterical. As I held Asher's arm I pinched him until I was sure he had bruised.

"Now be quiet," I said, dropping his arm and wrapping both of my arms around Naamah again. "Don't upset her any-more. Fill the bucket again so we can have another drink and wash our faces." I looked in his eyes, defiant in his pale face.

"I mean it, Asher," I said. "*Now.*"

♦

The dust of the weary path clung to our sandaled feet. I'd decided to avoid risking passage through the strange town—where we might incite curiosity with our presence—and instead circle the outskirts of the town by following the city wall. Asher walked on in silence, and once Naamah stopped crying, she squirmed to be set down and then began walking without com-plaint. She was remarkably quiet and seeming willing to embark on whatever adventure lay before her. I wondered how much of Asher's and my dialogue she'd understood. When she finally stumbled and fell to the ground, I passed our bundle to Asher without a word, and picked her up and kept walking.

"Why can't we stop here for now?" Asher asked. "Where are we going, anyway?"

"I don't know where we're going," I answered. "But we need to put as much distance between ourselves and our old home as possible. We need to find a place where no one recognizes us as the children who were abandoned when their mother died."

I looked at Asher, who seemed to accept my explanation. I didn't want to tell him that we were running away so our father could never find us—that he hadn't in truth gone away, and that I was taking them someplace he'd never look. I needed to know that our father could never hurt me again, or hurt either of them. If I'd known where we were going I would have told Asher—but I didn't know anything.

Long after the sun set, the dust began to grow cool under our feet and I turned to Asher. We were in a disheveled grove of olive trees outside the wall of the city, a grove which must have sprung up from seedlings that fell from the trees within. As I looked up toward the wall I could just make out their branches, stretching stolidly toward the night sky. I looked again at the trees surrounding us. It wasn't yet time for olives, and the trees should have been covered with the delicate white flowers that precede the fruit. But they weren't, and as I looked closer I saw new branches shooting out of the gnarled, ancient ones. The olive trees were dying. Yet something about the roughness of their bark made me feel like we could rest here and be safe.

"We'll stop here for the night. We need to rest before we keep walking."

I pulled some flat cakes out of our bag, the first I'd eaten all day. As I slowly chewed the small pieces I broke off, I was surprised at how much better I felt.

"Don't eat too much," I cautioned Asher. "I took everything we had but it's not a lot, and Naamah won't understand that she can't eat as much as she wants."

Naamah had both fists filled with the cakes and was nibbling from the end of a closed fist, soaking the cake with her saliva and turning it into a sticky paste that clung to her little hands.

Asher and I ate in silence. The moon was beginning to shine down on the path, and I thought of the kinds of people that usually traveled at night. We probably weren't the only travelers with reasons for remaining out of sight of the townspeople, and I wondered if we'd have been safer trusting ourselves to the mercy of an innkeeper somewhere within the town. But it was too late to go back to the gated entrance. I made Asher and Naamah as comfortable as I could, and we slept.

In the night I saw my father and my body froze, not knowing if it was a dream or reality. He was there again; I could smell the pungent goatskin and feel his rough hands catching in my hair.

"You're beautiful," he whispered to me. "Even more beautiful than your mother."

I woke with a scream caught in the back of my throat. The cold ground was hard beneath me, and I was drenched with sweat. The morning light wasn't far off, and Asher and Naamah lay sleeping curled up against each other. I rose and walked a little ways away from them, deeper into the grove of trees.

Pushing my tangled hair away from my face as I walked, I suddenly hated it. My fingers caught in the knots and I began to pull until I thought my scalp would rip and bleed. I wanted my hair gone—it had made him hurt me and now I had to get rid of it. Grabbing a sharp stone from the ground beneath me, I threw myself onto the twisted roots of a dying tree and began sawing at my hair as hard as I could, scraping the stone across the hair splayed out in the dust and dirt. I wanted it gone. I ripped and hacked and tore, sobbing, until at last a clump came free. I flung it into the air and it landed not far from me. As if possessed, I kept at my mission until I was on the last few strands of hair, tearing and cutting them off.

"What are you doing?" I sat up and saw Asher, awake, staring at me. "You've gone crazy, haven't you?" He bit his lower lip, serious.

"I don't know," I sobbed, trying to catch my breath and control myself. "Asher, I just don't know."

I held my breath, forcing my sobs to succumb to a calmer hiccoughing. I tried to look reasonable as I pushed the jagged edges of my now-short hair out of my eyes. "If we're going to live on the streets for a while, it's too much to look after you and Naamah and keep my hair. So...." I looked at the pile of brown strands on the ground. "So it's gone," I finished lamely. "Help me get Naamah up before it's fully light."

Two days later, our bread was gone. We hadn't journeyed even half as far as we'd made it the first day, because both Asher and I were growing weak and Naamah's cough had returned in full force. She couldn't even walk now, and taking turns carrying her slowed our pace considerably. We were beyond sight of the foreign city we'd passed, and the unchanging landscape stretched limitlessly along the lonely path ahead of us when I gave Asher and Naamah the last of our bread, whispering to myself that it was gone. Asher heard me and took the bag out of my hands, peering inside.

"*Achot*," he called, holding up a small wooden item. "Why'd you bring father's flute?"

I grabbed it away from him. I hadn't even remembered that I'd taken it the morning we left.

"I don't know," I said, the wood cold in my hands. "Here— take it. Break it, do whatever you want with it. It's yours; I don't want to see it again."

He took the small flute from me. "Maybe we could sell it for food," I said, turning my back toward him.

"Maybe you could play it."

Naamah finished her flat cake and started crying for more.

"No," I said. "I don't ever want to see that thing again. Come on, let's go find something to eat . . . something to do . . . something."

That night as we bedded down alongside the road, I wondered how many days we could continue on. Naamah was scarcely more than a toddling baby, and her cough wasn't getting better. Without food, Asher and I wouldn't last much longer. I whispered a prayer to Yahweh, wondering why I thought he listened to me anymore, and pressed my fingers against the backs of my eyelids until I fell asleep.

◆

"Is this them?" a coarse voice disrupted my dreams.

Then a childish grunt. "Why don't you at least ask them who they are?"

"I don't like the way they look. I say kill them before they wake up."

I kept my eyes shut and tried to guard my breathing, hoping it would sound regular and asleep.

"They've got a *baby*? Who travels with a baby?"

"I say you're right. We don't need these people."

It sounded like we'd been surrounded in our sleep. Yet the voices were children's voices. I finally opened my eyes to find I was staring straight into a pair of brown eyes belonging to a filthy, reeking boy not much older than me, hovering directly above.

I sat up, almost knocking my head into his. "What do you want?" I asked him in a voice that I hoped didn't shake.

He straightened, and motioned for me to stand. He looked like someone who was used to being obeyed. I stood.

"I'm Baruch," he said, "and these are mine." With a gesture he indicated a group of children of various ages, standing around him in a semi-circle. He seemed to be the oldest. The youngest was but a few years older than Naamah. All of them were dirty, snot-nosed, ragged, and mean-looking. Baruch had a cut above one eye, and glancing around I saw similar cuts and bruises among the masses of tangled hair and stained clothing that surrounded me. I stifled an involuntary shudder, then wondered what I looked like to them.

Baruch surveyed my sleeping siblings with a practiced eye. "We heard you were here. We're from the town not far up the road." One of the boys in the group pointed helpfully in the direction we'd been traveling, and a girl about my age slapped him across the face.

"So," Baruch continued, raising his thick eyebrows as he questioned me. "can you do anything?"

"What do you mean?" I asked.

He sighed. His breath was foul.

"If you're going to make a living on the street, you have to be able to do something. I'll offer you a place with me and my people, but you have to be able to do something." He ran a dirty finger alongside his nose, scratching it.

"I can do something!" Asher's voice startled me. He was awake and surveying Baruch with frighteningly cold eyes.

"I can fight," he said, and clenched his fists. I heard the girl who had slapped the boy giggle, and I wanted to slap her back.

Baruch stepped over to Asher, grabbed him by the ear and forced his face upwards until the boys were eye to eye.

"You don't look like much," he concluded, "but if you're stubborn, I can train you." He let go of Asher and looked back at me. "And you? I'm still waiting."

"I—I can learn," I finally said. "I can do anything you can teach me to do."

The nasty-looking girl giggled again and now I really wanted to hit her.

After what seemed an age, Baruch broke off his gaze with me. "All right," he said. "Come along and I'll show you where you can sleep. But she stays," he added, pointing to Naamah. "We don't have room for babies."

Hot anger surged through me. "Then we don't come," I said, and reached out to grab Asher's arm. "Who do you think you are, anyway, intruding on our lives? Did we ever say we wanted you? Did we ever say we needed you?" I yanked Asher over next to me and turned to look Baruch full in the face. "You can take your filthy band of starving *children*," I spat out the word, "and leave now."

My head bent sideways under the sudden crack of an unseen hand.

"That's what happens when you talk back to the leader," a voice said.

"And don't you forget it." Baruch leaned in closer. He reeked.

"Don't you touch me," I hissed back at him. "Ever."

We stood in silence, facing each other. Blood was pounding behind my eyes, but I glared at Baruch without blinking.

The children, loosely grouped around us, waited to see what would happen next.

"I like you," Baruch finally said. "You're tough. Bring the baby then, if you want to, and come."

And he turned around and started walking away in the darkness. Asher looked at me. I didn't know whether to follow Baruch or not, but as I bent down to pick Naamah up, I realized it was the best—and only—chance we'd been offered since leaving home. Naamah wrapped her sleepy arms around me and snuggled into my chest.

"Come on, Asher," I said. We hurried after him in the pre-dawn light.

"Glad you've decided to join us," Baruch said without turning around. "We can teach you and the boy to steal. But the little girl's your problem."

The ground was cold as we marched on, going where, I didn't know. I bit my lip and tried to decide if life with Baruch and the other children was actually going to be better than watching my siblings starve on our own.

◆

The busy street thronged with people as I skulked behind buildings, trying to remain invisible on a crowded market day. A sharp tap on my shoulder made me turn around, and Baruch was standing there, holding Naamah by the hand. She was smiling up at him with the same smile she used to bestow upon our father. The sight of it made me sick. Since we'd met Baruch two moons ago he'd gone from resenting Naamah to having an odd sort of affection for her. He'd even stolen something for her cough. I hated him for it, but it was good to see her feeling better and breathing easily again.

"Watch this," Baruch said. "Time to start her training." He was grinning.

"Naamah!" he leaned down so his face was only inches from hers. "You see those pomegranates there in that stall?" He pointed out from around the corner of a building, into the main

street where vendors had crowded their wooden carts in until
the people could barely move around them. The market was
filled with noise as buyers haggled with sellers, trading everything from jewels to fish. Naamah didn't say anything, just
stood there with two fingers in her mouth and reached for
Baruch's hand.

"See them? Right there?" he repeated.

She nodded, her fingers entwined with his.

"I want you to see if you can bring me one. Can you do
that?" Baruch's voice was low, conspiratorial. Naamah's eyes
were beginning to shine. She was loving this; she adored games.

"But you *can't* let anybody see you—that's part of the
game!"

Naamah's eyes went round and she stuck another finger in
her mouth and squealed with delight as she stomped her feet.

"Shhhh . . . " Baruch leaned in even closer. "Now, *go!*"

And with a scamper, she was off. I watched her thread her
way through the crowds, her fingers still in her mouth, looking
for all the world like a little beggar's child. This thought made
me cold as I realized that was indeed what she was—a beggar.
And Baruch was turning her into a thief.

Naamah crept quietly along to the stand of pomegranates,
her little head not even clearing the display. She took her fingers
out of her mouth and reached out her hand, catching a juicy
pomegranate between her fingers. She was back at my side before I knew it.

"See?" she called out happily. "See?" She held the pomegranate up to Baruch, who lifted it to his lips and kissed it.

"We're never going to be hungry again!" he roared, and
slapped me on the back. I jumped away from him and glared at
him warningly. He didn't notice, caught up in the ecstasy of
Naamah's success. "She's smaller than any of us, and she learns
quick. They'll never even see her coming."

I didn't know whether to laugh or cry as Naamah pranced
and twirled around him, pleased with her success at his game,
until suddenly he caught her around the waist.

"Naamah," he said crouching down again. "Since you won the game, you get the first bite." He lifted the fruit up and tore it in two with his dirty fingernails. Scooping out a sweet chunk, he held it to Naamah's rounded mouth and she sank her teeth into it, dark pomegranate juice spilling out of the fruit and staining her chin. My mouth watered. Naamah's eyes were bright as she slurped up her bite of the fruit, and she looked at Baruch adoringly. He'd just won himself a slave for life.

"*Achot*," I heard a voice right next to my ear, startling me.

"Asher! Where have you been?" Since joining Baruch's gang I'd seen less and less of Asher. He tended to spread out with the other boys his age, scouting for food, places to sleep, and things to steal. His pockets were filled with the small trinkets of a young boy's whims, trinkets I knew he hoarded and traded with the other boys in exchange for bits of food or shared alliances. When I did see him I felt sometimes as if he was ashamed of me, but I never had a moment alone with him to talk about it.

"Where were you?" I repeated.

"Around," he replied. He didn't look at me.

"You smell like stew." I bent closer to sniff him and he stepped back.

"I do not."

"Yes, you do—where were you? Did you find food?"

Asher said nothing, then glared at me. "If you hadn't made us leave, we'd have stew every day," he spat out. Then he turned and ran away from me. I saw him cuff a small boy about his age from our group on the back of his head, and the two of them ran off together. I wanted to call out to him, but I held my tongue. I'd thought he was old enough to understand, but maybe he wasn't.

I turned back to look at Naamah and Baruch. They were sharing the pomegranate, sucking the juice out of the fruit as it ran down their chins. They laughed together. I felt like I was losing both my brother and my sister.

Before the passing of the next moon, no one could admire anything without Naamah stealing it. We traveled from town to town with Baruch and his group, following the market days, stealing what we needed to live and, thanks to Naamah, anything else that caught our fancy. In a town twice the size of the one we'd grown up in I saw a vendor selling flutes, everything from small wooden ones like my father's to ornate instruments fit for royalty. I hurried up close to Asher as we passed the stall.

"Look, Asher," I said as I caught up with him. "Doesn't that flute remind you of father's?" I was desperate for any sort of connection with him. I understood his anger; I even understood why he blamed me for what had happened to us. But I couldn't stand to lose him completely.

"It does," he finally admitted, turning to look at the stall.

Not even a moment later Naamah ran in front of me, holding her hands behind her back and giggling.

"Naamah, what do you have? Show me," I instructed.

She stuck her arms out in front of her, unclenched her fists and held out a small flute.

"Naamah! We don't need that! Go and put that back right this instant," I said.

"What are you telling her to do?" Baruch appeared out of nowhere. He treated Naamah as if she were his own child, his and his alone. Anytime anyone else tried to talk to her or order her around, he got nervous.

"She doesn't take things back," he said. "She brings things to us. Don't you, *yaldah*." He tousled her hair and she smiled.

"What do you have?" he continued. She held out the small flute.

"Ah, a flute! Do you like music?"

She nodded and stuck her fingers in her mouth. I glared at her.

"She doesn't know what she's talking about. She stole that flute because it was pretty. And because you've taught her to take everything she sets her eyes on." I looked at Baruch accusingly.

"She stole the flute because it reminds her of our father," Asher interrupted. "And yes, she loves music. Our father used to play sometimes. And we still have his flute."

He hadn't spoken that many words to Baruch since we'd met him. His eyes bored holes into me. It was a challenge.

"We do not," I replied. "I lost that old thing ages ago. And I don't want to hear about it again."

Baruch looked at me for a moment. He knew I was lying. Then he turned his attention back to Naamah.

"Did your *abba* play the flute?"

She nodded again. Baruch looked at me, a gleam in his eye I didn't like.

"And who else plays the flute?"

Naamah pulled her fingers from her mouth with a sucking sound, and pointed a finger at me. I felt my cheeks inflame.

"She doesn't know what she's talking about," I told Baruch again, putting an arm around Naamah. "And I don't want to talk about it."

To my surprise, he looked at me but didn't say anything.

◆

At night, we set up crude makeshift camps not far outside the walls of the closest city. We never slept within city walls if possible—Baruch said it was too dangerous—but we also took care to avoid the unclean people that could sometimes be found outside the city gates. So every night we'd collect our spoils and leave, stopping at a well along the way. Tonight, I left the bickering, squabbling bunch behind me and went to look for Asher. He'd settled into our routine as adroitly as Naamah, perhaps even more so, and I saw him less and less. But now, I was worried. Too many long days had gone by without my seeing him. I almost expected his pale form to pop out suddenly and startle me, his eyes ever wider in his thin face, accusing me silently whenever he spoke.

Outside the city walls the night air seemed cooler, and more expansive. The dusty trail along which we bedded never changed; the trees and small shrubs were ever constant as we journeyed on, always on the move, always looking for another market to plunder.

The children tonight were in disarray as the older ones tried to start a small fire and the younger ones cried until they were cuffed. Earlier that day we'd left the city in a hurry when one of the vendors selling jewels caught Naamah with her sticky fingers wrapped around something brilliantly colored and precious. As he was roaring at her I had grabbed her in my arms and run, knowing we'd meet up with the others outside the city. Now, as the children began to settle down and huddle in groups, whittling sticks with sharp rocks and boasting about their days in the busy market, I couldn't find Asher anywhere.

"Baruch, have you seen my brother?" I hated to initiate a conversation with him, but he was the likeliest person to know where Asher went.

"No." He was rifling through the small knapsack he carried, looking over his spoils from the market. I crouched down on the ground beside him.

"You're lying to me."

"You lied to me about the flute. Why won't you play?"

"That's not what I came to you to talk about," I said, sitting down hard and pulling my knees into my chest. My body felt tough, beaten and bruised by our lifestyle that was constantly on the move. I wrapped my arms around my knees.

"You'd be pretty if your hair wasn't so awful," Baruch said suddenly, dropping his knapsack to look at me. I blushed furiously and felt an old pain begin slinking through my body.

"I will never be pretty." It was a promise. "Tell me where Asher is."

Baruch stretched and looked over the rest of the children he called his own. "He'll have to tell you that himself."

The night air felt thick against my exposed skin. I watched the boys Asher was usually with as they whittled away at their sticks, occasionally challenging each other with them as if they were swords.

"Baruch, tell me."

He didn't respond. Furious, I got up off the ground and walked over to where Naamah was sleeping peacefully, close to the small fire, stretched out on my robe. I lay down between her and the fire, tensing every muscle in my body to keep from crying. Where was Asher? The long nights since we'd left our home flew backward through my mind in rapid succession, ending with the night before we left. I thought about my father. I was floating again, above our flat roof, away from him, gliding peacefully over the close-nestled houses around us. Children were sleeping and their baby noises filtered up into the night. Stars rained like tears. I was shaking my mother; her body turned and I saw the raw stiffness of her unresponsive face. I tried to run, but I couldn't. I screamed.

"*Achot!*" I hadn't realized I'd fallen asleep.

"Asher!" Opening my eyes, I saw him bending over me, on his knees beside me. The dying embers of the fire cast an unearthly pallor on his face. I struggled to sit up, my own face wet with tears. My hands hurt from clenching them. Beside me, Naamah lay soundly asleep, undisturbed. I wondered how often I cried out in my sleep—had she grown used to it, just as she'd grown accustomed to stealing?

"Asher, where were you? Why are you always wandering off? I need you here—you should stay close to Naamah and me."

His eyes loomed huge and watery in his bony face. I reached out a hand to brush back his shaggy, unkempt hair; he leapt away from me. The moonlight shone off of his agile body.

"Don't touch me," he said, backing away slowly as if I were an animal. "I want to talk to you, but don't touch me."

I rose to my feet slowly.

"I won't," I said uncertainly, cautiously stepping closer to him. He backed away from me, his eyes wary.

"Don't come any closer." He held out his hand. We stood there for a moment in silence. Finally, he took a deep breath. I saw the bones of his ribcage heaving.

"I'm leaving," he said quietly. "I wanted you to know."

"Leaving?" My mind couldn't process the word. "What are you talking about? Where are you going?" Did he think he could go back home?

"I have to go back to the last village," he said, wrapping his arms around himself. "To the people outside the gates." He scuffed one sandaled foot in the dust. "I. . . . " He hesitated. I tried to encourage him to go on, without saying anything.

"I have to go," he finished lamely. "I can't stay here."

"Asher, we need you. *We* are all we have left. . . . " The tears were starting again and I didn't know if he'd understand.

"Listen to me!" His voice exploded and startled me. "Can't I make you understand? I have to go back!" He was crying now. I tried to walk up to him, to put my arms around him, but he ran away from me again.

"Don't touch me!" he screamed.

The rest of the children were waking up now, watching our quarrel with practiced indifference.

"I had some stew," Asher babbled. "They offered me some stew. I was hungry and I ate it. And now I have to go back." He looked up at me, panic in his eyes. "I can't stay with you. I don't want to make you or Naamah. . . . " He trailed off.

"Asher, you're not making sense. Just come here. Where do you think you'd live if you left us?"

"The people . . . the people outside the gates."

"The *unclean*? Asher, you can't go live with them! They're sick! You'll get sick—do you understand me?"

His eyes seemed to grow even larger as he took one step toward me and flung out his skinny arm. In the moonlight I could see it was covered with sores, red scabs showing dark against his pale skin. Inadvertently, I recoiled and jumped back.

"You see? I *am* sick, and I have to go." He was crying so hard I could barely understand him.

"*Achot*," he finally choked out, but then turned and ran.

"Asher!" I screamed, running after him. He was quicker than I, and I knew if I paused a moment, he would get away. "Asher, stop!"

A scream made me stop my pounding feet and turn back toward the camp. In my absence, Naamah had rolled over and the edge of her tunic had caught fire in the dying embers.

"Naamah!" I raced back to her, clapped my hands around the small fire licking at her hem and then clutched her to me. The danger passed as quickly as it had begun, leaving Naamah frightened but unhurt.

"Oh, thank Yahweh you're safe. You can't sleep that close to the fire—even when you're cold. Promise me that? Promise me, Naamah?" I stroked her hair away from her face as I rocked her and held her tightly. When my heart slowed down, I turned to look away from the camp.

"Asher . . . " I whispered into the night.

He was gone. I'd lost him.

As my eyes began to swim with tears I saw a small dark object on the ground not far from where I sat with Naamah. I put her down and went over to pick it up.

My father's flute.

♦

Later that night, after having moved Naamah further from the fire and held her hand as she fell asleep, I lay on my back and looked at the stars. I didn't cry anymore—I felt like all my tears had fallen, leaving me with a great emptiness inside. I rolled over. The coarse leather strap of the bundle I'd been carrying since we left home brushed against my skin, and I let my fingers glide slowly toward the knot. Without seeming to follow my will, my fingers untied the knot and slid inside the bag to curl around the flute and bring it out.

The smooth wood felt good against the skin on my palms and I held it for a while, thinking about my father: how he used to frighten us, how he used to make our mother cry, how he used to make us laugh. I curled my legs in toward my body and lay there for a moment. Then I got up, quietly so as not to disturb Naamah, and walked back toward the city we'd just left.

I looked at the flute. Then I raised it to my lips and closed my eyes.

I didn't play my song. I played a new song, one for sleepless nights, stolen food, and broken dreams. This song was for lost children who might not grow up, and for all the pain that brought them to the streets. I played for Baruch, for all of his group, for Naamah, and for Asher. As I played, salt stained my pursed lips. I played until there was nothing left of me to play.

♦

The next day, as we entered a new city, I didn't waste any time. I'd decided what I had to do, and now I was going to do it before I lost my resolve. Asher was gone, and if we stayed with Baruch, I was going to lose Naamah as well—I didn't know to what, but I knew she was slipping away from me as certainly as Asher had. Baruch had done a lot for us in his own way, but it was time to move on. I left Naamah with him and approached the first vendor I saw in the market.

Running my fingers through my matted hair, I tried to look less like a dirty, hopeless child and more like a woman.

"*Boker tov*," I said with a forced smile. "Could you tell me where I might find the city musicians?"

The vendor was a graying man, selling a variety of wooden boxes with intricately carved designs. As he lifted a finger to point, I saw the knobs of age disfiguring his knuckles.

"There's a woman living in the third house up that next street," he said, indicating it with his gnarled finger. "But I doubt she wants anything to do with you."

"*Todah*," I murmured, and ran off before I could change my mind.

The courtyard was small but neat outside the house the man had indicated. I clutched the small bag I'd tied around my wrist and walked slowly toward the doorway, forcing myself to breathe evenly. The heavy wooden door stood open, and as I approached it I could hear soft music from a lyre. I stopped in the doorway, hesitating.

"*Boker tov*," a woman's gruff voice called from inside. "What do you want?"

"Please," I said, furious at how my voice wavered. I tried again. "Please, I was looking for the musicians. I was wondering if you needed an apprentice—I play the flute." I fumbled with the bag and procured the wooden instrument, holding it out toward the form ensconced in the darkness of the house.

The woman didn't answer for a moment. Finally she replied, "Come in."

I stepped over the threshold and breathed in the smell of stone, wood, and cloth. I screwed up my eyes to keep from crying. I couldn't succumb now.

"Well, let me see then."

The woman was seated on a small three-legged stool, her lyre balanced against her legs. I couldn't tell how old she was as her covering nearly hid her face. She could be as old as my mother, even my mother's mother, or she could be very young. I lifted the flute to my lips and then paused.

"What would you like me to play?"

She didn't respond, merely gazed at me, so I took a deep breath and played the first note of my song. The image of my father overwhelmed me and I stopped.

"One note isn't going to get you an apprenticeship, child, with me or with anyone else." The woman rose from her stool.

"Wait!" I called, desperate. "I can play. Listen."

I lifted the flute to my lips again and started playing the tune I'd played the night before. The notes tumbled from the wooden cylinder and caught in the air, haunting and sad. I played for Naamah, for the only chance we had left. I played for Asher.

When I finished, I lowered the flute and looked at the ground. The woman stepped over to me and caught my chin in her fingers. Her grip was strong. Forcing my face upwards, she looked at me.

"You're not much to look at."

Since it was a statement, not a question, I didn't answer.

"You should answer when someone speaks to you. You're an orphan?"

I nodded, and then said, "Yes." It was close to the truth.

"Where'd you learn to play?"

"My father."

"Pity he died, then. He must have been a wonderful musician."

I couldn't say anything.

"How many of you are there?"

"Three," I said without thinking, and then lowered my eyes. "Two now."

The woman held my chin, considering.

"I might be able to use you for mournings. That was a moving piece you played—and you're pitiful to look at. You'd bring tears from an ox."

I felt myself beginning to smile. I wasn't sure I was supposed to, but I couldn't help myself. Surprisingly, the woman laughed.

"I don't meet many girls who smile when they're told they're ugly. Might be better for a lot of them if they did. What's your name?"

"My name is. . . . " I faltered. "I will answer to whatever you call me."

She looked at me again, closely.

"I'll call you Michal," she said.

"*Todah*," I answered. "My sister's name is Naamah."

"And my name is Yocheved. I'm getting ready to leave for a mourning right now," she continued. "The young daughter of one of the rulers has died. She was probably about your age. I'll take you with me, and if I like what you do, I'll take you on as an apprentice."

I wanted to throw my arms around her, but I didn't. She looked at me again.

"I want you to make the people cry."

I followed Yocheved through the narrow, twisting streets of the city, almost running to keep up with her. Her gait was long and she moved quickly, carrying her lute in a soft leather case. She didn't speak to me as we walked, but I noticed her back was strong and she was taller than I'd realized. I thought she was unlike any woman I'd ever seen before, and I was starting to like her. I wondered if Naamah would, too.

It was still early, but the vendors were out in full force plying their wares through the main street. As Yocheved and I walked, we were joined by three other women—the hired mourners. They accepted my presence without question, and seemed accustomed to following Yocheved without query.

"She was so beautiful," one of the women remarked to Yocheved as I hurried along behind them. I walked closer; I wanted to hear about the girl who had died.

"Her father was heartbroken," another woman continued. "He loved her so much. He would have done anything to keep her from being hurt."

"Why does Yahweh take a young girl from us who is so loved, and yet leave. . . . " The third woman's voice trailed off, but after she finished speaking I saw her glance back at me quickly.

"Keep walking," Yocheved said firmly. "We can't be late."

"I heard her father went to see the man Yeshua to see if he could heal her. But he didn't get there in time . . . she was dead early this morning."

"Her poor mother."

Unbidden, a picture of the girl started to form in my mind. Rich, beautiful, loved—I probably would have hated her. I thought she probably deserved to die just for having so much when other people had nothing. I remembered my flute and my mission, and thought to myself that I might begin to have something more than nothing, if today went well.

As the path meandered along, Yocheved lifted her hand and pointed to the house that would be our destination. The ruler's home was bigger than any I'd seen before, standing two stories high and looming over a huge courtyard surrounded by a low stone wall. The courtyard was packed with people, and even though we were just arriving, some women had already begun the mourning wail, keening the ancient death songs. I looked around for the body of the girl but didn't see her.

"Where is she?" I asked Yocheved. We were pushing our way through the crowd and closer to the house. I wanted to see her.

"Her body is still indoors," a man answered, and I instinctively shrank back, away from his nearness.

"The man Yeshua is here," another voice added helpfully. "The ruler just returned with him, only to find she is dead and he is too late."

I couldn't help but smile—the irony of a father who would do anything for his daughter, even persuade a miracle man to come and heal her only to find he is too late on arrival. It seemed cruelly just, somehow.

As Yocheved and the rest of the mourners arranged themselves in a small semi-circle by the doorway to the house, a group of people pushed by us carrying bundles of lovely white cloth. I could smell their delicately perfumed scent and knew they were the burial shrouds for this girl. I had to restrain myself from reaching out to touch them; I couldn't remember the last time I'd seen anything so beautiful.

Yocheved began to strum her lyre gently, and the women started to mourn. Their eerie, hollow voices sent chills up my spine and I glanced at Yocheved. The melody she'd chosen was simple enough, and I could follow along easily. I might even be able to weave my new song into her melody—I wondered if Yocheved had thought of that and chosen the piece on purpose.

I watched her face intently, waiting for a signal to join in. I was gripping my flute so hard I had to relax my hands for fear it would break, and my mouth felt as if I'd been eating dust. This was it—the moment that would decide our future. I thought of Naamah running through the market with Baruch, her fingers closing on anything she could find. I had to get us away from him. It was too late for Asher, but I could still save Naamah. All I had to do was play.

Yocheved nodded at me, and I took a deep breath and raised the flute to my lips.

"Silence!"

A man's voice cut through the noise of the crowd. The mourners stopped wailing, and Yocheved motioned for me to pause. I held my flute, suspended a breath away from my lips. What was going on?

"Go away," the voice continued, firmly.

No, I thought frantically, I need to play. I need to show Yocheved I am worthy of an apprenticeship. I need to save Naamah. I looked around for the source of the voice. Did the family not want mourners? Perhaps they had their own wealthy mourners. Perhaps common folk such as Yocheved and her troupe were unwelcome. I clenched my teeth together and felt a fury rising within me. I'd found a woman who against all odds had agreed to give me a chance, and I wasn't going to let anything ruin this opportunity. I turned with a glare as the man who'd spoken began speaking again.

"The girl is not dead, but asleep," he said firmly. His words fell like stones around my ears.

"Yeshua," I heard a voice whisper near me. Someone started laughing, callously, and soon the assembled people were shouting. The sound seemed cruel in the wake of the mourner's cries, but I forced myself to laugh, too. Of course the girl was dead. This man was merely a sham, trying to get the crowd to believe in a false miracle. But it wasn't true. The girl had to be dead.

I stared at him with as cruel a gaze as I could summon. He was tall and plain, dressed simply. His hands looked worn from work. I was not going to let this man destroy my chance to save my sister.

Shouts continued to mix with laughter over the heads of the crowd. Some people were mocking Yeshua; other whispered that it could be true, it could be a miracle. I didn't want a miracle. I looked at Yocheved desperately, wanting her to tell me to play. But she shook her head and looked back at Yeshua.

And then, from behind his robe, a small form appeared. It was a girl about my age, and from the gasp of the crowd I knew it was the ruler's supposed-dead daughter. She *was* beautiful, standing there in the morning light, the sun glinting off her soft brown hair and the small, sparkling jewels encircling her neck. Her robe was simple yet made from a beautiful, soft, expensive-looking fabric I didn't recognize. It fell from her shoulders in gentle ripples as she looked over the crowd and smiled, tears trickling down her face. She reached for Yeshua's hand and beamed up at him.

The crowd's shock exploded in exuberance—the girl was alive! Cries of joy rang from lip to lip.

I was blinded by a hurt so intense I couldn't see. I threw my flute to the ground and tried to stomp on it, missing in my rage. I was crying, too, but not tears of joy. We had missed our chance. I had failed Naamah just as surely as I had failed Asher, because this Yeshua raised the perfect little girl from death.

"Why?" I cried, out loud. Why did she get to live? Her life was going to mean my death. I hated her, almost as much as I hated Yeshua. I clenched my palms until my nails dug deep into my flesh.

"You dropped this."

The voice was so quiet I almost missed it. My vision cleared momentarily and I saw a hand holding my flute out to me. It wasn't Yocheved. I wondered where she'd gone—had she left me already?

"*Todah*," I murmured, and then looked up to see who was speaking to me. It was Yeshua. Startled, I backed away from him without taking my flute. Why was he talking to me? I wanted him to leave me alone; he'd already done enough.

I stammered, unable to find coherent words, and continued backing up until I bumped into someone. Yeshua laughed. I wanted to spit at him.

"Why don't you play something happy?" He was still talking to me. "Play something for the joy of life, since there won't be a funeral here today."

And something in me broke. I stopped backing away from him and stood my full height to look him in the eye.

"Why should I play something happy?" I challenged him. I could feel people moving away from me, uncomfortable. So stone me for speaking back to my elders, I thought. I don't care anymore.

"You saved her, but what about everybody else? Why her? Why is she special?" The rage was blinding me. I wanted one last fight before I met my fate. "What about all the other children?" I was screaming. "They're dying on the streets! They're living with the lepers! Save them! Save somebody who actually needs it!"

I turned to run, but Yeshua's strong arms stopped me from behind. I was fighting, kicking, crying. I hadn't been held by a man since my father, and I was infused with remembered pain.

"Go away!" I screamed. "Don't touch me!" I kicked back as hard as I could.

To my surprise, Yeshua let me go. His release was so unexpected that I stumbled, then turned back to face him. My breath caught in ragged gulps as I stared at him.

He was crying.

His tears looked odd, running down the face of such a young, strong man. It unnerved me. I looked at his face and, together, we cried. The crowd seemed to have melted away, and all I could see was Yeshua.

"Don't you know, little one," his hand reached out toward me and traced the curve of my face without touching me. I didn't step back. "Yahweh weeps for the tears of his children."

I was sobbing as I watched the crystal drops run down his face.

"His tears rain down like the stars in the sky." His voice was gentle, almost trembling. "Whenever you cry, little one," his voice broke as he touched a tear on my face, "Yahweh is weeping with you."

I stood there and looked at him, crying stupidly. Slowly I became aware that he was still holding my flute. I reached out for it, brushing my hand against his. Suddenly I wanted to play.

I wiped my face and my nose on the sleeve of my robe, and lifted the flute to my lips. I wanted to play a song for this strange man, and with a breath, I began. The melody was familiar, the song my father had taught me. Yet it was different, for in and out of the melody I wove my new song, the song for the pain of the children. Sorrow and joy, leaping and dancing together, twirling around in the notes of my music. I watched Yeshua's face, and felt as if something warm was being poured through my body, healing my old pain without taking it away. It would be a part of me forever, like the sorrow in the tune I played, but somehow I knew that it wouldn't always hurt. I tried to smile at Yeshua, and lost the note I was playing.

He laughed. Then he gently placed his hand on my arm and began to sing out my wordless melody. I lifted the flute to my lips again and joined him.

6

The First Stone

I crouched in the dust, the perfumed sheet wrapped tightly around my naked body, eyes riveted on my feet. So clean, I thought, as my eyes traced the line of my little toe against the sand. So clean, so free from dust. Even hauled away to this place, I somehow kept them clean. . . .

But I stopped that thought with a force that made me retch. *No*, I silently screamed. *No thinking. No thinking. Look at your feet.* My feet, curious devils, so rough yet so clean. I'd scorned sandals and run barefoot since I'd learned to toddle, and the telltale signs showed on the soles of my feet. But the nails, so clean, and the small, arched toes . . . I could feel his lips as he nibbled along them, whispering kisses that would make me laugh. . . .

And again I stopped. *No thinking. No thinking.* Above me I could hear my accusers. The memory of their faces, filled with cruel glee as they hauled me from his arms, now flickered over my feet like remembered flames. I was caught in the act, and I knew I would soon be stoned.

No thinking! I almost sobbed with the desperation of trying to shut down my mind. Months of living in sin had left me skilled at shutting out guilt. But that's not quite the same as shutting out impending death. My toes squirmed into the dirt of their own accord, as if wishing to bury themselves in memories before sharp stones would cut them, bleed them, break them. I summoned all my strength to shut my mind to the imminent blows, and took myself back, away from this place, away from this guilt, back to the day I first met him.

♦

He was young, so very young. When my husband brought him home that night I couldn't stop staring at him, the curves in his face, the boyish stubble barely gracing his cheekbones. His eyelashes glinted golden as he turned to look at me, and when he smiled I noticed a smattering of freckles across the bridge of his nose. Standing next to him, in the light from our courtyard, my husband looked even older. Gray hair dusted his temples, and although his hands were strong, they were speckled with the first marks of age. I stared and stared at the young man as my husband greeted me, his wife, asking if he could bring another one of his fishermen to dinner. I smiled at him graciously and set another place at our small wooden table.

The procession of men through our home had been a common occurrence; my husband owned many boats in the fishing industry and made his living lending them out to new fishermen who were too young and poor to own their own. My husband would often befriend these men, always variations on young and scraggly, and bring them home like so many stray dogs to be fed and entertained before sending them along on their way. I had grown accustomed to this procession of strange men, but never one like this. He was so young. So very, very young. He barely looked a season older than me.

I married my husband, a man twice my years, shortly before my mother died. My father had already passed on, and when Aharon came to my mother and spoke to her, saying he would take me as his wife, she immediately consented and we were married before the passing of the next moon. I was terrified of him. I had barely even begun to think about marriage, to look at the young boys in our community and wonder which one Yahweh intended for me, and then suddenly I was promised to a man old enough to be my father. He was kind to me as he spoke of our upcoming union, towering over me and folding both of my hands into one of his own, but his size and his years frightened me deeply. I had heard just enough from the older girls about men and weddings and wedding nights to be scared.

On our own wedding night, I clutched my hands in fists to keep from crying out. Perhaps he was gentle; I don't remember. All I remember was the sight of his body next to mine, dwarfing me, engulfing me. When it was over, I shut my eyes until his rhythmic breathing next to me assured me he was asleep, then rolled as far away from him as I could in our small wedding bed. I pinched my thumbs and fingers together the entire night to keep myself awake; I couldn't bear the thought of sleeping beside him, of him trying to touch me again.

As time passed, he tried to be with me less and less. We never spoke of it, but it was obvious, to both of us, that I hated his touch. I pled my moon bloods over and over again, feigned sickness and sleep, until one day I realized he hadn't tried to touch me in two moons. I assumed he had taken a lover, and I was happy.

Without the physical aspect of a marital relationship, Aharon and I soon became the best of friends. It surprised me, at first, that this grown man wanted to hear the things I had to say, would ask for my opinions and laugh at my humor. Under his encouragement I warmed to him, first only trying to please him, then slowly realizing I loved our conversations, loved every moment I could spend with him. I filled my days with thoughts of things I could tell him—the women's gossip from the well, the look of sunlight dancing over our freshly swept floor—waiting eagerly until he came home at night and I could regale him with the little stories of my day. He would bring home one of his stray fishermen; I would feed them one of the meals I soon became known for, and listen to their tales about fishing. Then I would impersonate the visitors for my husband after they left.

"But the net! It had a *hole* in it!" I would say, wide-eyed and incredulous, mimicking a fisherman with more aspiration than skill. My husband would roar at my performances, and I would blush with pride, secretly delighting in his obvious approval of me. We would stay up late on the nights he was home, talking and talking and talking, about fishing or anything or nothing at all. I would have happily sworn he knew more of the women's gossip than any other husband in our town, and he remembered and asked after all of my friends.

As for me, I learned more about the trade of fishing, the boats, the tides, the men and the fish, than I ever thought I would care to know. But when Aharon spoke to me of these things I was riveted. He could make any subject fascinating. So we would eat and talk until the lamps sputtered, and then take ourselves to bed. Once there, I would curl up beside him, almost touching him, content to lie in the heat of his body beside me. The absence of contact grew so familiar, it became comfortable. And I was comfortable. With myself, with my husband, and with our life together.

And then he came.

◆

Hunched over in the dirt, I felt my back starting to ache. I desperately wanted to rewrap myself in the sheet I still clutched, awkwardly, to my body, but to let go of it for a second would be to risk nakedness. And I had already been seen naked by more than enough people.

◆

The first time he touched me it was as if by accident, catching his foot against mine as I walked from the table to the courtyard to bring in our dinner. By this point, his face was a regular feature in our home, and I should have been used to his loose curls, the sun on his skin, the light that played constantly in his eyes. But I wasn't. Every time I saw him, I all but gasped. The force of him was physical, as if he'd already touched me a thousand times, as if he knew every curve of the length of my body and I knew the lines along his. I wanted to be near him, to breathe his smells and run my fingers along the hairs on his arm. The sensation was all at once so new and so strong, it overwhelmed me. I had never wanted a man before, but I wanted—I needed—Zamir.

That night, when his foot brushed against mine at dinner and I turned to look at him, he smiled at me quickly before casting his eyes at the floor. "I'm sorry," he said casually, as if a thousand winds hadn't rushed at me the moment we touched, as if all the noises of the creatures of the night weren't howling in my ears all at once. I couldn't say anything, merely stumbled out to the courtyard and crouched down over the fire until my head had time to clear. The fire that cooked our nightly meal was so much cooler than the fire of my brow at his touch.

◆

"Teacher, this woman was caught in the act of adultery."

The rough voice shocked me back to the present. My hairline was beginning to sweat, exposed in the hot desert sun, and a drop of perspiration started to roll ever so slowly toward my eye. But I didn't move, didn't raise a hand to wipe it away. I heard my accusers talking to the man Yeshua; he must have been summoned to pass my sentence. It seemed a trivial matter with which to occupy such a notorious man; the law clearly stated that I was to die. I wondered why my accusers bothered to involve Yeshua—surely they didn't need his sanction to carry out my sentence. Perhaps there was more going on that I realized, but all my mind could hold onto was the fact that I was about to die.

The drop of sweat made its way into my eye and started to burn.

◆

My husband was leaving on a long journey. As his fishing business had grown and prospered, he had begun to buy up boats and nets in other towns along the sea coast, some near our home and some many leagues away. The men who worked for him ran the businesses that were too far for a day's journey, but several times a year my husband would travel to see them, inspecting the boats, meeting the new men who used his supplies, and collecting the money he was owed. I was used to his trips by now; they were as regular as the change of the seasons or the rise and fall of the tides. I had grown to enjoy my time alone, stretching my mind into the quietness of the night as I stretched out my body alone on our small bed. But this time, it was different. Aharon was leaving, and Zamir was not. I was afraid of the burning inside me, afraid that when my husband left I might lose myself, rush to Zamir's house, embrace him in broad daylight and beg him to have me.

The night of my husband's departure I set out the evening meal for myself: cold flat breads and leftover lentils from the night before. It didn't seem worth it to light the cooking fires in my husband's absence, and I was doing everything I could not to raise the temperatures of the fires already burning within me. As I pulled out my usual chair, I heard a soft knock on the door. My heart started beating faster. *Don't let it be Zamir*, I prayed, and then *oh please, oh please, oh please be him*. I hesitated, waiting, my body fighting with my mind as I looked at the door and wondered what I was going to do.

Then I pushed my chair back. It was Zamir, somehow I knew it. I stood by the table for a moment, straightened my covering, pinched my cheeks to bring the color. I steadied myself against the table with my left hand, and then, careful footsteps denying the turmoil in my heart, I went and opened the door.

His hair was alight with the night, tumbling off his brow in unconcerned waves. He smiled at me, looking directly into my eyes. I was overpowered by the nearness of him, by the absence of my husband, by what I knew we could do.

"I was wondering if you might be able to spare a bite to eat for a poor, hungry fisherman?" he asked me quietly, then crossed over the threshold into my home. My heart was beating so hard that when I glanced down, I was surprised to see my robe hanging still over my chest, unmoving and undisturbed by the hammering within.

"I. . . ."

I started to answer him, and then stopped. I couldn't do this. I couldn't allow him into my home when my husband was gone. It wasn't proper; it wasn't how my mother had raised me. That thought made me step back from him for a moment, away from the heat of his body creeping ever closer to mine.

What was I thinking?

"I think you'd better come back when Aharon is home," I finally managed to mumble, looking at the ground to avoid his eyes.

"But *ahavah*," Zamir whispered, moving ever closer to me, reaching out one strong hand to lightly stroke the side of my face. "I'm hungry tonight."

At his touch, the fire raging within me burned out of control. In one movement I pushed the door closed and grabbed him. I pulled him toward me, touching him, touching every inch of him, a longing I had never known overtaking me, drowning me. I tasted the salt of the sea on his skin, I kissed him until I felt my lips bruise. I dragged him over to the pallet and pushed him down, hard, tearing at his robes until I scratched his skin. I had to have him. Now.

In the morning when he left, the guilt in his wake was so strong I couldn't stand. What had I done? I lay on the floor, feigning sleep as I listened to him collect his robe and cautiously push open the door, heading out for an early catch before the full sun of midday. I didn't say a word. After I heard the door scrape quietly shut, I waited until I knew he'd be at the water and I was truly alone. I tried to push myself up to stand, but his scent was everywhere. It overpowered me. He was clinging to my body as surely as if he were still there, and I didn't know how to get rid of him. I stumbled off the pallet only to fall to my knees again, shaking until I retched all over the clean floor.

The day passed in a blur of agony. I dozed, fitfully, but in my dreams he came to me again. In my dreams, free of my waking guilt, I held him, embraced him, covered every inch of him with myself until I was frenzied with longing. The thrill of his touch flooded over my skin, through my body, and I cried out again with wanting and pleasure and pain. Then I awoke. Guilt slammed into me like a fist, and I couldn't rise. I huddled on the floor. I didn't know what to do. I couldn't even breathe under the weight of my guilt, and yet in the deepest, most secret places within, I could feel my wanting for him still growing, now flickering, now burning, now raging once more like a midsummer fire.

◆

My accusers' voices rang out around me, heckling this man Yeshua.

"In the law Moses commanded us to stone such women," I heard a man's voice call. "Now what do you say?"

I didn't understand what he was asking. The law was the law, there was no other answer. The tears I'd been fighting since I was pulled from Zamir's arms now blurred my vision, mixing with the sweat trickling off my brow until I could barely see. I wished I could barely feel. I steadied my breathing, focusing on the one truth I knew could still bring me joy: Zamir had gotten away. Somehow, he had managed to escape. I would die here, but he would go free. I clung to this thought, repeating it over and over again while the men stormed and questioned around me. I waited for Yeshua's answer, waited for the cut of the first stone.

My little toes still dug in the dirt, still trying to escape of their own accord, when all of a sudden I started to cry in earnest. I didn't want my little toes to die. A thought flitted through the back of my mind, a tiny black bat almost unseen in the darkness.

It's not fair, the thought whispered into the ears of my mind. *It's not fair that I alone should be punished, when Zamir also sinned.*

No! I yelled at the thought, banishing it. I was happy that Zamir got away. I was happy. I was happy . . . wasn't I?

Through the tears and confusion, I was startled to see Yeshua now crouching down beside me in the dirt, tracing something with his finger. Despite myself, I looked over to see what he was doing.

◆

I awoke in the night from dreams of Zamir, my body sweating, shaking, pleading for him to touch me. Yet when I rolled over, reaching for him, my fumbling hands grasped not my lover, but my husband. Instantly I was awake, fully, sitting up on the pallet and wriggling back as far away from him as I could. But it was too late; he had already woken up.

"*Isha?*" Aharon asked me sleepily, looking surprised. Then a slow smile began to creep over his face; he reached out his hand to me, tentatively.

"Did you want something?" he asked quietly.

"No!" I almost shouted. Then, softer, "No. No, I had . . . I had a bad dream." My voice sounded unconvincing in the darkness, and he looked at me, puzzled.

"A bad dream," I repeated, more strongly this time. "I think I need some fresh air." I got up off the pallet and hurried outside.

The winds that blew in from the sea brought me the smell of Zamir, and I was bewildered. I had dreamed of him and reached for my husband in my sleep. What if I had done more? What if I had touched him? What if I had reached for him and called out Zamir's name? The panic I'd been fighting since my first night with Zamir swelled through me again. How could my husband not notice? Couldn't Aharon sense him, wandering through my mind at all hours of the day and night? Didn't he smell him, clinging to our home each and every time my husband returned from his trips? Didn't he notice my barely concealed joy when he went away, the excitement, the yearning, the expectation? How could he live with me, sleep beside me, eat the food I prepared while dreaming of Zamir, and not know I was an adulteress?

Eventually, I knew, I was going to get caught. I paced the courtyard around the remains of our fire and promised myself, not for the first time, that the next time I saw Zamir would be the last.

◆

The strange markings Yeshua inscribed into the dirt meant nothing to me, yet I watched him draw. In this surreal moment, waiting for my life to end, this simple action had grown to contain all of the meaning in the world. I looked at him, crouched down beside me, and judged him to be of average height when standing. Shorter than my husband, and smaller, not as broad. About the size of Zamir. The sun beat down upon my head, and still Yeshua drew. And still I waited.

The crowd around us was growing angrier, and I wondered that the stones didn't fly. Perhaps they were unwilling to stone me with Yeshua so nearby, perhaps they were still waiting for answers as they pestered him with questions of riddles. I wondered where Zamir was, wondered if he was thinking about me, wondered how much he cared that my life was going to end. The questions rained down around me, and still Yeshua drew, silent.

After what seemed an age, Yeshua stood, and I felt every muscle in me tighten. This was it. Whatever he had been doing was accomplished, and my waiting time was over. I closed my eyes and thought of things I loved: warm bread made from lentils, the smell of the sea, sunlight in the morning, Aharon, Zamir. I waited for the first blow.

"If any one of you is without sin," I heard Yeshua say, "let him be the first to throw a stone at her."

And I waited.

Nothing happened.

I waited.

Yeshua stooped down beside me once more, and again began drawing in the dirt on the ground.

◆

My feet felt like weights as I dragged them to the door, the knock barely a breath. I'd known he was coming, just as he'd been coming now for months. I had to end this, now. If I could just find the strength to end it tonight, to tell Zamir I didn't want him anymore, the nightmare could end before my husband ever found out it had started. If I could just make it right, now, tonight, it would be as if it had never happened. I could resume my life with Aharon, a life free of guilt and fear and the stench of betrayal, a stench I still marveled he couldn't smell on me, on my hair and my skin and my toes. I pushed open the door.

"Zamir, I need to talk to you," I began breathlessly, before my eyes could fully take him in, before my body was flooded with desire.

But his mouth was on mine before I finished the sentence. His kiss ignited me, and as we fell into each other I heard my mind query, *What's the harm? What's done is done, and you might as well enjoy him one last time before it has to end.*

So *one last time*, I told myself, as my body rose against his on the pallet. And *one last time*, when I snuck out to his house in the middle of the night two days later. And *one last time*, every time, as wanting overtook my guilt the moment I laid eyes on him. Guilt and wanting rose and fell together like waves, playing in and among each other, ever stronger. But the result was always the same, and no matter what I resolved to do I always ended up naked in Zamir's arms. I hated my body for the way it betrayed me, but I cultivated my desire just the same, fed it and freed it and unleashed it on Zamir.

◆

Beside me, Yeshua was still drawing. My back was aching so much I straightened up, involuntarily, my sheet slipping away from my body. As I grabbed at the sheet I looked around me. The crowd had dispersed. They were gone.

I looked at Yeshua, bewildered. He raised his eyes from the dust to meet mine, and his steady gaze was serious. I skimmed over his face, taking in his firm jaw, the set of his mouth, and then again the expression in his eyes. I had to look away. Out of the corner of my eye I saw him stand up and extend his hand to me. With one hand I reached out and took it, with the other I tried to hide as much of my body as possible behind the sheet.

"Woman, where are they?" Yeshua asked me. "Has no one condemned you?"

I looked around me, but we were alone, the empty space still charged with the flickering anger of the departed men.

"No one, sir," I faltered.

"Then neither do I condemn you," Yeshua declared. "Go now and leave your life of sin."

I blinked. What had he said? My mind was reeling. What had just happened? Where were my accusers? Why was I not to be stoned? And how—*how?*—having been granted my life, could I possibly hope to disentangle myself from Zamir? I thought about the days before he came, before I understood lust and longing. I didn't want to go back. I didn't know who I was without him.

"You must tell Aharon," I heard Yeshua say, and I looked up at him, startled.

"How do you know my husband's name?" I asked him.

Yeshua didn't answer, merely looked at me. His eyes were almost hypnotic, a brown so deep I could swim in them.

"You must tell Aharon," he repeated. "Tell him that I have forgiven you, and ask him to forgive you as well."

"Ask him to . . . tell him you. . . ." The nonsense of the words impressed itself upon me, and I fought the urge to laugh. I didn't know which part was most impossible: the thought of telling Aharon about Zamir and asking him to forgive me, or the fact that this strange man, who meant nothing to me, told me that he forgave me.

"I . . . " I faltered again. Then I looked up at Yeshua. "I can't," I said simply.

"You must," he replied, not angry, not unkind. Just a statement. Insistent.

And so I promised. I owed this man my life; what more could I do?

◆

"Aharon, we need to talk."

The words came out in a rush, before I could stop them, before I could rethink what I was going to do. He paused, one foot still over the threshold of our doorstep, and looked at me.

"About what?" he asked, kindly, gently. His gentleness moved me to tears, and I found I was shaking so hard I feared my knees would give way.

"Aharon. . . . " There was a pause in which all the earth held its breath, a pause in which I relived my wedding night, my life with my husband, Zamir, Yeshua.

"I'm an adulteress," I said.

7

Only a Woman

I wasn't always a cripple. When I was young I was strong and tall, taller than my brother and stronger than his friends. I remember days filled with laughter and games, running through dust-packed streets as if nothing could ever be more important than the pounding of our toes into the earth. My father used to laugh at me and call me his misfit, mussing my hair and shaking his head. My brother Eliahu, a year younger, accepted me as I was and we played together with his friends.

Only my mother disapproved; at night after I'd fallen asleep on the mat next to my brother, I would hear her talking to my father through the thick curtain that separated our rooms. She pleaded with him, remonstrating that it wasn't right for a girl to run wild as I did. She feared both for me and for herself; reputations were all women had in a small community like our own.

"She'll never marry," my mother prophesied. "No man would ever wed a woman he wrestled as a youth."

My father's laugh punctuated my mother's gloom.

"There once was a time even you weren't so meek as you are now, *isha*," he'd remind her.

Yet she said it was different. It is one thing to have the fire, I heard her say. But it was another to let it burn.

"Things will change when the boys go to synagogue school," my father would say. "She'll lose her playmates and settle down, and then you can train her in the gentler ways of women."

I shifted on my mat, pulling my robe more tightly around my body. Beside me, Eliahu snored into the darkness, suffused with deep sleep.

It isn't fair, I thought to myself. *Why should Eliahu get to go to synagogue school, and run and play and have fun, and I can't?*

I tossed on my mat. My mother's words gave me a glimpse into the drudgery of the days ahead, carrying water and standing quietly around the neighborhood well while the women talked softly amongst themselves. In the still night, as I picked at a bloody tear on one of my toes where I'd lost a nail in a race that morning, I willed Eliahu never to grow up, never to attend synagogue school. I would die cooped up in the house all day with my mother, I thought. I loved her, but she was so quiet. I didn't think I could stand it.

Out of the darkness I heard a small sigh from the next room, and I instinctively knew my father agreed with me. Much as he respected our customs and traditions, part of him would mourn his little fiery one being snuffed out as she grew into a woman.

♦

On the morning of Eliahu's first day of synagogue school, I sulked in the doorway as I watched my mother prepare his midday meal in our small courtyard. She was bent over the fire, heat rising from the dark bricks and causing perspiration to course down her face. She looked happy, and sang as she worked. I knew I could never do that, bend my back to provide food for a man as he went off to school and left me behind. I hated Yahweh for making me a girl.

Inside the house, my father spoke with Eliahu. I listened to their words, the descriptions of the synagogue and the cautions about the master, and I wanted to run free from my mother and follow my brother. But I couldn't.

The transition to life without Eliahu was difficult. In the morning and afternoon I worked with my mother, learning how to tend our home. My mother taught me to carry our earthen jars of water on my head without spilling a drop, and to my surprise, I found my strength and size an advantage. Although I was one of the youngest girls at the well, I could carry almost as much water as a girl nearly grown. For the first time, I saw my mother gently boasting to others about her overgrown, misfit daughter. I basked in her praise and ran her words over and over again through my mind as I waited for Eliahu to return home each evening.

"Time was I worried about her," my mother would confess at the city well as the women waited their turn to draw water.

"But look at her now, so healthy and tall. She's a blessing to have around the house, she's so strong." And my mother smiled. I loved to see her smile at me. It almost made the work I had to do bearable. I let the coarse rope supporting the bucket sink back into the well and drew up a full bucket with one hand. I wanted my mother to be proud of me. As I filled the earthen jars we carried to the well each morning, she smiled.

Her smiles disappeared, however, the night I decided to learn everything my brother gleaned from his lessons at the synagogue. The late sun was beginning to fade into the night, and my mother and I were finishing cleaning up after the evening meal. I placed the clean crocks into a small wooden chest we kept against the wall, underneath the carved wooden shelf my father had made to hold our prayer shawls. Eliahu's small, rough scroll rested there when he was home from his lessons. This was the scroll on which he copied out lines from the Torah each day as he learned to read and write the sacred words.

As I looked at it, I thought of the Torah in the synagogue, the strange markings on the stretched skin that I craned my neck to see every time I was close enough to look at it. I wanted to be able to understand them myself. If Eliahu was learning how to make sense of them, so could I.

"Teach me to read," I announced, sitting down beside him as he began his lessons that night. "Teach me to read the Torah."

He laughed as he pushed the small scroll he was working on away from him. Then he nibbled on his reed pen, considering me.

"Girls don't read," he finally said.

"Why not?" I challenged.

"They just don't." He paused. "But I bet I could teach you anyway. I'm good at my studies. The master told me today that I know more of the Torah than any other boy in the synagogue."

I felt something swelling in my belly when I heard him say that. I was so proud of him, but I wanted to be able to learn for myself.

He laughed again. "How funny would it be if we had a girl in our family who learned to read? I could show you off to my friends."

I was more than willing to be his latest novelty, if only he would teach me how to make sense of the strange lines and patterns that marked the surface of his scroll.

After a moment, Eliahu unrolled his scroll reverently and then spread it on a cloth at our feet. He lit the small oil lamp that hung on the wall beside us, and together we crouched down to look at the scroll. His fingers played lightly over the hand-drawn characters as his lips murmured words, looking for a place to start my studies.

"Look here, *achot*," he said, resting his finger on a section of the scroll. "Do you know what this says?"

Of course I didn't, but I looked at him expectantly and he began to read.

"Hear, O Israel," he read out in his strong, treble voice, "the Lord our God, the Lord is one."

"The *Schm'a*!" I said. I felt as if the cold well water I drew for my mother each morning was trickling down my back as I joined him in reciting the verses, the first I'd remembered hearing as a child, the first I could lisp at evening prayers.

"Love the Lord your God with all your heart and with all your soul and with all your strength," I joined with him. "Oh *ach*, is that what is says? Are those the words, right there?" It seemed almost mystical, watching him make sense of the strange characters and finding them to be something so familiar in the end.

"Yes, that is what it says," he told me, his tanned face flushed with the thrill of imparted knowledge. "And you can keep reading it with me; you already know what it says."

Together we worked, my brother reading, and I reciting, trying to understand how the lines on the scroll corresponded to the words in my heart.

"These commandments that I give to you today are to be upon your hearts," we chorused together. "Impress them upon your children. . . . "

Behind me I heard my mother's sharp intake of breath followed by the crash of splintering shards of pottery. I whirled around to look at her.

"What are you doing, *banim*?" she cried, clasping her hands together as if wringing out a cloth. "Women don't read. You don't teach her the Torah. Your lessons are for you, for your friends and other boys. Not for girls. Not for women."

My mother's face was twisted in tears as I saw all the smiles she'd given me at the well fading away, snuffed out like a candle after Sabbath prayers.

"But *em,*" I protested, "I'm learning to read the *Schm'a*! Listen!"

I found a place on the scroll and began moving my fingers as I'd seen my brother, reciting the familiar words. "Hear, O Israel, the Lord our God, the Lord is one!"

I wanted to keep going but saw my mother had rushed out of the room and behind the curtain that covered her sleeping area.

I looked at Eliahu, who shrugged. Yes, she was upset, but she was often upset at me. I had thought she was beginning to like me, but. . . . I looked back at my brother's scroll. Losing her smile was a small price to pay for learning to read.

"Teach me more, *ach*," I pleaded with my brother. Teach me everything you know."

"I will, *achot*," he promised. "Every evening after chores I will teach you what I learned that day. I will be your teacher—and you can call me *moreh*."

That night as I lay on my mat listening to the sound of Eliahu's snoring, I recited the *Schm'a* to myself and tried to recall the strange patterns and figures that somehow held the meaning of the words. They didn't make sense yet, but I knew someday, if I kept working, they could. Through the noise of my thoughts I heard my mother's voice again, whispering over the floor of our house to reach not only my father's ears, but mine.

"She can't learn to read," my mother stated, in a voice even stronger than the one I was accustomed to. "This cannot continue. She will never marry, and you will lose your place of honor as an elder."

My father seemed loath to agree, his voice coming deeper but more softly to my ears.

"*Isha*, I don't know," he said. "I think she's smart enough both to learn to read and to keep it a secret. Besides, doesn't the *Schm'a* itself say to impress these lessons upon your children? She is, after all, my child."

My mother's silence was louder than her voice. My father's unorthodox statement was all but heretical. Finally the silence was broken, but I had to strain to hear her next words.

"It is not the way things are done. She will bring shame to our family, and she will be cursed."

◆

The twisting did not begin until almost a year later. I continued on in my nightly lessons and took to calling my brother *moreh* when out of earshot of others. He taught me to read the words from the Torah, to understand the prayers, and to sing the chants passed on from father to son since the time of our ancestors. Together every night we would read, sing, and pray. My father smiled and my mother scowled as my brother and I read aloud: "I lift up my eyes to the hills—where does my help come from? My help comes from the Lord, the Maker of Heaven and earth."

By day I did my women's work in solemn respect for my mother, and at night when my Eliahu came home, he would teach me all the things he'd learned that day. The nightly repetition of his lessons helped to solidify them in his mind, and he soon became one of the quickest students at the synagogue.

"He will be a man of great learning," I overheard the elders say as I walked through the dusty streets of our town with my mother. I grinned to myself for the sheer pleasure of being Eliahu's secret cohort.

But then the twisting began. It was scarcely noticeable at first, merely a mild pain in my back when I would straighten after reading the scroll. One night as I straightened up after reading, my back felt like it was about to spasm. I pressed my hand against it and looked at Eliahu.

"*Moreh*, have you ever had pains after reading?" I rubbed my closed fist against the bony knobs of my spine.

"I get pains in my eyes sometimes," he admitted. "It's difficult to work with only the light from the lamp. The light in the synagogue during the day is much better." He paused. "Sometimes I really wish you could come to the synagogue with me. I can only teach you what I've learned myself, but if you were there, you could learn from the master. He's so wise." He stopped talking when he saw I was preoccupied. "Are your eyes hurting, too?"

"No, it's my back," I said, stretching. "Sometimes it feels like I can't straighten up again."

"Perhaps all this learning is too much for a weak woman, *achot*?" He laughed. I still cleared the top of his head by almost a handspan, and so I cuffed him lightly. I laughed with him as we wrestled, and decided from then on to keep my pains to myself. Perhaps it was because of the hours I spent bent over the small scroll—perhaps my body, although strong, was unable to handle the strain. I was, after all, only a woman.

As the new moon passed into fullness I fastened my lips into silence and continued on in my studies. Together with Eliahu I read the ancient tales of how Yahweh was faithful to our ancestors, and of the promised Moshiach who would come to save our people. My back grew stiffer but my heart was happy. In silence we studied on.

♦

Eventually I couldn't hide my twisting from others. Carrying water with my mother one day I slipped with the effort of trying to straighten my shoulders. The jug I was balancing fell off my head and narrowly missed breaking into a thousand pieces on the hard, dry ground. Clutching the rim of the now-spilled jug, I looked up at my mother.

"I don't know what is wrong with you now," she said to me. "You used to be so strong, and now you can't even stand up straight. What is the problem? You read, and now you cannot walk?"

Her words stung me and I made no reply. I trudged back to the well, redrew our water, balanced the jug on my hip, and silently made my way home.

♦

The years passed. I was almost old enough to marry. But as I watched other girls my age become promised to the young men of our community, we could no longer disguise my deformity. Hunched over like a gnarled olive tree, my uneven shoulders and the curve in my back meant I had to distort myself even further to look up at people. For a while I staunched myself against the pain, forcing myself to straighten as much as I could and look people in the eye. But eventually it became too much effort and I grew accustomed to my huddled posture, looking down at the ground at the feet, the dust, and the tracks left by children who could run and play as I once did.

My father said nothing about my deformity, and although my mother said nothing as well, her silence screamed in my ears. I recalled the words heard long ago as a child: "She'll never marry," her prophecy echoed through the intervening years. "No one will want to wed her . . . she'll be cursed." Was I cursed? I questioned myself daily. Was this God's punishment for learning the Torah with my brother? It didn't make sense. Yet the ways of Yahweh are ineffable, I knew, so I kept my musings to myself and continued to read. I could no longer stand or walk without pain. I had become a burden to my family and I knew I would never marry. Yet I couldn't give up my reading.

"*Moreh,*" I asked Eliahu one night as he rolled up his scroll after our studies.

"Yes?" He didn't turn to look at me when he spoke. He'd seemed preoccupied all evening.

I walked over to the small oil lamp and winced in pain as I struggled to straighten my back enough to reach and blow out the tiny flame.

"What's going to happen to me?"

"What do you mean?" He placed the scroll on its shelf and turned to push aside the curtain to our bedroom. I didn't follow him.

"When you marry."

He stopped, and then turned. "Who said I was going to marry?"

"You're getting close to the age . . . I know you will eventually. But I never will."

"That's not true," he started. It was no secret that my father had been asking young men who lived nearby about possible betrothals, offering almost obscene dowry prices. No one wanted an overgrown cripple when there were pretty girls available. Unless an old widower took pity on me, I had nowhere to go.

"Eventually you're going to marry, and our parents are going to. . . . " my voice trailed off. "Then what will happen to me?"

"I guess you'll continue to live with us," Eliahu replied with a sigh. I could see his broad shoulders sagging in the narrow light. He didn't want to have to take care of me forever.

"Us?" I tried to lighten the moment, teasing him. "Is there an 'us' already?"

He wasn't in the mood to jest.

"Eliahu, I'm sorry." I crossed over to him as quietly as I could, and, with some effort, twisted myself around to look him in the eye.

"Don't be sorry," he answered. "It's my fault. I never should have taught a woman to read."

♦

On a warm spring night, just when the shepherds were moving to the hills to help the sheep birth their lambs, Eliahu woke me with a shaking.

"*Achot*, wake up—quickly."

"Eliahu, what's wrong?"

"It's father. Come now."

He turned and ran from the room.

I rolled onto my left side and struggled to push myself up. My wrists felt weak on my mat, and as I struggled I heard small noises from the next room. My mother was weeping, and I could hear Eliahu trying to comfort her. I wanted to call out to him to help me, but I knew my mother needed him. I fell back down, my wrist pinned beneath me. I couldn't raise myself to standing again. I was helpless.

"*Achot*, come on!" Eliahu called from beyond the curtain.

"I can't," I gasped weakly. "I can't move."

With footsteps like the pounding of a drum Eliahu came back into the room, flinging the curtain aside. In the dim lamplight I could see his face as he looked down at me, alternating between sympathy and fury. Finally he crossed over to my mat and, with one easy movement, swept me to my feet.

"Now come," he said without looking at me again.

I struggled to maintain my balance and then followed him out into our main room. My father's cot lay unrolled on the floor, his body spread out across it, stiff.

"*Abba?*" I whispered.

"He can't hear you," Eliahu answered. "He's already gone."

I heard a wail escape from my mother's tightened lips. I wanted to sink down to my knees, wrap my arms around my father, and cradle him—but I couldn't. I knew I wasn't strong enough.

I caught my mother's eye, glaring at my hulking body swaying over the remains of her husband.

"Take her out of here," she hissed to Eliahu. "I don't want to look at her right now."

After the funeral, I waited until a day came when I was feeling strong, and then I dragged my mat out into the streets and placed it along the path to the synagogue. This was where the beggars sat, hoping passersby would toss them a coin while on their way to prayers. I hadn't told my family I was going to beg; I merely decided one morning and went. I didn't care if it was shameful, I didn't care if our family's status in society could never be regained. My mother hated me and even my brother now resented me; with my father gone I had nothing left to lose. So I dragged my mat into the streets.

"Alms," I tried to call as the first man passed me. But when I saw his face, I realized that I knew him. He had been a good friend of my father's, and as he stared at me now, I lost my voice and lowered my gaze. A crimson heat crept up toward my hairline and I watched his sandaled feet as they hurried past.

"You'll never get even a mite that way," a rough voice assailed me.

I raised my eyes to see a man I recognized as a local beggar. He had dropsy, and as he unrolled his mat next to mine I watched him twitch. It seemed odd that this person, whom I'd often crossed the street to avoid as a child, was now rebuking me. I swallowed my shame.

"Alms!" he yelled coarsely at the next passerby, and was rewarded with a copper assarion. He threw it at me.

"Don't say I never did anything for you, *ahavah*." His leering gaze made me turn away, and for a moment I reconsidered my hasty decision to beg. But just as I was thinking about trying to stand up and shuffle my way back home, I heard another voice, one younger and higher-pitched.

"Hear, O Israel," the voice squeaked out, "the Lord our God, the Lord is one."

The boys in the temple! I hadn't realized I was close enough to the synagogue to hear their lessons. I glared at the old beggar and stilled myself to listen.

♦

The moon passed into its next cycle, and each day that I felt strong enough I dragged my mat to the crossroads in front of the synagogue. I couldn't bring myself to ask for alms, so I merely sat in silence with palms outstretched and listened to the voices inside. The deep elders' voices carried in the arid, listless bustle of the town, and the echoes of the young boys followed close behind. I moved my lips with the words they learned. Bent and huddled as I was, no one could see my face and I was thus safe from scorn. The old beggar soon tired of me, as many who stopped to heed his cry would toss me a coin as well. Feeling that I was bad for his personal business, he soon left me for another corner near the marketplace.

Alone and muted I sat and watched the feet pass in front of me. Dirty feet, sandaled feet, young feet, crippled feet—I soon came to know all the people of our small community by their feet and the tracks they made walking through the town. I sat in stillness, listening to the synagogue elders and watching the feet. Many days I went home without a coin, as most of the passersby continued to give their alms to the noisier, rowdier beggars. Still, I was content on my mat. It was almost as if I'd been granted permission to sit for lessons in the synagogue.

♦

My brother's marriage brought joy to our family. My aging mother was particularly pleased when his young wife moved in with us and began to share in the burden of my care. Although she had continued to care for me all these years without complaint, my mother's resentment hung in the air like heavy cloths. I had moved to a mat in a corner of the house—the bedroom I'd shared with Eliahu now belonging to him and his new wife—and tried to be as unobtrusive as possible, spending most of my time keeping quietly to myself. His wife soon discovered that I could read, and although disconcerted, didn't begrudge me my hours with the scroll alone in the shelter of my corner. She was small and simple, her delicate feet pattering in the dust like a child's. But she was honest and kind, and my brother loved her.

Above all I wanted him to be happy with his wife, so I tried as best as I could to keep out of the way.

I continued to try and help with small tasks around the house to lessen the burden of my care. It was difficult, though, as with each passing moon my pain seemed to grow even stronger. My back felt as if some wild animal were crouched upon it, forcing me ever lower into the painful abyss that would be my future. When the babies came my brother's wife let me hold them, and she taught me to swaddle them and care for them as they grew. Such marvels, the babies. My childhood *moreh* had grown into a man and was now having children of his own—children with tiny feet and toes like buds in springtime.

On the day of the birth of my *moreh's* third child and second son, I was swaddling the new one to present to his mother. The air was torpid and the smell of birthing hung heavy in the air like a cloak. I felt bent down even further, and struggled to tear the strips of white cloth to wrap the lusty, yowling baby. As I lifted his softly scrunched body onto the cloths, a spasm of pain trumpeted through my body. I gasped and fell, the baby narrowly avoiding the floor as I managed to clutch him to my chest. His mother screamed.

That night as I lay awake on my mat and listened to the whispers between my brother and his wife, I thought back to the times I'd lain and listen to my own parents talking. The conversations were frighteningly similar.

"We can't keep on like this," my sister-in-law protested weakly. "I don't know what I'm supposed to do with her. She hurts everything she touches, and I have young ones in the house now!"

My brother tried to shush, to comfort, but I heard in the deep tones of his voice the same feelings.

"My *isha*, you know she is only trying to help. She loves you and the children. She can't help her deformity." His placid words belied his tone, but the sharpness in his voice left an acrid taste in my mouth.

Even in the silence that followed I knew my gentle sister-in-law was unmoved. She was a loving woman, but like all mothers, she loved her children more than she loved any outsider. I was only bringing her grief and pain.

"Perhaps your mother was right," I heard her say at last . "Perhaps she is cursed."

After that I never touched the children.

♦

My days on the mat in front of the synagogue grew longer, and my time at home grew shorter. I knew my brother and his wife cared for me, but with a growing family of their own I was becoming more of an encumbrance, so I stayed away. It was now almost eighteen years since the twisting began, and I was afraid for the remainder of my years on this earth. I was bent, useless, and without hope.

Talk in the synagogue, meanwhile, was bubbling, fierce. The elders were arguing about the teacher again, the new teacher named Yeshua. A simple carpenter from Galilee, this man had caused more foment in the temple than any issue since a proposed ban on ceremonial hand washing shortly after I'd started begging.

"He's a fraud," I heard a deep voice proclaim.

"He heals by way of a demon," another asserted.

The young boys knew to keep quiet in the face of such discussions, and so the deep voices continued to roll out unadorned by high treble counterparts.

"He claims to be the Son of God!" one man finally called.

"Now, now, do you know if any of these accusations you make are true?" I recognized the gentle voice of the eldest priest. "Perhaps he is just a great teacher—or a prophet. No son of Galilee would be foolish enough to call himself the son of God." His slight emphasis on the word "Galilee" made me smile, and I wondered what the other elders thought.

His point seemed to still them, and shortly the discussion turned back to the Torah and the young boys' voices rang out again.

But as I listened I kept musing over the talk of the teacher. Everyone who passed, it seemed, was talking about him. The sturdy feet carrying men home from work, the narrow feet of the women, even sometimes the running feet of the children—all seemed to be walking under an interminable discussion of this Yeshua.

I wondered.

Could this man be the Promised One, *Elohay Yishi,* God our Salvation? It didn't seem likely. The prophecies were all there in the Torah, to be sure, but it seemed improbable they would be fulfilled in our time. I thought about the discussions I used to have with Eliahu, before his resentment grew so strong he stopped talking to me. After all, he used to say, hadn't the children of Yahweh been waiting immeasurable years for the Moshiach? Why would He choose to come now?

I missed the nights spent in study with my brother.

♦

News that this Yeshua was coming to our town, to our synagogue, spread like fire. The children ran shouting through the streets, women murmured quietly at the well, and men debated in the synagogue. Was it an honor? Or the prelude to a curse? If this Yeshua was truly a great teacher, we should afford him the respect such a title deserved, some argued. But if he really was claiming to be God, he was an impostor and as such deserving of death.

The people argued.

I pondered and read.

In anticipation, we waited.

The week before Yeshua was to arrive I brought home more coins than any week before. The number of people loitering around the synagogue continued to grow, and the beggars were profiting from the ensuing rows. The air grew hot and repressive as the talk of Yeshua incensed every lip—what would he be like? What would he teach? A beggar gleaned a host of coins when he called out, "Alms for the waiting, until Yeshua will heal!" Shouts of laughter followed, and a rainbow of coins chased the sound.

But *was* this Yeshua a healer? I wondered and waited.

On the Sabbath that Yeshua came hordes packed into the synagogue; those from neighboring villages who couldn't fit inside sat with me out in the dust surrounding the building. Hunched on my mat, I listened.

Voices inside were raised in a familiar psalm: "I lift up my eyes to the hills—where does my help come from? My help comes from the Lord, the Maker of Heaven and earth." And then Yeshua began to teach.

His voice was quiet and confident. He spoke the Hebraic lessons with grace and alacrity, and though I listened for blasphemy, I heard none. The synagogue inside was quiet. The waiting men outside were quiet. Even the beggars were quiet. Perhaps this Yeshua wasn't going to be that exciting after all—from the low tones gently rising and falling in swells from inside the synagogue, it sounded like the people's anticipation was going to be met with disappointment.

When the service ended I watched countless pairs of feet leave the synagogue in droves. People were quiet, bored that Yeshua turned out to be merely a teacher after all. Talk was turning to other things. The daily smatters of conversation that made up our lives scampered along like leaves in the wind. Tiny feet ran up to mine and a child threw down a coin. An old man, judging by the calluses on his feet, threw another. Two sets of young, sturdy feet walked by accompanied by a discussion of the teaching. Life was resuming its normal pace.

But just then a set of brown, sandaled feet stopped in front of me. A worker, no doubt. I waited for the coin.

Instead, all was still. A deep silence penetrated my ears and rang like nothing I'd ever heard before. My head was filled with a silence that by its very nature was music. I made the effort to look up.

Twisting my head and craning my neck to see the man standing in front of me sent my gnarled back into a spasm. He looked like an ordinary man, dark and leathery, with rugged features that spoke of hours of hard work. I dropped my gaze—and then looked again.

Something in his face was arresting. I felt forced to look at him, compelled to stand up. I struggled to my feet, my twisted posture making it almost impossible for me to look him in the eye. The pain was intense, searing. Yet I couldn't look away. Awash in a sea of pain and silent singing, I looked at the man. His eyes, his face, were coming closer. Was he stooping down to look at me? Or was I standing up to look at him?

His eyes were drawing me in, deeper. I looked him full in the face, weak from the pain I was almost certain would overtake and kill me. And then I realized I was standing up, straight, eye-to-eye with the strange brown man. He looked about my brother's age, with deep brown eyes just beginning to crease in the corners.

He reached out his arm and touched me, and then I heard him speak.

"Woman, you are set free from your infirmity."

Instantly, the pain was gone.

A wall of sound crashed upon my ears as the pain left and the musical silence was torn. I was aware, suddenly, of the people around me—children were screaming, women were babbling, men were beginning to yell. I didn't care. I stood, for the first time in eighteen years, face to face with a man roughly my height, and simply stared.

"Who are you?" I tried to ask, but my question was lost in the rumble of the crowd.

"He's magic!" the children yelled.

"He has a demon!" called a boy.

A girl screamed for her mother and I became aware of the undercurrent of female whisperings bolstering the deeper men's voices.

"He healed on the Sabbath! He healed on the Sabbath! The penalty for such is death!"

Finally the eldest synagogue ruler stepped forward and looked first at the man, then at me. The crowd grew still.

In this eternity of a few seconds, time paused as we waited for the synagogue ruler to speak. At last, he turned to the man.

"There are six days for work," the ruler said. "Heal on those days, not the Sabbath."

Then he turned to me, and in terror I began to stoop. Was my healer going to be sentenced to death? Was it by a demon I was standing? Would the pain and the crookedness return? Having tasted barely a breath of freedom, I choked on the thought of returning again to my crippled, useless body.

But the healer was turning away from me to look at the crowd. He considered the assembly quietly. And then he raised his voice.

"You hypocrites!" he cried, in a voice that scarcely seemed his own. This voice was an indignant thunder, and I straightened again to watch him.

"Doesn't each of you on the Sabbath untie his ox or donkey from the stall and lead it out to give it water?"

Not a whisper was heard. The legions of feet were stilled in the dust. Women shrank back against their husbands, but the children didn't seemed frightened at all, edging unbelievably closer to this incensed man.

"Then should not this woman, a daughter of Avraham," the man continued, his voice softening and almost breaking, "whom Satan has kept bound for eighteen long years, be set free on the Sabbath day from what bound her?"

I felt tears dripping on my clothes, though I was unaware of my crying. The children, eager for any sort of spectacle, began to cheer as if it were Purim. Some in the crowd began to join in. Others stood there, uncertain, hesitant. The elders remained unmoved, and I could hear their low voices murmuring dangerously against my healer.

The man turned to go.

"Wait!" I gasped, and almost stumbled as I took my first upright step since I was a child. "Who are you?" I reached out and grabbed the back of his cloak.

The man turned around and smiled at me with his eyes.

"Have you not read about me?" he asked, turning again to go. He almost looked like he was laughing. "I believe you should know who I am."

With that, he was gone. Looking after his retreating form I began to sing that ancient psalm: "I lift up my eyes to the hills—where does my help come from? My help comes from the Lord, the Maker of Heaven and earth."

For I knew I'd just seen *Yahweh-Rophe* . . . Yeshua, the God who heals.

As I sang out the ancient hymn, the dancing children joined in my song.

8

Bartimaeus the Blind

The evening meal set, I turned and got the broom from its resting place in the corner of our small house. With a practiced hand, I carefully swept the dirt floor from the table to the doorway, looking, as always, for any stray bits of detritus that might trip up my brother as he walked into the house. It was my nightly ritual, performed every evening for so many years I did it unthinkingly, as I did so many things for my brother.

The floor was swept, the table set, the chairs and bowls in exactly the same places as they were last night, the night before, every night. Not far from the table my brother's pallet was made up, neatly, by my hands; the same fold in the top cover, the same angle of the smaller cover across the foot. My own pallet, smaller and shabbier, I never made up. What was the use? The only one who ever saw it was me—for I, unlike my brother, could see. As I'd recently passed the age when girls would marry, I was starting to acclimate to the fact that I would indeed spend the rest of my life caring for my younger brother. Thankless tasks like making up my pallet were quickly falling to the wayside.

With my evening chores finished, I pulled out my usual chair to wait for my brother. He was seldom late; a life of endless repetition caused him, if nothing else, to be punctual. I listened for his halting steps on the road outside our door, the scrape of the walking stick he carried in front of him to ward off unseen dangers. I looked around our small house as I waited. Everything was in order.

"*Achot!*" I heard my brother calling to me, loudly, followed by the sound of pounding feet. I rose from the table and hurried outside. To my astonishment, Bartimaeus was flying up the road, his robe streaming out behind him, his walking stick gone.

"Bartimaeus!" I screamed. "What are you doing? Be careful! Stop running at once or you'll fall!"

But my brother didn't stop until he reached our doorway, colliding with me, almost knocking me over with his weight.

"*Achot,*" he panted, grabbing me by the shoulders. "*Achot,* I can see."

His breathless words meant nothing to me; they were completely incomprehensible.

"Bartimaeus, what are you talking about? Why are you late? And what on earth were you running for?"

To my astonishment, he let go of my shoulders and ignored me, raising his arms to the heavens and twirling around in front of the house.

"*Bartimaeus!*" I hissed. "What are you doing?"

"*Achot!*" he repeated as he stopped his spinning. "I told you. I can see. I've been healed, I can see."

I shook my head at him, bemused.

"Come inside and eat your dinner."

I didn't know what he was playing at, but I was not going to have our neighbors start thinking him crazy, spinning around in front of our house and declaring that he was healed. I was going to get him inside and feed him his dinner. I reached for his hand to guide him into the house; without the aid of his walking stick I knew he would need me. But he flung my hand aside, walking across the threshold without tripping or stumbling, and strode inside to the table and his waiting, customary chair.

He then turned to me, still radiant.

"I never knew how nice our home was." He turned his head as if he could actually see the small, cramped quarters where we lived. I suppressed a snort. We were lucky to have this house, yes, especially when so many blind beggars lived in tents. But it was far from nice, and my level of annoyance with him was rising.

"Sit down," I said. "Eat your dinner. Quit talking foolishly."

He pulled out his chair and sat, and I took my place opposite him. I waited for him to extend his hand along the surface of the table, reaching for his food, but he was still lolling his head around like a crazy person.

"I never knew my pallet was green," he said, looking over at the corner where he slept. "I think I always supposed it was brown."

I stared at him. What was going on?

He continued to turn his head, sweeping across the room, down and around and over and back, and then suddenly he turned his face toward me.

"But why," he asked, "have you made up my pallet so neatly, when you haven't touched your own?"

I dropped the lentil loaf I was holding, and it rolled, unnoticed, to the floor.

◆

Later that evening, I plied Bartimaeus with questions as he recounted his story once again.

"So you were calling to him," I repeated, still staring at my brother as if I, too, was seeing for the first time. "Why?"

Bartimaeus shrugged. "He's a healer," he replied, unconcerned. "What could be the harm?"

It was this attitude of his, this brazenly cheerful, impudent demeanor that netted him so much money begging. While others beggars sat despondently, some not even raising their voices to cry out, Bartimaeus treated begging like his personal one-man show. He claimed he could tell women from men by their scent, and once he determined the gender, he was off. He'd call to the women, extolling their beauty with fulsome praise for their hair, their faces, their clothing. He'd tell them they were the prettiest sight his blind eyes had ever seen. He lauded the men for their cleverness and skill, lavishing them with accolades for the great deeds he falsely attributed to them. He was really quite funny, and when his descriptions were even close to accurate, the people laughed and threw him coins. When he admired a short, stocky man for his tall, feminine grace, the laughter and the coins flew even faster

I guess I shouldn't have been suprised to hear that my brother had been sitting by the side of the road, calling out to healers, telling them he wanted to see. I could picture it as easily as if I'd been there. What happened next, though, was strange beyond words.

"And then he called to you," I prompted, hoping to hear more. But Bartimaeus, obviously preoccupied, pulled out the smooth pebbles he always carried in a pouch around his waist and held them up to the light streaming through our one window. He looked at them, then closed his eyes and ran them through his fingers as he used to do. When he opened his eyes, he looked at them again, as if trying to reconcile what he knew with his fingers to what he now saw with his eyes.

"Bartimaeus?" I interrupted his reverie.

"Yes," he said, dropping the stones back into his lap. "He called for me, and I went to him, and he asked me what I wanted. I told him I wanted to see."

"And then what happened?"

"And then he said, 'Go, your faith has healed you.' I didn't even know I *had* faith!" He laughed.

Typical. I shook my head at him, and he stopped laughing and looked at me in amazement.

"What?" I asked.

"It's just—I know that sound, the sound your covering makes against your hair. And now I can see it, when you're moving." He laughed again with delight. I shook my head.

"And then what happened?" I wanted to hear the details of the story over and over, as if impressing them repeatedly on my ears would make them somehow more believable.

"And then it was like all this light, and all these colors—except I didn't know they were colors—came rushing at me, and it was so painful I closed my eyes, and when I opened them again, I could see. And then," he said, getting even more excited, warming to his favorite part of the tale, "as I looked, I suddenly knew what things were. Yeshua was standing over me, looking at me, and I knew he was a man, and that the hair on his face was a beard. And as I looked down at the dirt I knew it had a color, and I knew it was called brown, and when I looked at the sky I knew it was blue."

"How?"

"I don't know. I just knew. And then Yeshua started walking away from me, and I got up, and left my stick, and followed him."

The litany was interrupted by a small knock at the door.

"That'll be Kitra," I said, getting up and moving toward the door. "She's bringing over some sewing." To supplement the money Bartimaeus made begging, I took in sewing projects for families who lived nearby and had too many children to keep up themselves. I didn't earn much money, but every now and then I would be asked to help sew for something important, new clothes for a feast, perhaps, or in this case, a wedding. Sewing for a special event yielded more pay, and between the little monies Bartimaeus and I made and the home our parents had left us, we managed to get by. And for that I was grateful. So many others in our situation simply lived on the corners of the street where they begged.

I undid the latch and swung open the door, and Kitra stepped inside. We sat down at the table, going over the details of the work, mending a tear in the veil her mother had worn on her wedding day. Kitra's head was bent low over the fabric as the light began to fade, and she didn't hear Bartimaeus walking up behind her.

"Kitra," he breathed, and she startled. I looked up at him. He was standing there, transfixed, an expression on his face I'd never seen.

"You are the most beautiful woman in the world," he exhaled all in a rush, then grabbed her hands and held them to his chest. "Will you be my *isha*? Now?"

The look in his eyes was like an animal.

Kitra stifled a scream as she stood up and pushed him back, all but running toward the door and out of the house. I hurried after her and caught up with her on the street.

"I'm so sorry," I panted. "Forgive Bartimaeus. He's had a difficult day."

"What was he talking about?" Kitra asked, her voice shaking. "I'm *airusin* to Tzviel. Everyone knows that!"

"I know, I know," I said, speaking soothingly as if to a frightened gazelle. "Bartimaeus doesn't know what he is saying. I think he might have a fever."

I calmed Kitra with soothing words until she quieted down and left for home. Then I turned around and stormed back in to Bartimaeus.

"What in the name of all that Yahweh has sanctified do you think you were doing?"

Bartimaeus stopped his examination of the texture of the mud that made up our walls, and turned toward me. His expression was still not quite like him.

"*Achot*, she's beautiful. I never knew!"

"Bartimaeus, you scared her out of her wits! Do you want me to lose this project? Everyone knows she's *airusin* to Tzviel; that's why I have the veil in the first place." I gestured toward the table. Bartimaeus walked over and picked up the fabric, running it through his fingers, now closing his eyes, now opening them.

"She'll look so beautiful in this," he said, turning it over and over. "She must wear it for me!" He looked at me again, now with an expression of frightening sincerity. "Did you see her hair peeking out under her covering? The way her hands turned when she spoke? The way she walked, and moved?"

"Bartimaeus, she's a woman," I snapped. "All women look like that. *I* look like that. Stop being so ridiculous."

I felt his eyes upon me, appraising me; I turned away. *At least I used to look like that*, I thought, moving over to shake out the covering on my pallet. *I used to look like that before I couldn't take a husband, before I wasted my entire life taking care of you.* I had never resented my blind brother as much as I did at that moment.

♦

Long after darkness had fallen and we'd lain down to sleep, Bartimaeus was still awake, talking on his pallet into the darkness. I was only half listening, waiting for him to finally be quiet so I could fall asleep. He was rhapsodizing about his new life, no longer as Bartimaeus the Blind, but just Bartimaeus.

"I can take a wife," I heard him saying as I tossed on my pallet. "I can marry, and have children and raise a family. I can do anything now!"

Good for you, I thought uncharitably as I rolled over. *Can you possibly go to sleep?*

"I can start a trade!" he continued to gush, happily. "I can be a carpenter or a fisherman or a merchant!"

"Bartimaeus," I finally said, wearily pushing myself up on my elbows, "How do you expect to start a trade when you have no training, no skills, and no apprenticeship?"

I felt, rather than saw, my brother deflate. "I hadn't thought of that," he said, his voice a little more subdued. "Someone will take me on, don't you think? I mean, I can see!"

"Everyone can see," I answered, lying back down on my pallet. "Everyone else could always see, and everyone else has been training to work since they were boys."

The moment of silence stretched so long, I began to wonder if Bartimaeus had finally fallen asleep. I readjusted myself on my mat and closed my eyes.

"But I can't go back to begging," a quiet voice said eventually. "I can't be a beggar now that I can see; I'm healthy and strong and whole." He paused for a moment, then his voice drifted out again over the darkness. "What am I going to do?"

I didn't admit this to him, but the thought suddenly scared me. Of course he wouldn't be able to continue begging; no one would give him a single coin now that he'd made his way home this evening proclaiming to all the world that he could see. Why hadn't I thought of that? He had no training or skills, and was far too old to begin looking for a trade. He was useless. In granting him sight, Yeshua had taken away the one and only skill he possessed.

And taken away our money, I thought, suddenly cold. What *were* we going to do? Bartimaeus lay breathing quietly on his pallet. Like me, he lay awake, and I wondered what he was thinking. What had Yeshua done? What kind of a miracle was it to grant a fully grown man his sight, and rob him of the ability to feed and clothe himself?

Bartimaeus could now see, and yes, it had been a miracle. But at what cost? It wasn't as if he'd been born seeing and then had it taken away; he was blind from birth. He'd never known what he was missing as a blind man, but he would know what he was missing now that he was sighted. I shifted in the darkness, unable to find a comfortable position in which to curl my body. What would this mean for us? We couldn't live off of the tiny money I made taking in wedding veils and torn robes. And what was Bartimaeus the Sighted supposed to do? Mope around the house, forever useless, fawning desperately over any female who came his way?

I sighed again into the darkness, louder this time, and rubbed my knuckle against the space between my eyes. Perhaps our lives would have been better if Yeshua had simply left us alone.

9

The Remnant of Our People

The night heat clung to my skin as I peeled my robe off my body. I rolled over for what seemed like the hundredth time that night, my skin sticking to the mat, my tunic, and the air surrounding me. Through the baked mud walls of my home I heard the cry of a baby next door—my neighbor Chaya had borne a daughter with the passing of the last moon, and the tiny girl hadn't stopped crying since. *I'd be crying, too, forced into this stifling heat*, I thought, and sat up in the darkness. It seemed ages since my own son, now grown, had been a tiny infant, and I sighed as I thought of those tear-filled nights that I once thought would never end.

The high, small window in my room revealed a flickering light that bounced off the walls in Chaya's home, through her window, over the narrow passageway between our houses, and straight into my eyes. I sat up and pushed my sticky hair away from my face with weary hands. There was no escaping the night; I felt as if I was going to scream. Just as I was contemplating going next door and offering to take the baby for a spell so Chaya could sleep—since it was obvious I wasn't going to—a harsh pounding echoed through my room.

"Open!" The pounding continued. "Open in the name of Caesar! You are housing a thief!"

Instinctively I reached for my robe and draped it around my

sweating skin. The male voice outside was strong.

"Open!"

The tone was insistent, and I listened to see if I could hear more than one voice. The last time they came there had been five of them, and I didn't like feeling so overpowered in the middle of the night.

"I'm coming," I called softly, hoping not to wake any neighbors. Then Chaya's baby screamed again and I realized no one in this section of the city could possibly be asleep anyway.

"I'm coming!" I yelled louder over the pounding.

I raised myself off my mat and pushed back the curtain hanging over the doorway to my bedroom. The main room was slightly cooler, and as I felt my way around the table and chairs, I considered moving my mat out there for the night after I saw to the men at the door. Slowly, I lifted the latch and swung the heavy wooden door inward just enough for me to see the guards standing outside in my small courtyard. The outside air was just as hot, and the light from the stars blazing out of the dark sky seemed relentless. Two young guards stood there, cruel determination etched onto their otherwise expressionless faces. Their highly polished helmets shone in the starlight, and as I glanced down I saw the high, bracing spats of their sandals crossing and recrossing their way up thickly muscled legs. Members of Caesar's army. One of them had a long, aquiline nose, jutting out harshly from his face in the starlight. But the second guard. . . .

"Avishai?"

The younger guard turned away from me, in embarrassment or confusion I could not tell. The older guard, the one who had been pounding on my door, snapped around to face him.

"You know this woman?"

"No . . . yes," Avishai stammered softly. "I knew her when I was growing up."

"You are a member of Caesar's army now!" the tall guard yelled at him. "Who you knew when you were growing up doesn't matter."

He turned back to me, his searching eyes covering me swiftly. With one hand I pulled my robe tighter around my body.

"You are housing a thief," the Roman guard repeated. "I charge you in the name of Caesar to give him up to us, or stand back and we will search your house."

"Please," I intoned, leaning my head against the door. "Please, I know of no such thief. I have been awake for hours listening to the *yeled* next door, and I would have heard someone enter my house. Please, I am an old woman and an *almanah*— my husband is long dead."

If they had any shred of decency, I thought, they would leave me alone and turn back into the stifling night. But Caesar's guards were renowned for their cruelty, so I held my breath for a tense moment.

The guard pushed his body into the doorway and I looked up at him, unwilling to step back. He peered over my shoulder into the darkness, and I could smell the astringent polish he must have used on the metal of his uniform. I knew as well as he did that he couldn't see anything in the darkness, but I said nothing.

Finally, he took a step back and looked at me again.

"*Takif.* . . . " Avishai started to speak, his voice wavering.

I stole a look at him and gave what I hoped was a barely perceptible shake of my head. I didn't want him getting in trouble with his leader for my sake. Besides, the tall guard had backed off, and I was certain it would be only moments before he abandoned the search attempt and left.

I was right. The guard turned and spit on the ground, and then looked back at me.

"Leave!" he called. "There's no one here but an ugly old *almanah*. Or if there is. . . . " He leaned closer to me until I could feel his breath, even hotter than the night air. The threat went unstated, but we both heard it as clearly as if it had been spoken.

The two men turned around and stomped through the narrow courtyard. The older guard kicked at the small brick oven in the middle of the courtyard and muffled a curse as the bricks held fast against his foot. Avishai turned once to glance at me, but I pretended not to see him and he continued on with the other guard down one of the zigzag streets that ran between the houses.

I closed the door and leaned against it, sweat dripping in runnels down my face. Then I felt my way back around the table and chairs, past the curtain sectioning off my bedroom, and on toward the back of the house. Through the walls I could hear the baby still crying next door. I reached my hand out in the darkness and pushed against another, thicker curtain. I grabbed it and flung it back.

"You!" I hissed into the darkness, my calm resolve melting with the exodus of the guards. A small flame sputtered into being, and I was face-to-face with my son, who was holding a lamp in his one hand while he pushed his hair out of his face with the other. In the lamplight he looked young, even though he'd been old enough to marry for several years now, and when he looked up at me, his shaggy brown hair fell into his dark, sleep-crusted eyes. I stood still as he got up off the floor and began to pace. Suddenly feeling weak, the vacated mat unrolled on the floor near the curtain called to me. I had to fight the urge to sit down.

"That is the last time," I continued, my voice rising. I don't know what you did now, but I am not going to cover for you, ever again."

My son stopped his pacing and gestured toward the two high, small windows in the back wall of his room. He motioned for me to be quiet.

"Quiet?" I roared. "*Quiet?* You have the audacity to tell me to be quiet? I just saved you from the Roman guards, and I've half a mind to march back out there and tell them you're here! I don't know how you grew into this, a common thief, an *Ish HaMufkarut!* This is not what I raised you to be! If your father were alive. . . . "

My voice trailed off in the darkness. I was tired deep within my bones. Even my anger couldn't give me strength. I sank down on my son's mat.

"What did you take this time?"

His laugh startled me as he crossed back over to the mat and reached beneath it with one hand to pull out a small silver anklet, made in the Roman style and adorned with multicolored jewels. When he shook it in front of the lamp, it made a gentle tinkling sound.

"My liege's lady won't be needing this anymore," he said mockingly as he swung the trinket around. "I didn't expect her to notice it was gone until morning."

He sank down beside me and dropped the anklet into his lap.

"I'm sorry, *em*," he said. "I just can't help it. They have so much, and we have nothing—nothing!"

I resisted the urge to slap him.

"Nothing is what we *will* have if you keep stealing from the people who are giving you work! Nothing? You have a roof over your head and plenty of food and clothing and more than most! Nothing? You call this nothing?"

My son set the lamp on the packed clay floor and flopped back onto his mat to stare up into the darkness at the ceiling.

"Our *people* have nothing," he said.

Chaya's baby wailed on.

"The *Yehudim* are being desecrated by the Roman filth living among us," he continued. We must drive them out! Restore the remnant of our people!"

In the flickering lamplight his dark hair curled across his sweaty brow. He smacked one fist into the palm of his other hand, and then punched the darkness. Caged-up strength oozed from his every pore. I resisted the urge to lift the hair off his brow and kiss him as I'd done when he was a child. I held myself still—my boy had become a man.

"And you're going to restore the remnant through petty theft?" I asked, my voice gentler but still pointed. He didn't answer. I placed my hand on his knee.

"If you get a reputation for being a common *ganav* it will be the end of your floor-laying. This is the third time, *beni haahuv*, and the guards know it's you. You have to stop. You can be put to death for theft under this Roman government."

A fist flew into the air again.

"But I work all day in their filthy homes, scraping the flesh off my fingers as I lay stones for their floors. Mosaic floors!" He sat up abruptly, knocking my hand away. "Some of our people don't even have floors! The Romans are laying mosaic floors over the sweat and the blood of the *Yehudim* in our own land!"

I sighed. "No, actually, *you're* laying their mosaic floors over the sweat and the blood of your *Yehudim*. Think about that the next time you want to steal something."

I leaned over and blew out the lamp, rendering the room black as pitch. In the sudden darkness I realized Chaya's baby was finally quiet.

"I'm going to bed," I whispered. "I'll see you in the morning."

◆

With the earliest light of dawn the heat became even more unbearable. I woke in a sweat from a dream where Avishai came again in the night and shackled my son, laughing, as his nose twisted and morphed until it was distinctly Roman. As I sat up on my mat, panting, I flung away the robe I'd been clutching to myself during my night terrors.

The city outside was already awake and beginning to churn with daily activity. Mothers called to their children, fathers bid their families goodbye until the close of the day. I sat bolt upright on my mat, still feeling the paradoxically hot chills that had swept over my spine the previous night. Finally, I got up and draped my robe over my body before I rolled up my mat and tied on my sandals.

From the doorway into the main room, I could see that the curtain to my son's room was flung back. Behind it I saw his pallet still lying unrolled on the floor, but he was gone. From a small chest on the floor next to the table I took a few pieces of yesterday's flat bread sweetened with date honey, and collected both of my water jars for the daily trip to the well.

Outside, the morning was blazing. Not even at its zenith, the sun was so hot it felt like midday already. I looked down at my sandals with gratitude and relief: I wouldn't want to walk to the city well—located close to the edge of the city—in my bare feet.

As I joined the throng of wives and daughters going to collect their daily water, female voices bounced off the hot, dusty trail with a mild chatter, while children scampered around the women, picking up small stones from alongside the trail to play with. Although the trail snaked its way through close-built mud houses, countless years of the daily trudge of women's feet had worn it into a wider path, one of the widest in the city. At the same time, the courtyards that bounded it had grown ever smaller. A short ways ahead of me I saw my good friend Yehudit, and balancing one empty jar on my head while steadying the other with my hip, I made my way toward her.

"Yehudit!" I called. "*Boker tov!*"

Yehudit turned around and a smile of recognition lit her face as she saw me.

"*Boker tov!*" She returned the morning greeting. "And how did you fare on that miserably hot night last night?"

Yehudit was younger than I, almost young enough to be my daughter. She and her husband had moved to our section of the city when they'd married, and since then, an odd sort of friendship had sprung up between us. Sometimes we were merely good friends; other times, our friendship deepened until I felt I was almost a mother and she the daughter I'd never borne. Her family was far away; having married her off to a distant cousin, they didn't concern themselves with her well-being anymore. Still, Yehudit never spoke ill of them; according to her, being one of five sisters meant she was lucky to even find a husband.

"I'd be happy if the only thing bothering me last night was the heat," I muttered to her as we walked together.

"Oh, not again. . . . " Yehudit's eyes seemed reticent as she swiftly glanced in my direction, and just as quickly looked away.

"Yes," I admitted. "Yehudit, I don't know what I'm going to do. He's a grown man, and far too old to act like this. I don't know what I did to raise him so wrong."

The heat was oppressive as we walked.

"Maybe it wasn't anything you did," Yehudit suggested tentatively as she shifted the weight of one of her jars to her other hip. "You said his father died right after his *bar mitzvah*; that must have been so hard. . . . " Her voice trailed off like dust.

"It was," I agreed. "But that's no excuse. He's grown into a common thief, an *Ish HaMufkarut*." I paused. "I called him that last night."

Yehudit laughed. I smiled with her, and then became sober.

"But it's nothing to laugh about. Three times now he's stolen something quite valuable, and twice the guards have come to my home. It's only because of their overconfidence I've been able to keep them away this long. If it happens again they're going to look for him until they find him, I know it."

The well was visible in the distance. Around me the women's daily chatter of husbands, children, and food preparation seemed trivial compared with my own fears.

"Would it really be so bad if they came and took him?" Yehudit asked cautiously. "Perhaps some time in the Roman prison would cool him off."

"Oh Yehudit," I said. "You're so young. Wait until you birth a *yeled*; then you'll understand. A mother can't just stand there while guards from some foreign government drag her only child to prison. And besides. . . . "

We'd entered the cloister of women waiting to draw water from the well.

"I'm not afraid of them taking him to prison." My voice was so low Yehudit leaned in closer to hear me. "I'm afraid of something far worse."

"They wouldn't," Yehudit began to protest, but I interrupted.

"They *will*. The Romans are fed up with us, all of us. Think about how many people have been unjustly punished lately. They're sick of the whole lot of us, and now with this false moshiach proclaiming himself king, they're looking for people to make examples of. They want us to know the *Yehudim* have no power under Roman rule."

Yehudit was silent as I bent to grab the rope that held the bucket inside of the well. The thick rope, once coarse, had been worn smooth from many pairs of hands raising and lowering it over the years. I silently let the soft braided camel hairs slide through my fingers.

"So how were the Romans last night?" A mocking voice made me raise my head. "I assume you're getting quite friendly with them; this was the second time they've come to visit since the last moon?"

"Chaya," I said, shielding my eyes from the sun with one hand. "How's your *yeled*?"

"Fine, thank you. We couldn't sleep last night wondering what an old *almanah* could be doing to bring the Roman guards back to her, again and again, in the middle of the night, no less."

Chaya could be cruel with her words, but having lived next door to her since her wedding day, I'd grown accustomed to her acerbic tone.

"Oh, you know," I said casually. "Once upon a time I was the best-kept secret in Yerushalayim, but ever since I plied my trade among the Roman guards, apparently the secret's out." I grinned.

Turning away from her stunned expression, I raised the full bucket of water to pour into my first jar. Chaya didn't reply.

On the walk back home from the well, Yehudit rebuked me for my words.

"She hasn't recovered from the birthing yet," Yehudit chided me. "She has to adjust to new motherhood."

"Chaya's been like that since before you moved to the city, birthing or no birthing. Besides, what would you know about bearing a child?

Yehudit blushed to her roots. It was no secret that she longed for a child; she'd been trying to conceive since the night of her marriage.

"Nothing, yet. But I just think she's having a difficult time. We all know how much she longed for a son, and Yahweh gave her a daughter. We must be patient with her."

I sighed and shifted the heavy jars.

"Not a day has gone by lately, Yehudit, when I wouldn't trade my son, my darling *beni haahuv*, for a daughter like Chaya's. At this point I'd even take a screaming infant."

We smiled at each other as we parted ways to head back to our respective homes before the heat of midday.

♦

That night my son came home early. The meat stew was still sizzling over the fire in our small courtyard, and I had just checked the lentil and olive flatbreads in the adjoining oven to see if they were ready. I shifted my weight. My proximity to the fire was unbearable, but I wanted my son to have a cooked dinner waiting for him after his hard day of labor.

"*Em!*" I heard him call as he walked up the street toward our house.

"Home so soon?" I asked, rocking back on my heels away from the brick oven. I didn't want to ask if his early arrival meant he was also in more trouble.

"Don't worry so much," he laughed, coming closer. He smelled of sweat and plaster as he bent to kiss the top of my head.

"Worrying will give you lines and then you will look like an old woman."

"I *am* an old woman, and I *do* worry."

He laughed again.

"Well, you shouldn't. The only thing I stole today was the heart of a general's young wife, and I suppose I can't help that."

He stretched to his full height above me, flexing his muscles like a gladiator. Although I wanted to remonstrate him for his blasé attitude, it was so good to see him cheerful and relaxed that I held my tongue.

"I *did* bring you these, though," he continued as he untied a small leather pouch from around his waist. He fished around inside and closed his hand over something before bending down to show me the contents. I hesitantly peered into his open hand, where several small, brightly colored stones twinkled against the rough lines of his palm.

"Oh *beni haahuv*," I began, reproachingly.

"No!" he cut in. "These were given to me! The wife of the general—I told you she was taken with me—she gave me these after my work today. They didn't fit into the mosaic pattern, and I'd told her so much about you, and she said I could take them home with me as a gift to my mother."

For a moment, the towering, muscled man before me disappeared and instead I saw a small boy, overjoyed at his first discovery of amaranth. He was running toward me, clutching a bundle of the scarlet blossoms, tripping over himself in his delight.

"*Em! Em!*" he called. "Look what I found for you!"

His dark eyes were so bright and so pleased with his gift that I scooped a small amount of water out of our large earthen jar and placed his flowers in a small clay pot.

"They're beautiful, *beni haahuv*," I had said, admiring his gift. "The most beautiful flowers I've ever been given."

I ran my fingers through his rumpled hair and didn't tell him that in about a week, the entire city would be cursing the invasion of amaranth into every tilled plot of ground we worked. The blooms had been a gift of love to a mother from her young son.

Now, my son bore a striking resemblance to that child he'd grown out of.

"These are bdellium," he said, pointing with his thick index finger to a creamy, smooth-colored stone. "And these . . . " he swirled the stones around and separated out a small, light green one. "These are chrysoprase. And this one," he grasped a yellow-orange stone between his thumb and forefinger so I could barely see it anymore. "This one is jacinth. It's my favorite because it reminds me of the way the sunset looks from up on the roof. Here. . . ." He poured the pile of stones into my cupped hands. "We can put them on the shelf with the prayer shawls, and then you will have beauty in your home just like a mosaic."

I smiled up at my son, then wordlessly indicated for him to bring the meat stew inside for our dinner.

◆

The moon passed into its next cycle without incident. The hot spell broke and the days began to seem like any other spring in Yerushalayim. Since the nights were cooler, Chaya's baby didn't cry as much, and without the Roman guards beating on my door I began to sleep sweet, restful nights. My son's foray into thievery seemed a thing of the past.

One night I startled awake in the utter darkness, clutching my robe. The dream had returned—the one of Avishai putting my son in shackles. I lay still for a moment and listened to the sound of my breathing, reassuring myself that everything was all right. It was only a dream, the dream of a foolish old widow. But through the stillness I heard what sounded like scratching, and it sounded like it was coming from the door. I held my breath and listened more closely. It definitely wasn't knocking, but something was out there. I pulled my robe around my body and got up.

At the door I paused. It sounded as if someone was running fingernails up and down the splintery wood of the door.

"Hello?" I called softly, wondering if I was too soft to be heard. "Is anyone there?"

The scratching turned to a small tapping, and curiosity overcame fear long enough for me to open the door. Standing there, in a dark cloak that all but concealed his face, was Avishai.

"Avishai? What are you doing here in the middle of the night? Come in!"

The look he gave me was one of pure terror as he pushed me

aside, stepped over the threshold, and quickly closed the door behind him.

"Shhh," he said. "We must speak softly and be quick. If I'm caught here. . . . "

"What's wrong? Why are you here?"

"I think you'd better sit down," Avishai replied as he took my elbow and guided me over to the table. The chair made a small scraping sound against the clay floor as he pulled it out from the table. Then he put his hands on my shoulders and pushed me gently down to sit.

"Avishai, what's going on? Shall I wake my son?" The fear evident in his face was beginning to unnerve me.

"*Eishes chayil*, I wish I could tell you to go and wake your son. But. . . . " Avishai pulled out the other chair and sat down, facing me. "He's not here."

I felt my brows knit as I turned my puzzled face toward Avishai.

"But where is he? He was here when I went to bed."

"*Eishes chayil*, your son is away most nights." He paused, and I looked at him in disbelief. I'd thought my son's indiscretions were over.

"I'm sorry I had to be the one to let you know," Avishai continued, "but. . . . " He placed his hand on my knee. "Tonight there was something of an uprising."

"Oh Avishai, no," I breathed, my voice trailing off.

His hand on my knee tightened until I almost winced.

"Yes," he continued. It was at the home of the guard where your son has been laying mosaic."

"And he was there?" I interrupted. Avishai kept speaking without answering.

"There were several of them there, all *Yehudim*, mostly men who work in the Roman homes like your son. Petty thievery is one thing. . . . "

He quit speaking. I slid my hand under his chin and lifted his face until his eyes met mine, silently imploring him to go on.

"They ransacked the place," he finally said. "They took

everything that wasn't part of the foundation and broke anything that was. When I got there the wife was standing on her bed screaming, clutching the few garments she had left. They terrorized her."

"They didn't . . ." I choked. It was too awful.

"No, they didn't touch her. They just tormented her until she was absolutely petrified. When I slipped away she was still screaming; not even her husband could comfort her."

"Avishai, tell me who was there."

"It was a group of about ten men." His voice was thick in the darkness. Most of them got away by the time the guards got there, but. . . ."

He didn't need to tell me, but he did.

"They captured your son."

I was aware of so much. The rough spot on the edge of the chair that we could never seem to hone to perfection; my son always took this chair at meals so it wouldn't bother me. The swirls in the grain of our table, marred by the dent where my son had struck the wood with a rock after his first Torah lesson. My husband had been so angry with him. I slowly turned to view the room as if seeing it simultaneously for the first and last time. The light curtain to my room, flung back. My son's curtain, also open.

Why hadn't I noticed? Why hadn't I heard him, stopped him? As these thoughts assailed my brain, my eyes alighted on the carved shelf that held our prayer shawl, at eye-height on the wall at the back of the room. The blue-and-white prayer shawl my mother helped me make when I was engaged to be married, so many moons ago, lay reverently folded on the shelf. The small colorful stones my son brought me lay sparkling beside it, and even though I couldn't see them in the darkness, their glistening beauty hurt my eyes.

"What do I do," I said simply, turning back to Avishai.

"I don't know."

He reached out and wrapped his arms around me, bringing my head to his chest as if I were a child. Holding me there in the silence, I could feel unshed tears rising up in a foment until I began to shake.

A small scuffling sound outside made Avishai jump. I startled.

"I must go," he said, rising and pushing his chair back. It scudded against the mud floor.

"I must go," he repeated. "If they find me here—

"Tell me where he is."

I grabbed Avishai's cloak desperately as he turned to leave. He pivoted on a noiseless sandal and clasped both of my hands in his.

"*Eishes chayil*, he's in prison. But. . . . " His hands tightened around mine.

"I don't want to tell you this. . . . " He swallowed. "He's with the condemned. There are three others, sentenced to crucifixion. The guards put him with them."

◆

"Drink this."

A woman's hand cradled my head and I opened my eyes to the smell of a rich goat broth. A gentle light from a window revealed my own room, my mat, and as I looked up, Yehudit.

"Yehudit . . . " I struggled.

"Shhh. Don't talk yet. Just drink this."

I did as I was bade and let her bring the crock to my lips. When I parted them to drink the broth I realized they were dry and painfully cracked. The broth was pungent, and as the savory liquid trickled slowly down my throat I laid my head back in Yehudit's arms. I was beyond tired.

"How did you get here?" The croak of my voice unnerved me, and I realized that the light coming through the window was early light. I struggled to remember what had happened.

"Shhh," Yehudit said again. "Don't try to think just yet. Finish your broth."

I rested in her arms and let her feed me. She gave me a piece of lentil flatbread and with effort I wrapped my lips around it.

Lying in her arms, gazing up at the underside of our flat roof, I felt contented. I didn't know why she was there, or why I was so weak, but it didn't seem to matter. I felt as peaceful as a small child. I smiled, remembering the way my son's head would fall back after he'd fed at my breast as an infant, his body suffused with sleep. He would lie in my arms, heavy and warm, his mouth still working against the small traces of milk left in his mouth.

My son.

Abruptly I sat up, startling Yehudit and causing her to drop the crock of broth, which shattered on the floor. Hot liquid spattered my face as I clutched Yehudit's robes and fought to stand.

"My son! My son—they took him, there was an uprising, the Roman guards put him in prison and sentenced him to . . . to. . . . "

Yehudit interrupted me.

"Shhh, *eishes chayil.* Avishai told me. He came and woke me when you lost your senses. He told me the whole story before he left, and then I came and stayed with you all through the night."

Her words didn't make sense to me. All I could think of was my son.

"Yehudit, I have to go," I said, pulling myself to my feet. "I have to see him."

Yehudit stood with me and placed her hands on my shoulders. Her eyes locked with mine.

"You are my dearest friend," she said. "You have been a mother's strength to me since my marriage brought me to this city, and where you go now, I will go with you."

Her brown eyes were serious. The words of Ruth to Naomi. Whatever ordeal I was going to face, I would not face it alone. I pulled Yehudit to me and held her tightly for a moment, our arms wrapped around each other in a silent embrace. Then without a word, we turned to go.

◆

The streets were crowded with people pushing and jostling. In the pain of the night before, I had almost forgotten that the culmination of the Feast of Unleavened Bread was drawing near. The entire city had turned itself inside-out in preparation and Yehudit and I could barely make it through the crowded streets. Sidling along the rough stone walls of the buildings that seemed to almost meet overhead yet somehow did not block out the sun, we navigated the paths as quickly as we could.

The prison lay near the center of the city, but every street we walked on seemed to have turned into a market in preparation for the high feast day. Small children screamed, old women sang. Although the air was still mild, I had begun to sweat.

"Yehudit, what if he's gone by the time we get there?"

Yehudit laughed as she sidestepped a small child, being sick at the side of the road.

"Somebody got into the consecrated wine?" she asked the small boy, and he looked up at her with a weak smile before his mother grabbed his hand and hurried him onward to wherever they were going so quickly.

"Don't worry." She turned back to me, her strong voice full of confidence. "The Romans may be cruel, but we know they're not fast. They'll use their bureaucracy to its fullest advantage and leave him there for weeks. It will provide an example to the others."

And then, I thought . . . but I didn't say it. I was panting, trying to keep up with her pace. She reached back, took my hand, and squeezed it gently.

"Are you sure?" I queried at last. The prison was a horrible place, but as long as my son was there, he was alive.

Just then a vendor leapt out from behind a stall, thrusting a fresh, gutted fish into my face. No wonder that small child had been sick—the excitement alone was enough to unsettle a stomach, even without every other vendor trying to crowd you with fresh fish or raw meats. I assured him I didn't need any fish and we hurried on.

The light-colored stone walls of the prison soon loomed in

front of us, and I felt my resolve dwindle. Two guards stood sentry outside the entrance dressed in full Roman regalia, intimidating any Yehudim who would come to see their loved ones in preparation for the high feast. They were both young, and for a moment I wondered what it must be like to be stationed in Yerushalayim during a high feast, with your mothers, gods, and customs so very far away. Through the prism of my thoughts the guards looked even younger, softer, and I let go of Yehudit's hand and approached them.

"Please, *shomrim*, I wish to see my son."

The guards didn't move.

"Please," I asked again. Still the guards ignored me, their eyes boring straight ahead into nothingness, their spears crossed over the small cutout in the stone wall that served as an entrance.

"Please," I tried one more time. I moved so that I was directly in front of one of the guards, the one with the more pronounced nose.

"If your mother was coming to see you, would you want her to be allowed to pass?"

The guard's strong shoulders relaxed ever so slightly, and he lowered his eyes to look at me. Without a word to me, he issued a harsh command to the other guard and the two of them raised their spears, permitting me to pass.

I stepped inside the prison. At the sound of clanking metal behind me, I turned to see Yehudit held back by the now crossed spears.

"No!" I said, addressing the guards. "You must let her pass. She is . . . my daughter."

The spears raised and Yehudit rushed past with a quick glance at me, and then we were together in the prison.

The small enclosure reeked of filth, unwashed skin, waste, and despair. A narrow cobbled path ran down a flight of twisting stone steps, and it was to these that I turned. The prisoners condemned to crucifixion would be below street level, and that was where I had to look if I wanted to find my son. Small cutouts in the walls of the prison held dark metal bolts that had been driven into the stone, menacing and virtually impossible to break. To each bolt a man was shackled—the place was full for the up-coming feast.

Yehudit and I walked quickly down the row of men toward the stairs, trying to ignore their stares and jeers. One man's spit-tle reached my foot, prompting a host of yelling and similar ges-tures from the other men.

"I never should have brought you here," I hissed to Yehudit as one man tried to grab her ankle.

"*Ahara!*" One man yelled at her. "We are poor prisoners who are condemned to die! Give us something to remember when we go!"

Yehudit blushed and focused her gaze on the floor.

"*Almanah!*" Another yelled at me. "Why would you bring your daughter here if she wasn't come to share herself? Unless of course you're giving it out!"

Laughter and the sound of clinking chains rumbled over the stones.

"I'd take even the *almanah* now," another man yelled.

The noise mounted as we reached the stairs and hurried down, holding our robes up off the filth-covered stones. I couldn't bear to think of my son alone in this place, with all these people. But when we reached the bottom, quiet assailed our ears. The iron-bolted walls, identical to the ones above but fitted also with manacles for the feet, were empty.

"They're gone!" Yehudit gasped.

I didn't know what to say.

"If you're looking for the prisoners, they were taken away this morning."

The strange voice made us jump; a man was indeed shackled to the wall in the far corner. In the quiet and darkness we had missed him. His matted, grey hair hung over his almost-naked body, and he swung against his chains as if he were a child at play.

"Oh, they didn't take me," he continued speaking more to himself than to us as he swung. "Never, no rest for the *ish evyon*.

The *chaiyalim*, they take everybody to trial . . . everybody but me."

"He's crazy." Yehudit grabbed me. "I know who he is. They locked him up because he has no family and they didn't know what else to do with him. My husband told me about it when he was put away."

I looked at the old man, swinging almost happily.

"Where have they taken the prisoners?"

"I will die here," he laughed in a singsong voice. "I'm alone and no one wants me! But I will come back." He looked up at me with an unnatural light in his eyes. "Yes, I will come back. Back with the Moshiach."

"Where have they taken the prisoners?" I repeated.

"They caught the Moshiach and they brought him here," the man continued. "He was beautiful. He was like light. But they took him away . . . all away."

I looked at Yehudit desperately.

"To Pilate, to trial!" the man yelled gleefully.

"To the Roman governor?" Yehudit looked at me. "Can he know what he's talking about?"

"To Pilate!" he repeated.

His eyes rolled around in his head, spinning crazily. He bared his teeth. I quit questioning him and turned to Yehudit.

"If there's any sense in him and this is true," Yehudit said, "that means they've taken them all to be sentenced. We should go."

The crazy man interrupted.

"Crucify them all! Crucify, quick before the Sabbath!"

Yehudit reached for my hand again.

"Come on," she said. "Let's go quickly."

◆

Throngs of people filled the open courtyard outside of the governor's palace. The air was full of sound and smell, and clutching Yehudit's hand tightly within my own, I felt like I was going to be sick. We were so far away I couldn't see what was going on, and the people were packed in against each other so tightly Yehudit and I couldn't move any closer.

"*Boker tov.*" Yehudit turned to a woman standing on the fringe of the crowd, near us. The woman was balancing a young boy on one hip, and as she turned to Yehudit the child grabbed a fistful of her head covering and ducked behind it. I smiled at him, and then thought of my son.

"Could you tell us what's happening here?" Yehudit continued.

"There are just too many people to be able to see." The woman waved her free hand in front of her, indicating the crowd. "They say Pilate is coming outside to judge the condemned, so we could all see the sentence—but there's too many people."

Pilate must be coming outside, I thought, because none of our people would enter the palace and be defiled this close to the end of the Feast.

"And what's happening now?" Yehudit continued to question the woman while I stood there, stupidly, holding her hand. Faced with the massive crowds of people in front of the governor's palace, the reality of the situation was beginning to take its toll on me. I didn't want to move or speak—I just wanted to hold Yehudit's hand and let her make everything be all right.

A man standing nearby turned around and began speaking to us.

"I think he's come out. The criminals are being led out too."

I realized my teeth were clamping my tongue so hard I wondered that it wasn't bleeding. Still I said nothing and clung to Yehudit. She turned to the man and the people packed tightly in front of him.

"This woman is mother to one of the condemned. Will you step aside to let her pass through and see her only son?"

The woman to whom Yehudit had been speaking made a noise between a moan and a sigh, and wrapped her arms protectively around her little boy. The man said nothing, but began to tap the shoulders of the people in front of him, asking them to move aside. The crowd unbelievably began to clear in front of us, leaving a small open space. Yehudit pulled me into it. I was two steps closer to my son.

"This woman is one of the criminal's mothers." Yehudit placed her hand lightly on the shoulder of another woman. "Will you let us through?"

Step by small step, we worked our way through the crowd. Men, women, and even children continued to push aside and clear a path for us to walk. I was aware of the smell of too many bodies in one space, the fibers of the clothes I brushed against. Many people murmured to me as Yehudit led me past, but I couldn't even turn to look at them. I felt as if I were very, very young again, alone, bewildered, and frightened.

It was hot and close as we pressed on, and I felt again like I was going to be sick.

"Yehudit," I tried to whisper.

She didn't hear me, and gently touching another woman's arm and explaining our mission, pulled me ever closer to the sentencing.

"Yehudit," I whispered louder. My voice, so strong in the prison, now sounded weak and strange in my ears.

"Are you all right?" She paused to look at me, catching my free hand with her own.

"I don't want to keep going . . . I want to leave. I'm going to be sick."

I couldn't explain what I meant, and as I looked at her, tears blurred her image.

"I want to go," I repeated.

Yehudit placed her hands on my shoulders and looked me directly in the eye.

"*Eishes chayil.*" She held me for a moment there. The crowd closed in around us as we stood still.

"We couldn't leave even if we wanted to." She spoke to me as I had once spoken to my son. Slowly. Simply.

"It would be just as hard to fight our way out as it is to push in," she continued.

I blinked, and the tears that blurred her image seeped out until I could see her clearly.

"I don't want . . . " I began again and then stopped.

"*Eishes chayil.*" Yehudit's fingers slid lightly alongside my face, tucking a strand of hair back into my covering. Her hand stopped to cradle my cheek. "You need to see your son."

After a moment, I nodded dumbly, imploring Yehudit to understand all the things I couldn't say. We turned and continued on.

Yehudit squeezed us past another clump of people, and another. All of a sudden we were pushed out into the open air, and standing in the front of the crowd, I could finally see my son. A strangled-sounding cry escaped my throat. He was standing with three other criminals, his head hung low. The dark hair falling over his eyes was matted as if with sweat or blood, and his body, wrapped only in a strip of cloth, looked as if it had been beaten. I began to sob, sucking in air and then choking on it as if it were dust. I couldn't stop. I couldn't speak. Supported in Yehudit's arms as she stood close behind me, I looked at my only son and wept.

As the governor began to speak, Yehudit pressed her hand gently against my lips to quiet me. I fought the urge to bite her.

"You brought me this man as one who was inciting a rebellion." Pilate's voice rang out in clear, cold tones over the heads of the crowd. He indicated one of the criminals. Forcing myself to look away from my son, I glanced at the man to whom Pilate pointed. He was wearing an ill-fitting purple robe, and through the opening I could see his body, beaten worse than my son's. The man returned Pilate's gaze, seemingly neither angry nor afraid. I felt my sobs quiet as I stared at him.

"The moshiach," someone in the crowd murmured next to me.

"About time someone caught him," I heard another voice respond.

Through the cloudy haze of my mind I felt a prick of curiosity, and I continued to look at this man I'd heard so much about.

So this is the moshiach, I thought to myself. *Some savior.* He was about my son's age, maybe a little older, with unremarkable features—plain brown hair, brown eyes. His body was muscular, toned with hard work, and even though he'd been beaten he exuded a quiet strength. I turned to see my son and my breath caught as I inhaled. My chest was in spasms. I looked again at the man.

"Who do you think they'll release in honor of the Feast?" A man next to me questioned the air. The crowd around him had several opinions, but most thought it would be this false moshiach. Yeshua, they said his name was. A plain name for a plain man. I searched his face and wondered what made him want to proclaim himself king. He didn't look like the sort of man who would. Although his purple robe did little to hide his muscular form, he seemed a gentle sort. I always imagined false moshiachs as men full of life and anger—men like my son. I tore my eyes away from this Yeshua and looked again at my boy.

"I want them to release my son," I said to Yehudit. My voice sounded plaintive.

"Shhhh." She tightened her arms around me. But I pushed her away before turning to face her.

"They have to release a criminal for the Feast," I said. "It's tradition." Somehow, in the horror of all that had happened, I had forgotten that one of the four men would be freed. "Why can't it be my son? He isn't a treacherous criminal, he's just a foolish boy."

Yehudit didn't say anything, didn't even look at me, and I realized she didn't want to give me false hope. Unreasonably, I wanted to hit her. Instead I turned my back on her to watch Pilate. He spoke again.

"I have examined him in your presence and have found no basis for your charges against him," he continued, looking at Yeshua. "Neither has Herod, for he sent him back to us; as you can see, he has done nothing to deserve death."

"How can that be true?" I said out loud. Everyone in the city knew this man had been traveling around, proclaiming himself a king and a god. He probably deserved crucifixion more than any man standing there.

"Therefore," Pilate paused, considering the crowd. "I will punish him and then release him."

"No!" I gasped. If he was the man chosen to be released, my son would be put to death. But my shout was lost in the sudden, surging noise of the crowd.

"He should be crucified," a strong voice said near my ear.

"Yes, yes!" I said, as loud as I could. "Crucify him! Crucify him and release my son!" My heart was beating faster.

"Crucify him!" someone else yelled.

"Away with this man!" another called.

"Crucify him! Crucify him!" I screamed.

I turned to Yehudit, entreatingly, begging her to join with me. There was hope. I grabbed her hands again. But I didn't need Yehudit's voice—the crowd was taking up the call.

"Crucify him!" they thundered, over and over.

And all of a sudden I was laughing. My emotions shifted so violently I became dizzy. Tears of elation spilled over my face and I wanted to spin around until I collapsed from relief. My son was going to be spared. "Crucify him!" I yelled with all the strength I had.

The crowd continued the cry. "Crucify him!" I heard in shrill treble voices from around my knees. A few small children had pushed their way to the front of the crowd as I had done, and were screaming and dancing even though they weren't old enough to understand what they were saying. But I didn't care— every voice that cried out was a voice that could redeem my son. I was dizzy now with joy. I leaned back against Yehudit and let the saving cries wash over me.

"Release Barabbas to us!" someone yelled. I whirled around, looking for the voice.

"No! Release my son!"

"Release Barabbas!" someone else called.

"No—*no!*" I screamed. I began pushing everyone around me, shoving them away as hard as I could in an effort to find the voices and stop them. But I couldn't move against the throng of humanity. I was trapped.

"I am the mother of that man!" I yelled, pointing helplessly at my son. "Release him—he's done nothing!" But the strength of the crowd, so welcome a moment before, now fought against me. I was one voice in a vast multitude, a single star in the night sky. My voice was worthless.

"No!" I screamed on in a frenzy. "No, release my son! Release my only son, my baby boy. . . . " And then something within me cracked and I was on my knees, sobbing, tearing at my robe and beating the ground. No one seemed to see or care.

"Crucify him!" the crowd continued to shout above me. "Release Barabbas!"

Pilate was speaking, but I couldn't understand him. I scratched my nails against the ground, over and over until they ripped and bled.

"Release my son," I said again and then buried my face in my knees, clawing at my head, the ground, my covering, my own skin. Everything felt thick inside of me and I wondered what it would feel like to die.

Suddenly, strong arms were restraining mine. Yehudit wrapped her body around my own and pinned my arms against me.

"*Em,*" she spoke directly into my ear. It startled me—I wasn't her mother.

"*Em,*" she repeated, more softly.

I felt my body go slack. I shifted my weight and slumped against her, and together we waited. Above us, the noise of the crowd carried on. Kneeling in the dirt, I felt removed, distant.

Eventually Yehudit pulled me to my feet. I looked toward my son and saw the Roman guards strapping a heavy wooden cross to his back. The man Yeshua already bore a cross, as did the other criminal. There were only three. Barabbas had been released. My senses felt numb, as if I were encased in a closed jar. I could hear my breath snagging through my lungs, and I could see my son, but that was all. I'd ceased crying.

Someone pushed me from behind, and I realized the crowd was moving. As my feet shifted underneath me, I became one with the mass of people, traveling from the open square in front of the governor's palace into the crowded city streets. We would follow the procession of the condemned out to the hill beyond the city gates, where we would watch them die. Somewhere in my mind I knew this, but it was as if I couldn't understand what it meant. Numbly, I followed the people as they crowded around my son.

I could see him, and then I couldn't, as we pushed our way through the narrow streets. My feet plodded on without my awareness. I could see him again. His bare shoulder scraped against the wood, and he stooped under the weight of the cross. It was obviously hurting him. I wondered why somebody didn't lift it off of him and stop the pain. I wondered why the wood wasn't sanded smooth, why the splinters had to lodge so fiercely in his skin. I kept my eyes fixed on his shoulder. I couldn't see his face.

The many vendors assembled in the streets in preparation for the Feast made the paths even more crowded. At times I could see nothing but robes in front of me; at other times when the twisting road turned I could see my son again. The cross was still hurting him. Why didn't somebody help?

As we neared the city wall the man named Yeshua stumbled, and the guards pulled another man from the crowd to carry his cross. I wanted someone to carry my son's cross. I wondered if I could.

Impressions whirled around me without leaving a mark on my mind. We left the city and trudged up the hill used for crucifixion. I was still waiting, stupidly, for someone to save my son. I didn't cry. I had forgotten how to feel.

The condemned reached the place where the crosses would be raised, and I watched as a guard grabbed my son's wrist. He held it against the wooden beam, and then drove a nail right through his wrist, binding him to the cross. I reached for my own wrist and suddenly became aware of Yehudit, standing beside me and holding my hand tightly. Had she been with me all this time? My mind felt as if it were slipping in and out of my body. I shook my hand free of hers and grasped my wrist, feeling the spot where bones gave way to something soft. I remembered the softness of my son's fingers when he first curled them around mine, the strength in his tiny fist. I clutched my wrist and watched.

As the guard nailed my son's other wrist to the cross, I saw his flesh tear and heard him scream in agony. I wanted to hold him, to feel his baby skin against mine again and smell the soft spot on the back of his neck as I rocked him in the darkness. I held my arms tight against my body, rocking my son. I looked at him being nailed to the cross, and held him in my arms . . . rocking . . . rocking.

The other prisoners were nailed to the cross; the crowd was screaming, mocking, jeering. I saw a sign above Yeshua's cross: THIS IS YESHUA, KING OF THE YEHUDIM.

That man is not my king, I thought. If he were my king, he would save my son. I searched his face for some clue to explain his behavior. Why he would make a claim that would inevitably lead to death, I wondered. No one who called himself moshiach was allowed to live—according to the law of the Yehudim it was blasphemy against God. I looked at the man nearly fainting under the weight of his cross and wondered when the true Moshiach would come and save us from the Roman rule. Would we know him? We had years of prophecies to rely on, but when he actually came, could we recognize him? What if the true Moshiach came and we killed him, too?

The crosses were lifted up and dropped into the earth with a sickening thud. I felt a spasm in my womb as I'd felt before I gave birth. I looked at the men on the crosses, Yeshua in the middle, my son to his right. His body thrashed and I heard him scream.

He screamed when he was a baby, I thought, oh how he screamed. I held him against my breast and rocked him. He writhed on the cross. I rocked him. He was crying; I could see the tears mixing with blood, running down his face. I began to sing his favorite lullaby. He hung on the cross. I rocked him and sang: "He will cover you with his feathers, and under his wings you will find refuge; his faithfulness will be your shield and rampart. You will not fear the terror of night, nor the arrow that flies by day."

Slowly I became aware that my son couldn't hear me. The noise of the crowd was too large, too intense for my small voice. Feeling was returning to me; I could hear and smell and taste again. I didn't want to. I wanted to drown out the noisy crowd. My baby, on the cross. I held my arms out to him and wept.

"*Beni haahuv!*" Why couldn't I save my baby?

The criminal on the left was speaking, and the crowd hushed to listen.

"Aren't you the Moshiach?" he screamed at Yeshua, who had been stripped of his purple robe. Someone had fashioned a crown out of thorns and pushed it onto Yeshua's head; blood was running in rivulets from the punctures on his forehead. I wanted to wipe the blood away.

"Save yourself and us!" the criminal continued.

The people roared in approval. The guards, casting lots for the criminal's clothes, called out as well.

"He saved others!" one of them asserted, and spat on the ground at the foot of the cross.

"Let him save himself if he is the Moshiach of Yahweh!" someone yelled back. Men were laughing.

I stared at my son, who was now struggling to part his lips. His face was smeared with blood, and he was looking at the criminal who had just spoken.

"Don't you fear God," he rasped out, "since you are under the same sentence?" I could barely hear him. He arched his back against the cross, pushing himself up to breathe.

"We are punished justly, for we are getting what our deeds deserve. But this man has done nothing wrong." He collapsed again, the weight of his body dropping down against the wood. The crowd mocked him and I saw the guard spit.

My son pushed himself up again, then turned to look at Yeshua, hanging on the cross beside him.

"Yeshua," he gasped, "remember me when you come into your kingdom."

The man named Yeshua turned his bloodstained face toward my son.

"I tell you the truth, today you will be with me in paradise."

I looked at Yeshua. He turned his head. His brown eyes were deep, filled with pain, and he seemed to focus them on me. I looked around to see who he was looking for, but it was me he looked at as he hung there. I didn't know this man at all, yet strangely, I started to wonder if I could believe him. He was nothing but a man being crucified as a false moshiach next to my son, but as I looked into his eyes I had the unbelievable thought that maybe he spoke the truth. If it was true, if this man somehow really were the Moshiach, the Savior, then today my son would be with this man, our true king, in paradise.

I took one more look at my son, then held Yeshua's gaze within my own and smiled.

10

On the Clouds of Heaven

"The body's missing."

"*What?*"

When I heard the words, I paused on my way up the curving staircase that led toward the second floor of the house. I looked down. My master, Caiaphas, was so intent on the breathless priest who brought him the news that he didn't seem to notice my presence. I held my breath, wondering if I could slip down a few steps closer to listen. I walked as lightly as I could, my bare toes alighting on each step first, followed by rest of my foot, slowly, cautiously. The way my friend Dassi had taught me. When I'd gone as far as I dared, I pressed myself against the banister and stopped, breathing as quietly as I could.

Three days had passed since Yeshua, who had claimed to be the Moshiach, was dragged from our courtyard by the Roman guards. He was sentenced to death, crucified, and buried in a borrowed tomb. After the tense days of plotting his capture and the flagrant display of hatred my master had exhibited toward him at the trial, the news of Yeshua's final end seemed to restore our household peace. My master resumed his impenetrable exterior, and I could feel the atmosphere in the house relaxing palpably. The menace was gone; Caiaphas could now prepare himself for whatever crises awaited him next. But by the look on his face as he stood in the entry hall, glaring at the priest who brought him the news, this was not the crisis my master had anticipated.

The priest was bent double, gasping for air. He looked as if he was going to faint. Caiaphas merely stared at him, his expression hard.

"Please," the priest gasped. "I ran all the way to tell you. It's true. You must believe me."

Caiaphas still said nothing.

I had been a servant in the household of the Yehudim high priest, Caiaphas, for almost as long as I had memories that I could trust. I knew I was taken from my family as a very tiny girl and brought to Yisrael as a slave, one among many of the spoils of war, but I didn't remember my family, or even the name of my homeland. I had adopted the customs of the Yehudim people as my own, having been raised by the women of Caiaphas' household as a Yehudim slave. Throughout my life my master was good to me; I was never beaten, nor was I ever hungry.

But sometimes at night I would dream of a woman's face, shrouded in shadows of the past, smiling at me, only inches away. I felt warm and safe when I dreamed of her, singing a song in a tongue I didn't know but could almost remember. My hands longed to reach up and caress her face, play with the lock of hair against her shoulder, but she was never really there. The warmth and the smile and the song and the woman were ever only a dream.

"Come," Caiaphas now said curtly to the visitor, sweeping him away to his private rooms where I knew their discussion would continue in earnest.

"Wine?" I asked quickly, arriving at the bottom of the stair just as the men began to turn away. I was the picture of an obedient, disinterested servant girl.

"Yes," my master replied as he ushered the man down a corridor leading away from the entrance hall. "Bring a new bottle."

The swish of his robe against the floor followed in his wake as he stormed out of the entry hall and away toward his private room.

I scurried down to the wine cellars, grabbed the first bottle my fingertips found, and blew the dust off as I raced back up to my master's rooms. I desperately wanted to find Dassi, but I didn't dare risk angering my master or missing any conversation.

When I reached the room, I knocked on the heavy wooden door tentatively, then pushed it open. The room was dark, the rich curtain having been drawn over the window, and I could just make out the outline of the visiting priest pacing back and forth, wringing his hands as he walked around the narrow space. He no longer looked as if he was going to faint; rather, his agitation was palpable.

"We had guards!" he moaned. "A stone! And a seal! How did anyone manage to break in and steal the body?"

I walked toward the low table in the middle of the room, unobtrusive as ever. I poured the wine into two stone goblets and listened as hard as I could.

"How do you know, for sure, that he is gone?" my master asked. I calculated how slowly I could pour before appearing to dawdle. On inspiration, I stopped when only a mouthful was in the first goblet and brought it to Caiaphas to taste. He held it up to his lips, not looking at me.

"I went and saw the empty tomb myself!" The frantic priest stopped in the middle of his stride, running his hands through his hair as if clawing at his head.

"It's empty," he continued. "Completely empty. And the women who claim to have seen the angel are running all over the town, telling everyone Yeshua has risen."

Women and angels? This was even better than I thought. I couldn't believe Dassi was missing this.

I heard my master make a small noise in his throat, as if choking, and glanced quickly up at him. He seemed to have forgotten I was there. I poured the wine into the second goblet as slowly as I possibly could.

"What are we going to do?"

Just then, there was a knock at the door, bolder than my own had been.

"Open the door," my master barked, and I got up quickly and opened it. Dassi was standing there, eyes wide as she looked at me, and behind her stood two Roman guards in full regalia.

Caiaphas got to his feet quickly and crossed to the door in two steps.

"Come in, please," he bid them, all traces of his former tension now gone. "*Shfakhot*," he called to me harshly, "bring more wine and two more goblets."

I nodded, then left the small room, Dassi on my heels.

"Stay here," I hissed at her as we pushed the door shut together. "Stay here and listen! I'll explain when I get back."

I took off running.

When I returned to the room, wine and goblets in hand, Dassi had settled herself in the hallway with an ear against the door and an expression of pure rapture on her face.

"You're not going to believe this," she said eagerly. "They're saying that the man Yeshua is alive again."

"What?" I asked, almost dropping the goblets I was carrying.

"He's alive. There was an earthquake, and an angel, and the moshiach is no longer dead!"

I couldn't even think of anything to say—surely there had been some mistake. He was crucified and buried. Perhaps the body had been stolen, but Yeshua was dead, I was sure of it. And yet I couldn't help but wonder, as I opened the door and poured out more wine for the men. The Roman guards weren't the sort to be given to flights of fancy. Why would they said there was an angel and an earthquake, unless somehow they believed it was true?

The two guards looked nervous as my master and the other priest discussed the matter, planning what to do.

"Are you sure he was dead?" the priest kept asking. "Are you *sure?*"

"I was there," my master replied tonelessly. "I saw the sword in his side; I saw the blood and the water flowing out. He was dead."

Silence for a moment. I sat on the floor by the low table holding my breath, hoping my small presence had been forgotten. But my master soon looked at me, and his eyes told me clearly that I was not welcome. I stood up and left the room, closing the door firmly and rejoining Dassi on the floor outside.

Voices dropped to mutters, and it was hard to make out what the men were saying. Finally my master raised his voice, questioning one of the guards:

"Did you actually see him yourself, walking and talking? Did you see him with your own eyes?"

"N-no," the guard faltered. "But the women—"

"Women," my master replied, that one word holding more scorn than I would have believed possible. "They're hysterical," he said simply, evenly. "The body has been stolen. It's unfortunate, but despite the steps we took to prevent it, it has happened. I thank you not to repeat anything you hear from *women*," he paused significantly, "to anyone else."

The sound of clinking. Money was exchanging hands. I looked at Dassi, and we got up quietly and ran away before the conversation was concluded.

But all the money in the world wasn't going to be enough to stop the rumors from flying.

That night, Dassi and I sat up late on our mats in the bedroom we shared with the other female servants, talking as quietly as we could so as not to wake them. The events of the past few days still had me reeling, and I was eager to discuss them with my compatriot. We talked until the first light graced the edge of the window, then she fell asleep. In the few remaining minutes I had until it was time to get up and start the day, my thoughts turned back to the night of the trial, remembering the strange visions I had seen.

◆

The sound of scuffling drifted in through my window to where I was lying on my mat, awake. I listened. The sound repeated itself, louder this time, and was soon followed by the clink of clanking metal. I sat up, hesitated, and then crawled around the sleeping servants and went to look outside.

I rested my fingertips against the edge of the window, but the night was too dark for me to see anything. Quietly, I turned around, looking for Dassi. She was nowhere to be found. I pulled my robe off the mat and draped it around my shoulders. I glanced toward the window one more time, then started to make my way downstairs. If the noise was caused by something my master was doing, I didn't want him to see me and think I was spying on him. But if the noise was an intruder, I didn't want my master to accuse me of being a lazy, neglectful servant.

I looked around the room for the small oil lamp, found it alongside Dassi's mat, then thought better of lighting it and began to feel my way toward the staircase in the dark.

Noiselessly, I slipped down the stairs, my hand tracing a familiar path down the curved wooden banister. At the foot of the stairs was the great entry hall, and I paused for a moment, listening, to see if anyone else was about. I strained to see into the darkness, but it was as thick as the night outside. Not even the inlaid gold of the mosaic floor, which spun and danced through the swirling patterns, could catch enough light to glisten up at me. As the chief high priest from a family of high priests, Caiaphas' home boasted of great riches, some even more splendid than those possessed by the Romans. But in the darkness, all was a void, and I relied on the texture of the mosaic pattern under my bare feet to guide me to the door.

I pushed the front door open, wincing as it creaked, and peered out into the courtyard. The darkness was still almost impenetrable, but I could now make out a great many men, gathered around in groups in the courtyard, talking quietly or simply standing as if waiting. The slight sound of clinking metal reached my ears again; I turned to my right and saw several Roman guards flanking a man whose face I couldn't see.

"*Shfakhot*," I heard my master's voice call out to me roughly, his robes brushing against mine as he passed me quickly in the dark. "Light the fire."

I hurried to obey him, kindling the fire in the large stone pit in the center of the courtyard. As the flame ignited and began to rise, I could see the groups of men moving closer to the flame. The night was cool, and the blaze provided not only light but warmth. I rubbed my hands together over the growing fire; I hadn't realized until that moment that I was shivering under my thin robe in the moonless night.

As soon as the blaze was certain, I moved away from the center of the courtyard and went to stand back in the shadows of the house. I didn't return to my bedroom, even though it was very late and I knew I would be up long before dawn, as was my custom. I stayed in the courtyard in part because I wanted to be available should my master call for me again, but mostly because I wanted to see what was going on to cause this great group of men to assemble in the courtyard of the high priest in the middle of the night.

Looking around, I began to see many faces that I recognized. Almost all of the high priests were there, accompanied by many of the elders and those who taught the law. The firelight gleamed off of hard faces, cold expressions standing in contrast to the soft weave of warm, expensive garments surrounding me. In the middle, now standing directly in the light of the fire, were the Roman guards and the man they encircled. Their spears and helmets glittered in the fire, and the reflected light caught my eye as I tried to peer through them and see the man they held prisoner. What was going on?

I scanned the courtyard. Toward the opposite end from the mass of people, hanging back as if he didn't want to be seen, was a man in plain clothes. Obviously not a priest or any member of the elite, he shifted his muscled body from one position to another, appearing to be intent on listening but desirous of not being seen. As the crowd pressed in, he remained by himself on the periphery.

After a moment, Caiaphas stepped forward to survey the crowd. If he was at all startled or taken aback by the strange group of men gathered around his house, he gave no outward sign. But I knew my master well enough to know that he rarely allowed anything to disturb his composure. Now, his stoic expression seemed even harder in the firelight, the flickering illumination glancing off the angles of his face as if they were carved in stone.

"Who can present evidence," my master finally asked, "against this man Yeshua, whom many have claimed is a false moshiach?" His deep voice rang out into the darkness.

I felt my eyes widen. So this was Yeshua, the man I had heard so much about. As the latest burden to weigh on my master's mind, Yeshua had been the subject of many whispered conversations I had been privy to around my master's large, ornately carved table. The council of priests had been plotting against this man for some time now, as he had grown from merely a nuisance to an absolute threat. But the priests had been planning to wait until after the Feast of Unleavened Bread to carry out their scheme, worried about inciting a riot among the people. Caiaphas feared that many might believe the man's claim to be the Moshiach. I wondered what had happened to make the priests change their minds, why they had decided to carry out their plans now regardless of the outcome. I wished Dassi was with me.

Such an arrest wouldn't be kept secret, even if the trial were held in the deepest darkness, in the middle of the night. Yeshua was notorious. Even those who didn't believe the claim of moshiach thought he was a prophet, and others said he was a great teacher. But it was the small but growing band of others, as my master had said, the ones who believed he was the Moshiach, whom the priests feared. As a servant in Caiaphas' household, I had seen firsthand some of the effects of such religious zealotry in the past, and I understood my master's concern.

I felt myself pressing closer to the crowd, out of the sheltering shadows of the house. I had never seen Yeshua myself, and I craned my neck to see this one who was causing such a ruckus and upset. I could barely see him for the surrounding guards, but from what I could see he looked unremarkable. A plain man, he seemed the sort who could blend easily into any crowd and probably escape unnoticed.

As I looked at Yeshua, scanning his face for hints of the uproar he had instigated, I saw all around me the priests and teachers exchanging glances and looking at one another uncomfortably. If I understood their unspoken sentiments correctly, no one wanted to be the first to testify against the man.

Hours passed. The shadows began to lighten to gray; the stone wall behind my back pressed the cold cusp of morning into my very bones. Yeshua's trial dragged on. My master had been questioning people since the middle of the night, and still he was not satisfied. I could hear several of the priests convening close to where I stood, discussing the trial and the suspected outcome.

"There's too much disagreement," I heard one say, a tall, well-dressed man with dark hair and a flowing beard. "No one concurs with anyone else; all the stories are too jumbled to reach a conviction."

"Do you think Caiaphas will let him go?" His companion looked worried. A shorter, stockier man, he seemed better fit for the rough work of a laborer than the mind's work of a teacher or a priest.

"Never," the first one replied. "He's taken it too far already. He can't turn back now."

Then with a sudden movement, as if deciding something instantly, he turned and began walking toward my master, his brisk, long strides leaving his friend hurrying in his wake. When he reached the other side of the courtyard where my master was hearing testimonies, he waited respectfully to be acknowledged. I noticed that, among the many who had spoken out against Yeshua that night, these two had held their peace until now.

"Yes?" My master turned to look at the two men standing next to him.

The tall one cleared his throat, then pointed at Yeshua and began to speak loudly. "This fellow said, 'I am able to destroy the temple of God and rebuild it again in three days.'"

A murmur went up around the priests. The Roman guards, bored, had settled themselves along the ground to await the end of the trial, but now they looked up, attentive, and I saw one of them put his hand on his sword.

The tall priest whipped around and looked at his shorter friend with a piercing gaze. His friend startled, then began speaking quickly in a voice neither as loud nor as elegant as his friend's.

"Yes, it is so," he asserted quickly. "It is as he says. I heard the man say it myself." He looked at Yeshua, nervously.

The murmuring among the assembled men had grown louder at the second man's corroboration, and now my master held up his hand for silence and looked at Yeshua, right into his eyes.

"Are you not going to answer?" he asked him. "What is this testimony that these men are bringing against you?"

Yeshua, who had been silent throughout the entire night, simply looked at Caiaphas. I could see my master becoming unsettled; the man's refusal to speak up on his own behalf seemed more upsetting than if he had railed and screamed and cursed. I saw the composure on my master's face slip for a moment, and the look he gave Yeshua was one of pure loathing.

"I charge you," he finally said, raising his voice and standing up tall, "under oath by the living God: Tell us if you are the Moshiach, the Son of Yahweh."

Yeshua continued to look at him, apparently unfazed. Then quietly, so I had to lean forward to hear him, he answered.

"Yes, it is as you say. But I say to all of you: In the future you will see the Son of man sitting at the right hand of the Mighty One and coming on the clouds of Heaven."

The murmuring among the priests escalated to a roar. They finally had what they wanted: a direct confession from the mouth of the false moshiach himself.

The Roman guards shook themselves, then stood. The priests were rushing at Yeshua, and I glanced over at my master to see how he would calm and control them, restore order. To my shock and horror, a transformation was taking place in my master's face, something like I had never seen. He glared at Yeshua, clenching his hands into fists by his side, and then started shaking. I didn't know whether to run to him or not; I didn't know if he was suddenly taken ill or if Yeshua's words had truly upset him that much.

Just as I was about to dart out from the house, my master reached a hand up to Yeshua's throat and tore his robes, in a single movement, clear to his waist. I clapped my hand over my mouth and took a step backward. My master was screaming in a high, strange voice I barely recognized:

"He has spoken blasphemy! Why do we need any more witnesses? Look!" He appealed to the mob gathering in quickly around him. "Now you have heard the blasphemy! What do you think?"

"He is worthy of death!" several screamed as they rushed at Yeshua. Fists were raised, and I saw the quiet man hit again and again, and spat upon repeatedly by the priests, teachers, and elders. I was horrified. Even my master had joined in the mêlée; rather than trying to stop the crowd, it seemed he was inciting them.

"Prophesy to us, Moshiach!" I heard harsh voices shout. A large man cuffed Yeshua behind the head, then ducked back into the crowd. "Who hit you?" he screamed from his hiding place. Someone laughed.

Fists were flying and I could barely see the man in the center of it all. I turned to run back into the house when out of the corner of my eye, I saw the man I had noticed earlier, the one in plain clothes. He was sitting by himself at the edge of the courtyard, and to my surprise he was watching the scene unfold with tears running down his cheeks. He made no attempt to hide his tears, and as I watched him he covered his face with his hands and sobbed. I was moved by his emotion, and instead of walking in to the house, I approached him.

When he saw me coming, he wiped his face with his hands, which, I could see, were enormous—rough and weather-beaten, covered with calluses, raw blisters, and stains. Unlike most of the men assembled in the courtyard, this man used the strength of his body to earn his wages. I crouched down on the ground next to him. I didn't know what I was doing, but his grief was so real, so palpable, that I couldn't let him grieve alone. I waited until he was quiet, and when he finally looked at me, I saw it in his eyes: he had known this man.

"You also were with Yeshua of Galilee," I said to him, my heart aching for the pain in his eyes. But his response startled me.

Standing to his feet, he called out to the crowd, "I don't know what you're talking about!"

His cry drew the attention of those at the outskirts of the mob. Yeshua was being bound and led away by the guards, and this unexpected declaration piqued the interest of those furthest away, who turned now to look at us. I was embarrassed; I wished I had left him alone. But the pain in his face made him look absolutely stricken. Yet he said he didn't even know the man. Why, then, was he crying?

The servants of the household were beginning to rise, and I knew I must leave soon to attend to my duties. The morning would be filled with the questions of all those who hadn't woken up during the trial, or who had stayed inside at the sound of the mob. I knew I would be telling my story over and over again for the rest of the day. With a sigh, I glanced at this strange man and began to make my way back toward the house.

As I walked away from the man, suddenly I saw Dassi's small form out of the corner of my eye. She must have risen and crept outside to stand by me, unheard. She was like a mouse, I mused, as I gesticulated wildly for her to come closer. I still envied her ability to walk among the others almost completely unheard, and I wondered how long she had been shadowing me. I wanted to fill her in on all the strange details of the night.

She glanced at me with a grin, then approached the man herself.

"This fellow was with Yeshua of Nazaret," she called out

loudly, her strong voice a stark contrast to her noiseless footsteps and slight frame. She raised her eyebrows at me. I gaped at her.

How could she know that? I thought, wondering if she was making it up. The strange man swore, then called out even louder:

"I don't know the man!"

The mob was moving toward us now, Yeshua having been dragged out of the courtyard by the Roman guards.

"Surely you are one of them," a voice called out, "for your accent gives you away!"

The strange man began to curse and scream, anger boiling up and engulfing any traces of his former grief.

"I don't know the man!" His voice was like an unsharpened knife, slicing through the air and swiping at my ears. Dassi was beside herself with glee, but suddenly I didn't want to watch anymore and I pushed past her to the doorway into the large entry hall. Behind me, I heard a rooster crowing, heralding the dawn with his raucous cry. Then a louder cry overtook his, and turning to look behind me I saw that the strange man had dissolved into tears once again. I shook my head and rubbed my hands over my tired eyes. It was going to be a long day.

♦

Memories faded into fitful dreams, dreams of the woman who sang to me. Her face was so close, her voice so sweet. I could smell her breath as it warmed me, I reached out to her in the darkness. My hands grasped cold air as I woke, alone as always, on my mat in the servants' room.

♦

"I saw him!"

Dassi's face was triumphant, announcing her news to the servants assembled in the kitchens.

"You *did?*" Several of the housemaids turned on her, and she was instantly the center of attention. No one even bothered to ask whom, exactly, she had seen.

"I saw him," she repeated. "Down by the lake. He was with the men who always followed him."

I looked at Dassi's earnest face; she was in no doubt about what she had seen. And she wasn't the only one. The days following the disappearance of Yeshua's body had been filled with rumors of sightings, servants who swore they saw him walking through the city, standing in the market, teaching in the temple. I didn't know what to think. These stories were deafening, while the coming and going of the chief priests and elders, who conferred constantly with my master, were barely audible. I felt caught in between the two worlds: my loyalty to my master, and my own curiosity and wonder. Could this man truly have risen from the dead?

With the entire kitchen focused on Dassi, I took the opportunity to slip away. As I rounded the corner I heard someone ask, "Could he have a twin, one kept hidden all these years until now?"

It was possible. If Yeshua had been born a twin, he and his brother could have schemed to claim the title of the Moshiach, as long as one of them was willing to sacrifice his life. But it was the other possibility, the sensational one, that wouldn't let my mind out of its grip. What if this man truly was the Moshiach, the man sent by the Yehudim God to redeem his people? I knew the prophecies, I knew of the one who was supposed to be coming. What if, in my lifetime, he had finally come?

And if so, what did it matter to me? I wasn't a Yehudi. The events of the past few days had brought this fact home to me in ways I'd never felt before, ways I couldn't explain, even to Dassi. This drama was a Yehudim drama, being played out by the Yehudim for the Yehudim people. It didn't concern the Romans, beyond the disruption it caused in the lands and the people they governed, and it certainly didn't concern me—though I found myself thinking, more often than not, that I wished, somehow, it did.

I reached my bedroom and lay down on my mat even though it was the middle of the day. The events of the last few days had left me shaken, my mind sore. The excitement of the people was tangible; many believed that Yeshua was the Moshiach. And if he was, he had come to redeem them. But what about me? Who was the God of my forefathers? Who was the God of my mother?

Being raised as a Yehudi I knew all the prayers; the songs, the chants, the promises of the Moshiach. But I wasn't a Yehudi. Though I loved the rituals for their haunting melodies and the beauty of the words, they were just that to me: empty melodies, meaningless words. I said the daily prayers and followed the customs and laws for the holy days because I had been taught to say them, taught to follow them, but on their own they held no meaning for me.

As the sun began to sink outside my window, I wondered what it would feel like to be someone for whom the blood of Avraham was a birthright. I wondered what it would feel like to know the God of my own people.

Unbidden, tears sprang to my eyes and I buried my face into the mat. I found myself praying, to the Yehudim God, to my own God, to any God who would listen, to bring my mother back to me in dreams. Let me hear her song, I begged of the growing darkness. Let me smell her scent. Let me touch her face. Just once.

Dreams of words that tasted of milk flowed over me, around me, through me. I woke in the night crying for my mother, for my homeland, for a God I never knew. Salt tears dripped into my mouth, their bitter taste drowning out the memory of sweet milk.

◆

The sun was not yet up as I hurried down the street, away from my house and toward the lake where the fishing boats would be heading out for the first catch of the day. I paused at a crossroad to make sure I knew where I was going; this wasn't my usual errand. Dassi was always the one to venture to the lake in the mornings to purchase fish fresh from the water, but today she had offered to let me make the trip in hopes I would see the risen Yeshua with my own eyes. It was uncharacteristic of Dassi to give up on a chance for excitement, but as I hurried along in the pre-dawn chill, I wondered if perhaps she had guessed at some of the torments running through my mind. Or perhaps, I thought, as the salt smell of the sea reached my nose, she simply wanted the extra time to luxuriate in slumber.

Despite the early hour, the shore was teeming with people—fishermen were preparing to head out in their boats, and the air rang with sounds of men and work and damp ropes being tossed against wood. I stood back a ways from the water, watching the men, their strong arms lifting heavy nets and dragging them into their boats. Some were pulling their boats back to shore, exhausted though the day had barely begun. Alongside the men a crowd had already begun to gather, people, like me, who had come to the water in hopes of seeing Yeshua. Embarrassed, I headed toward the water's edge and hid behind several boats. I sat down on the sand, tucking my feet up under me, and held my basket in my lap. I listened. I watched. I waited.

And then he was there. I could no more mistake him than I could mistake Dassi or my master, even though I'd only seen him once. I knew it was him. I watched him walk down to the water, this man who was supposedly killed, and felt a shudder when I noticed the red marks inscribed on the insides of his wrists. I couldn't say for certain that he had ever been dead, but I knew, right now, that he was alive.

Yeshua lifted his hand in greeting as he approached the water, waving at several men out in a tiny boat not far off. With a start, I realized one of the men was the stranger from the night of the trial. He and his friends looked tired, worn, their sopping wet robes slapping against their knees as they steered the boat in toward the shore. I noticed their nets were devoid of fish.

"Friends!" Yeshua called to them. "Haven't you any fish?"

The men looked up at him, shielding their eyes against the rising sun.

"No," one of the men called back.

"Throw your net on the right side of the boat," Yeshua advised, "and you will find some."

I scanned the water for the reflective, light-on-light flashes of silver that indicated a school of fish, but I saw nothing. Nevertheless, the men lifted their nets one more time and dropped them over the edge into the water. Suddenly, the boat began to tip.

"I can't lift it!" One of the men cried out. "There's too many fish—they're going to tear the net!"

Strong muscles strained at the net, struggling in vain to raise it back into the little boat. The man from the trial looked toward the shore again, shielding his eyes. One of the other men squinted into the sunlight and then exclaimed loudly:

"It is the Lord!"

In an instant, the man from the trial had pulled his outer garment from the floor of the boat, flung it over himself, and jumped right into the water. He slogged through the waist-high waves, running with remarkable speed, until he reached the shore. With a blazing look in his eyes he ran toward Yeshua, who stood there and simply looked at him.

"Bring some of the fish you have just caught," he said, and the man from the trial stopped running. He looked at Yeshua, emotions battling across his face, then wordlessly turned to go and help his friends drag in the fish.

The net was too full to be lifted, so they had to tow the boat to shore. But somehow, by the time they reached the sand and unloaded their catch, not a single tear had snagged the ropes of the net. I listened to the men remarking on this and watched Yeshua crouch down and light a fire. I stayed hidden behind the boat while they cleaned the fish, cooked them over the fire, gave thanks, and ate. The men were girlish in their giddiness at the sight of Yeshua, but the one who had been at the trial was silent throughout.

As the last scraps of fish were being eaten, the bones and guts scraped up and cleaned away, Yeshua turned to the man from the trial.

"Shimon son of Yohan," he asked him, "do you truly love me more than these?"

He held the man's gaze within his own for a long time, and nobody spoke.

Finally the one named Shimon answered, "Yes, Lord. You know that I love you."

As I watched the two men together, I slowly began to realize that I had been holding my breath. The other men surrounding the two had also grown silent, and we watched Yeshua and Shimon, and waited. Love was flooding out from Yeshua's dark eyes as surely as tears. I looked at Shimon and immediately understood what had happened, why he had been crying in the courtyard. I had been right; Shimon did know the man. He loved the man. But when questioned as Yeshua was being dragged off to death, Shimon had denied him out of fear. Now I understood the tears, the shouting, the strange change in his behavior, the curses. And as I watched the two holding each other's gaze so steadily, I understood, as I knew Shimon did, that he was forgiven.

But Yeshua spoke again.

"Shimon son of Yohan," he repeated, "do you truly love me?"

And again Shimon answered, "Yes, Lord. You know that I love you."

Yeshua looked at him, a gaze that seemed to take in everything down to his very soul. "Take care of my lambs," he said.

Yeshua reached out his hand, covered the big, heavily muscled hand of Shimon in his own. "Shimon son of Yohan," he asked him, now so quietly I could barely make out the words, "do you love me?"

I could see the hurt in Shimon's eyes at being asked a third time, yet he did not withdraw his gaze or his hand. Finally he answered, in a voice barely above a whisper, "Lord, you know all things; you know that I love you."

Yeshua grasped both of his hands. "Feed my lambs," he replied.

Again, I understood: three times Shimon had denied he knew this man; three times Yeshua allowed him to be redeemed. I was leaning out so far now from my perch behind the boats, the men could have seen me if they had turned around.

"Remember, you are Peter," Yeshua said, still holding Shimon's hands. "And on this rock I shall build my church."

And I was crying again, crying without knowing why, as the man named Shimon-Peter stood and pulled Yeshua to his feet and embraced him and wept. I didn't understand all that I had seen, but I knew that somehow, I wanted it. Sitting there in the sand with the sun rapidly rising overhead, the basket for the fish long forgotten in my lap, I wanted what Shimon-Peter had, I wanted what Yeshua had granted him. I wanted a God. I wanted a faith. I wanted to believe.

◆

Yeshua was gone. Those who had seen him leave told the story again and again and again, never tiring of the smallest detail, the tiniest nuance. I found I was hungry to hear it, and I asked the servants in the household who had been there or who had heard the account to tell it to me, again and again and again. Dassi had told the tale so many times that I think she almost believed she was there with the crowd, watching Yeshua being lifted up right into the clouds.

The fervor surrounding his departure was worse than the fervor surrounding his death. Those who had seen his ascension believed, wholeheartedly, that he was the true Moshiach. Many who heard the story from them believed, as well. My master hadn't slept in days, and his conversations with the priests and elders now took place in the doorway, in the entry hall, on the road to the temple. There was no need for secrecy anymore. The need for action had become too great.

Yet what was he going to do? If this man had not only risen from the dead but lifted himself into the heavens among a throng of onlookers, nothing Caiaphas could do was going to stop the story being spread, the people starting to believe.

I wondered about belief as I carried out my work within the house. Did the believers believe all of a sudden, did it come upon them in an instant like a sickness? Or was it a process, a gradual turning from one conviction toward another? I wanted to know what believing felt like, so I could know if I, too, believed. I thought I might believe Yeshua had been the Moshiach, the Chosen One sent by the Yehudim God. But still, he couldn't be my God. Faith in my own God was something I would never know. It had been ripped away from me just as surely as I was torn from my mother's arms and left adrift, motherless, godless.

♦

The Feast of Pentecost was upon us, and the city was full beyond bursting. The duties of a high priest were numerous at this time, and the additional stress made my master snappish and even more prone to temper. I felt he was changing before my eyes. I had known this man to be stern, but never unkind, and now he was increasingly harsh with his servants, nasty to his fellow priests, and cruel in his actions toward everyone. I didn't know what had happened to cause this shift in his personality, the shift that had started the night of Yeshua's trial, but I feared for what my life might soon become.

The market was overrun with faithful, God-fearing Yehudim come from many different lands to worship in Yerushalayim on the holy day. I was struggling in vain to make it from one vendor to another, lugging a heavy bundle of purchases down a busy street, when suddenly a commotion rang out behind me.

Turning to look, I saw a crowd of men, some of whom I recognized from the morning I spent at the water. These were Yeshua's followers, the men who first believed. And they were staggering down the busy street, bumping into people left and right—could they be drunk? It was barely midway through the morning. I watched in confused fascination as they drew closer, and I saw they were laughing, holding on to one another for support. One of the men fell down, another fell in his attempt to pick him up. I tried to step back from the crowd, but I was hemmed in on all sides. What was happening?

Just then, as I watched, tiny fires erupted over the heads of the seemingly intoxicated men. The crowd screamed. Suddenly, what had merely been another spectacle was now dangerous, and people were fighting each other to beat their way out of the crowd, away from the terrifying, burning men. I pushed against rough fibers as I tried to fight my way away from them, but it was of no use. The crowd was too dense, and I was too small.

I turned back to look at the men. There it was: a burning fire above each one of their heads as they laughed and fell against each other and struggled up the street. I was in shock and beginning to cry. I couldn't get away, and they were coming toward me. None of the events of the past two moons, strange as they had been, had come close to preparing me for what I was now seeing with my own eyes, and I desperately wanted to break free.

And then the men began to talk, shouting as they made their way down the street, shadowed by the tongues of flame. The words weren't words I knew. Streams of gibberish poured forth from their mouths as they gesticulated toward the crowds. Beyond frightened, I kept trying to squeeze my way out of the throng, but the press and the rush were too dense. I began to flail my fists and scream, slinging my bundle at the people blocking my way.

And then, I heard it.

The tongue. The language. The woman in my dreams, her whispering voice, the lullaby. Someone was speaking, in words I barely knew, yet when I heard them I knew that I understood. Memories of speech and cadences long forgotten came rushing at me with a force so strong I thought my knees would give way. But they held. I stopped fighting the crowd.

A man was rushing toward me, one of the followers of Yeshua. And he was speaking to me, in my own language, my mother-tongue. I dropped the heavy bundle I was carrying and ran toward him. Nothing mattered anymore, nothing but hearing that beautiful voice carrying me away on a river of words. I closed my eyes as he approached me, tilted my head back, and simply listened.

I don't know how long I stood there on the crowded street in the busy marketplace while people screamed and ran around me. I was listening to the man who spoke my mother-tongue. All I knew was that I wanted him to go on speaking forever. He spoke to me of a loving God, a God not only of the Yehudim, but of the whole world. He spoke to me of Yeshua, saying he hadn't come to redeem only the Yehudim people, but all people. My people. He was my God, the God of my kinfolk, the God of my mother. He spoke my language. He spoke to me.

Relief and hope and fear raced frenetically through my body as I listened to the man talk. Was this the beginning of belief? I wanted it, I wanted this God, this God of the man who knew my language. I wanted to believe in him, to follow him. I wanted to belong.

Lying on my mat that night after Dassi fell asleep, I didn't cry out to the darkness for dreams of my mother. I felt closer to her than I ever remembered, listening to the words she gave me, meeting a God who spoke her tongue. I was going to believe in this Yeshua, even though I didn't know yet what that meant. If he was indeed the God of all people, then he was my God. My God.

Tears stung against the insides of my eyelids.

I thought back over the events of the recent past, the whirlwind that had begun when I heard the crowd rustling outside my window in the middle of the night. And now here I was, lying on my mat again, and I felt different. New. I wondered, again, if this was belief.

I thought back over the things I'd heard about Yeshua, the things I'd heard him say myself. Sitting on the shore, looking so earnestly into Shimon-Peter's eyes. *Feed my lambs*, he had said. I wondered what it meant. He had spoken so intently, his brown eyes holding meanings I knew I had yet to discover.

Feed my lambs.

It was a place to start. I wasn't sure what it meant, but I

trusted that if I started there, the rest would come. I could believe that much.

Feed my lambs, I whispered into the darkness as I closed my eyes. The first step toward belief.

Author's Note

The preceding stories were based on the following verses from the New Testament. Although I have endeavored to be historically accurate to the fullest extent of my ability, a few deviations were deliberate, most notably with regards to the circumstances surrounding Jesus' birth. Recent scholarship gives us many varied (and sometimes conflicting) versions of this narrative; I have chosen to follow the one most common in current popular imagination. As such, I assume full responsibility for any errors.

This Crowded Night

In those days Caesar Augustus issued a decree that a census should be taken of the entire Roman world. (This was the first census that took place while Quirinius was governor of Syria.) And everyone went to his own town to register. So Joseph also went up from the town of Nazareth in Galilee to Judea, to Bethlehem the town of David, because he belonged to the house and line of David. He went there to register with Mary, who was pledged to be married to him and was expecting a child. While they were there, the time came for the baby to be born, and she gave birth to her firstborn, a son. She wrapped him in cloths and placed him in a manger, because there was no room for them in the inn.
—Luke 2:1-7

Constant Companions

Every year [Jesus'] parents went to Jerusalem for the Feast of the Passover. When he was twelve years old, they went up to the Feast, according to the custom. After the Feast was over, while his parents were returning home, the boy Jesus stayed behind in Jerusalem, but they were unaware of it. Thinking he was in their company, they traveled on for a day. Then they began looking for him among their relatives and friends. When they did not find him, they went back to Jerusalem to look for him. After three days they found him in the temple courts, sitting among the teachers, listening to them and asking them questions. Everyone who heard him was amazed at his understanding and his answers. When his parents saw him, they were astonished. His mother said to him, "Son, why have you treated us like this? Your father and I have been anxiously searching for you." "Why were you searching for me?" he asked. "Didn't you know I had to be in my Father's house?" But they did not understand what he was saying to them. —Luke 2:41-50

When the Light was Still New

On the third day a wedding took place at Cana in Galilee. Jesus' mother was there, and Jesus and his disciples had also been invited to the wedding. When the wine was gone, Jesus' mother said to him, "They have no more wine." "Dear woman, why do you involve me?" Jesus replied. "My time has not yet come." His mother said to the servants, "Do whatever he tells you." Nearby stood six stone water jars, the kind used by the Jews for ceremonial washing, each holding from twenty to thirty gallons. Jesus said to the servants, "Fill the jars with water;" so they filled them to the brim. Then he told them, "Now draw some out and take it to the master of the banquet." They did so, and the master of the banquet tasted the water that had been turned into wine. He did not realize where it had come from, though the servants who had drawn the water knew. Then he called the bridegroom aside and said, "Everyone brings out the choice wine first and then the cheaper wine after the guests have had too much to drink; but you have saved the best till now." —John 2:1-10

Sounds of Them

When Jesus came into Peter's house, he saw Peter's mother-in-law lying in bed with a fever. He touched her hand and the fever left her, and she got up and began to wait on him. When evening came, many who were demon-possessed were brought to him, and he drove out the spirits with a word and healed all the sick. —Matthew 8:14-16

A Broken Melody

A ruler came and knelt before [Jesus] and said, "My daughter has just died. But come and put your hand on her, and she will live." Jesus got up and went with him, and so did his disciples. When Jesus entered the ruler's house and saw the flute players and the noisy crowd, he said, "Go away. The girl is not dead but asleep." But they laughed at him. —Matthew 9:18-19; 23-24

The First Stone

The teachers of the law and the Pharisees brought in a woman caught in adultery. They made her stand before the group and said to Jesus, "Teacher, this woman was caught in the act of adultery. In the Law Moses commanded us to stone such women. Now what do you say?" They were using this question as a trap, to have a basis for accusing him. But Jesus bent down and started to write on the ground with his finger. When they kept on questioning him, he straightened up and said to them, "If any one of you is without sin, let him be the first to throw a stone at her." Again he stooped down and wrote on the ground. At this, those who heard began to go away one at a time, the older ones first, until only Jesus was left, with the woman still standing there. Jesus straightened up and asked her, "Woman, where are they? Has no one condemned you?" "No one, sir," she said. "Then neither do I condemn you," Jesus declared. "Go now and leave your life of sin." —John 8:3-11

Only a Woman

On a Sabbath Jesus was teaching in one of the synagogues, and a woman was there who had been crippled by a spirit for eighteen years. She was bent over and could not straighten up at all. When Jesus saw her, he called her forward and said to her, "Woman, you are set free from your infirmity." Then he put his hands on her, and immediately she straightened up and praised God. —Luke 13:10-13

Bartimaeus the Blind

As Jesus and his disciples, together with a large crowd, were leaving the city, a blind man, Bartimaeus (that is, the Son of Timaeus), was sitting by the roadside begging. When he heard that it was Jesus of Nazareth, he began to shout, "Jesus, Son of David, have mercy on me!" Many rebuked him and told him to be quiet, but he shouted all the more, "Son of David, have mercy on me!" Jesus stopped and said, "Call him." So they called to the blind man, "Cheer up! On your feet! He's calling you." Throwing his cloak aside, he jumped to his feet and came to Jesus. "What do you want me to do for you?" Jesus asked him. The blind man said, "Rabbi, I want to see." "Go," said Jesus, "your faith has healed you." Immediately he received his sight and followed Jesus along the road. —Mark 10:46-52

The Remnant of Our People

Two other men, both criminals, were also led out with [Jesus] to be executed. When they came to the place called the Skull, there they crucified him, along with the criminals—one on his right, the other on his left. Jesus said, "Father, forgive them, for they do not know what they are doing." One of the criminals who hung there hurled insults at him: "Aren't you the Christ? Save yourself and us!" But the other criminal rebuked him. "Don't you fear God," he said, "since you are under the same sentence? We are punished justly, for we are getting what our deeds deserve. But this man has done nothing wrong." Then he said, "Jesus, remember me when you come into your kingdom." Jesus answered him, "I tell you the truth, today you will be with me in paradise." —Luke 23: 32-34a; 39-43

On the Clouds of Heaven

Now Peter was sitting out in the courtyard, and a servant girl came to him. "You also were with Jesus of Galilee," she said. But he denied it before them all. "I don't know what you're talking about," he said. Then he went out to the gateway, where another girl saw him and said to the people there, "This fellow was with Jesus of Nazareth." He denied it again, with an oath: "I don't know the man!" After a little while, those standing there went up to Peter and said, "Surely you are one of them, for your accent gives you away." Then he began to call down curses on himself and he swore to them, "I don't know the man!" Immediately a rooster crowed. Then Peter remembered the word Jesus had spoken: "Before the rooster crows, you will disown me three times." And he went outside and wept bitterly. —Matthew 26:69-7

Acknowledgments

This collection began as the final project for my Masters of Fine Arts in Creative Writing from The Pennsylvania State University; as such, I'd like to thank my thesis readers, Josip Novakovich and Julia Spicher Kasdorf. Thanks also to all those who gave feedback on the stories as they grew, particularly Sharon Davis and Larry and Mary Beth Lake, and my father-in-law, Bill Evans, who had the idea for the thief's mother. Thanks to the women of *Literary Mama* who read and commented on earlier drafts, Susan Ito, Suzanne Kamata, Caroline Grant, and especially Ericka Lutz.

I'd like to thank my agent, Rachel Sussman, for seeing my vision for the work and helping me refine and focus it, and my editor at Cascadia Publishing House, Michael A. King, for bringing that vision to realization. Thanks always to my parents, John and Gwen Prestwood, my wonderful husband Bill, and my three children, Annika, Joshua, and Zachary.

The Author

Elrena Evans was born on April 19, 1978, in Houston, Texas, but spent most of her life living in Pennsylvania, and it is Pennsylvania that she now calls home.

After graduating from Delaware County Christian School, she attended Bucknell University where she majored in English and Russian. She then went on to receive her MFA in Creative Writing from The Pennsylvania State University.

Elrena found out she was expecting her first child during the second semester of a PhD program, but her plans to sail blithely through her pregnancy while continuing her studies were radically altered by serious pregnancy complications. After trying to balance recovery, new motherhood, and graduate student life for a semester, she realized she needed to take some time off and rethink her commitment to the academy.

Having left the confines of the ivory tower, she then proceeded to co-edit *Mama, PhD: Women Write About Motherhood and Academic Life* (Rutgers University Press 2008), a literary anthology about balancing motherhood and an academic career, with *Literary Mama* Senior Editor Caroline Grant.

Following a second (and complication-free) pregnancy, she decided to devote her time more fully to her family and her writing. Her work has appeared in the anthologies *Twentysomething Essays by Twentysomething Writers* (Random House 2006) and

How to Fit a Car Seat on a Camel (Seal Press 2008) as well as in *Books & Culture, Brain, Child: The Magazine for Thinking Mothers, Episcopal Life, Relief: A Quarterly Christian Expression, Literary Mama,* and *Christianity Today,* where she writes for the blog Her.meneutics. She is represented by Rachel Sussman of the Zachary Shuster Harmsworth literary agency.

She lives with her husband and three children, and a baby on the way, in a house with about 2,000 books. All of her children like to see their mama's name in print and find their own names in dedications.

Elrena is a longtime member of the Church of the Good Samaritan in Paoli, Pennsylvania, where she is involved with the children's ministry and the liturgical dance choir. Her website is http://www.elrenaevans.com.

Lightning Source UK Ltd.
Milton Keynes UK
UKOW02f0721291116

288725UK00002B/137/P